# CONTEMPORARY FICTION BY FILIPINOS IN AMERICA

Collected and Edited by

## CECILIA MANGUERRA BRAINARD

Published by PALH
(Philippine American Literary House}
P.O. Box 5099
Santa Monica, CA 90409, USA
PALHBOOKS.com

ISBN: 978-1-953716-09-5 (Paperback edition)
ISBN: 978-1-953716-10-1 (Ebook edition)

# INTRODUCTION
## Cecilia Manguerra Brainard

Contemporary Fiction by Filipinos in America, *which I collected and edited, was first published in 1997 by Anvil. The anthology was designed as a follow-up to my earlier book project,* Fiction by Filipinos in America. *This 2021 US edition of* Contemporary Fiction by Filipinos in America *retains the original biographies of the contributors.*

*I wish to quote my 1997 Introduction to this book which explains my vision of this book:*

~

Even while I was editing the earlier anthology, *Fiction by Filipinos in America,* I knew I would edit a similar anthology in the future. *Fiction by Filipinos in America,* released in 1993 by New Day Publishers, was not an attempt to include *all* Filipino American fictionists; I was well aware there were many other Filipino American writers aside from the ones included in that collection. I also knew there were more exciting and wonderful stories out there and that the output of these stories would grow through time, that in fact it would be impossible to coral them (so to speak) into definitive or comprehensive collections. One can only try; and hopefully with enough such attempts, one can look at the various collections and gather a larger picture from these little dents. *Contemporary Fiction by Filipinos in America* is my second attempt to document some of these writers and their stories. It is my hope that this documentation adds to the larger story of Filipinos in America.

While I was working on *Contemporary Fiction by Filipinos in America,* writers had asked me what kind of stories I was looking for. My standard reply was: I'm looking for good stories that reflect the theme of contemporary fiction by Filipinos in America. I did not elaborate but knew on a gut-level that I wanted first-rate stories written by Filipinos in America, or by Filipinos who had lived in America for a long time, and I wanted material that said something about Filipino or Filipino American history, experience, soul/psyche, or any other aspect to him. I was of course open to anything really, really good. I was not rigid about the Filipino American theme, that is I did not limit my selection to only stories about the Filipino American experience. That technique in editing would have assumed that I know with perfect clarity the definition of what is "Filipino American" or who is "Filipino American." I would not presume to know the exact definition of that term, which by the way is subject to numerous debates within the Filipino American community.

To me it is enough that there are Filipinos in America, immigrants as well as American-born, and that they have written stories. The job I had given myself was to gather the strongest stories into a collection that educates as well as entertains. I tried not to impose my idea of what is literature by Filipinos in America, but to allow the writers themselves to reveal this in their stories. In many ways, this anthology shaped itself. It is with deep regret that I had to reject some fine stories because they did not fit the dictates of the book. To strengthen the thread of the collection, I arranged the stories according to the chronological ages of the protagonists, from the young to the old.

The stories in this collection are varied. There are stories set in the Philippines such as Luis Cabalquinto's "The Fog," N.V.M. Gonzalez' "Confessions of a Dawn Person," Mar Puatu's "Valentinus," and Marianne Villanueva's "Sutil." Told with humor and a touch of pathos, Veronica Montes' "Of Midgets and Beautiful Cousins," tells about an American-born Filipina girl's Manila Visit. Eileen Tabios's "Negros" and John Silva's sultry "Dolly Rivera" hearken the Marcos years in the Philippines.

On the other hand, there are stories focusing on the

Filipino American experience-among them are Mila Faraon Heubeck's enchanting "The Pig-Slop Man," Lee Respicio Colomby's moving "The Lost Hero," and Alma Jill Dizon's mournful "Bride."

Eulalio Yerro Ibarra's "Paperback Dreams and Other Realities" jolts us with the contemporary gay/AIDS issue. Nadine Sarreal's "Hang, Man" reminds us of the Filipino migrant workers in Hong Kong and other parts of the world. The Filipino American gang issue is dealt with by Lilia Villanueva in her story "My Gang/My Family."

We have stories about women: the headstrong Glenda in Edgar Poma's "The Little Boy Who Fell in the Puka;" the overwhelmed balikbayan in Melissa Aranzamendez's story; the tormented wife in Linda Ty-CAsper's "Dark Star/Altered Seeds."

And we have stories about men: the cynical Bogey Reyes during the Vietnam years who finds peace in the homeland of his father; the puzzled young man in F. Delor Angeles's "Grandma and Spanish Women"; the down-to-earth ex-priests in Paulino Lim, Jr.'s "A Certain Failing."

To me the power of these stories come, not only from the tales themselves, but from the writers, too. Greg Sarris is in my mind. Sarris is the grandson of Eulalio Helario, from Panay, who married a Coast Miwok American Indian, Evelyn Sarragossa. Because of the anti-miscegenation laws in California, many Filipinos had married American Indian women. Greg Sarris the poet and the late William Oandasan, products of such intermarriage, have always been diligent in pointing out their Filipino background. Although Sarris's contribution, "Joy Ride," has a strong Native American point of view, I have included it in this collection because the writer's history adds to the greater picture of the Filipino in America.

# CONTENTS

# THE WHITENESS OF ANGELS

## Fatima Lim-Wilson

THE ISLAND of Marawak woke that June morning to the sight of angels.

At least, that is what most of its fisherfolk claimed to have first seen and as they shivered, still submerged under their thin blanket of dreams. Outside, the air was full of winged, white creatures that danced wildly before falling upon the wave-dashed sand.

Dawn never arrived gently to this island. The yellow drum of sun beat down upon the villagers. Sweat crowned their foreheads long after the dew blessing the thick carabao grass had vanished. But today, the angels brought an unknown chill that was like a dead man's hand wrapped round their hearts.

Only the retired priest, banished to this island for his dark misdeeds perpetrated behind church altars, recognized the angels and gave them a name. "SNOW!" he shouted, as he dashed out of his hovel, leaping on bare feet. Born in the midst of forest pine and white capped mountains, he welcomed this odd onslaught with crazed glee. To his prized rooster's astonishment, he proceeded to tear off his clothes until he stood naked before his parishioners, pale and bloated as a drowned baby, calling down upon the white wonder to bless or whip him, his extended arms shaped into a cross.

But the residents of Marawak did not have the time to look at the priest's live sculpture. They searched desperately through their pitiful pile of clothing as their teeth and bones jiggled drunkenly out of rhythm. Outside, the fish were leaping out of the water, landing with a metallic note upon the hardening crust of snow. The mayor hid among his wife's dresses hanging in the closet, keeping warm and keeping out of his townspeople's reach. He assumed he was to blame for had he not sold his soul and his fish-rich town to the devil himself? His wife did not miss him as she lounged in bed, blowing again and again the surface of her silver mirror that was misting over her cake-powdered beauty. Pulling out all her hairpins with a vengeance and tearing to shreds her lacy chemise, his favorite daughter ran outside, wrapped only in the robe of her own hair. She joined the island children who, by instinct it seemed, started making snowballs which they hurled against the mayor's house with frenzied delight. The mayor's much doted upon daughter threw against the biggest snowballs. In fact, she wielded them with such force she knocked down the plaster angel guarding her father's heavy doors.

Three houses away, the husband who had stopped speaking to his spouse for many years turned towards her in the dark. His hot tears fell upon her unmoving back. She let him sing praises to her navel, her moles, her shell-shaped toes for at least three hours before she slowly, very slowly turned towards him. As the snow continued to fall, their little house rocked back and forth on its stilts, making a whistling sound.

Everywhere, the fishfolk kept warm in each other's embrace. Wayward sons wended their way home, begging for their mother's healing fish-head broth. Winsome maidens who would never have let any man touch even the tips of their elbows jumped out of windows into the waiting arms of their faceless beaus. And the village spinster burned to death. Feeling colder than ever, she had surrounded herself with her hoard of tall, black candles. Her neighbors say her screams rose to the sky, turning into screeching bats.

The next day, there was not a single trace of snow. All that remained were the mountains of fish that were quickly spoiling in the sun. The priest had to be carried home, his body still bent into his life's penance. The mayor raised his fist to the sky, cursing the vanished angels for he had made grand plans in the night to turn Marawak into a tourist resort. His wife slept on, clutching tightly to her mirror, while her daughter ran off with a passing farmer who lovingly covered his naked bride with his harvest of hay.

Nine months later, many squalling babies would be born on the same day, at the coming of dawn. They all would have icy fingers and a tendency to walk a few inches off the ground. The whites of their eyes would glint, almost blinding those who stared at them too long. And from the ashes of the spinster would rise a leafless tree looking uncannily like the bony, brooding woman.

It is close to noon. The sun's drums thuds, sending dry echoes down the parched land. The spinster's tree creaks loudly as it dances by itself to the music of an indifferent wind. Under its sun-filled shade, the snow children look up, up, hungrily as if waiting for their next meal to come falling down from on high. The priest stands close by, a transfixed crucifix. His listless rooster stamps the ground. The enraged animal raises clouds of dust and ear-piercing cries, his and his master's lust spent as the emptied skies.

*Bio*: Fatima Lim-Wilson lives in Seattle, Washington, with her husband Adrian and son Francis and is an Academic Program Manager at the University of Washington. She has published two books: Wandering Roots/From the Hothouse and Crossing the Snow Bridge. Wandering Roots/From the Hothouse won the Colorado Book Authors Award and the Philippine National Book Award.

*Crossing the Snow Bridge was selected over seven hundred manuscripts as the winner of the Ohio State University Press Award for Poetry. Fatima has a Ph.D. in English from the University of Denver on a full scholarship.*

# THE PIG-SLOP MAN

Mila Faraon Heubeck

THE LEFT wing of the airplane dipped sharply as the pilot made his final turn, pointing the nose of the twin-prop shuttle toward the asphalt runway extending in the distance below.

From my view of the Hawaiian island a short distance above, I could tell that nothing had changed in the eight years I had exiled myself from this place. The two-lane highway adjacent to the airport was devoid of traffic. Young people had been leaving Moloka'i in great numbers for years. Who was left to drive on these roads?

The lonely roadway weaved through miles of shrub and brown grass dotting the dry earth, which lay useless and abandoned now that the pineapple plantations had given up and gone away, too. In the middle of this desert, one sagging, gray structure rose up from the landscape, almost blending in with its surroundings. The airport terminal looked as if it would be swallowed up by the earth. I wondered if anyone would care.

The tires of the airplane screeched on the pavement as we touched down. We stopped in front of the terminal, and I made the few short steps to the ground. I looked up cautiously, hoping that no one would be waiting for me as I had asked, preferring instead to rent my own car so I could leave if I felt like it. Thankfully, no one was there to meet me or the handful of horrified-looking tourists, who were undoubtedly cursing their travel agents for suggesting this place.

I would have loved to tell them that they should have skipped the place altogether. In the space of a day, I would warn them, they too would feel the slow pace of the island envelope them. They would sense the stagnant weight of an isolated world abandoned by progress and hope. And fearing that they would be sucked into the slow death of an island struggling for its last breath, they would run for the airport, desperate for the first flight out to anywhere, much as I had, eight years ago. And they too, would never look back.

It was only my mother's incessant nagging that finally brought me back to this place.

"Your father is old," she had said on the telephone, calling me every Saturday morning at 5:30, when she was sure I'd be home.

"He asks for you every day. You'll be sorry when he's dead, and then, too late, too late," she warned.

How could I tell her that I never wanted to see that island again? That I never wanted to remember their stifling, angry voices that followed me like a shadow throughout my adolescence? How could I explain that I was quite content with the maddening pulse of Los Angeles and its choking freeways, everyone flowing with purpose and direction?

Finally succumbing to the guilt, I made the long flight home, where I now found myself in a compact rental, making my way down the same road I had seen from the airplane. At three o'clock on a Monday afternoon, only four cars meandered past me in the ten miles I had travelled from the airport.

Nearing the eastern end of the island where my parents

lived, I breathed in the fresh, salt-sea air, feeling the trace of a memory scratching at the back of my head. I remembered a child sitting on her father's shoulders, grasping his bald head, as he waded in the ankle-high water in search of crabs. His voice echoed in my brain, "I cannot see the crabs if you cover my eyes." The memory dissolved quickly, and I had to fight to remember the times my father took me crabbing for good luck.

As I rounded a curve in the roadway, an old Dodge truck, marred by rust where it once was black, and faded by the hot sun, slowly crept to my left as it passed me. In the front seat, an old man, chomping on a smoke pipe waved to me and forged ahead, merging into the lane in front of me. In the back of the truck, a black, 55-gallon drum stood, wrapped firmly and tied to the truck with rope. As it moved ahead, a wall of undeniable stink emanating from the truck hit me like a wave. Pig Slop. There could be no mistake.

The pungent smell of slop instantly propelled me to my childhood, when I lived in the Filipino section of a pineapple plantation on Moloka'i with my parents, two sisters and two brothers. Immediately, I remembered the acrid sweetness of slop collected from the neighbors and those wonderful, early mornings I spent with my father, when it was 75 degrees cool but I was freezing.

The memory is faint, as dark as the mornings when I accompanied my father once a week in a borrowed Ford pick-up, faded to a chalky blue half-eaten by the salt that plagued most things on the island where I grew up. Each Saturday morning, before the sun came up, I awoke to the sounds of my parents in the kitchen, my mother fixing father a cup of Nescafe, sugared and lightly creamed with condensed milk; my father, silently shuffling through his deck of cards, playing solitaire on the kitchen table. The old transistor radio with the twisted coat-hanger antenna echoed the comforting sounds of the Filipino language station they listened to religiously.

From my bed, I would sniff the air for the smell of cooking pork or fish, a sign that it was a work day and my parents were preparing their lunch. But smelling only coffee, I would get out of bed, glad that it must be Saturday, and I could have my parents all to myself. Today, I would not be dragged off and left with Apo Masing, the old, deaf babysitter, for another silent and lonely day.

Reassured by the noise and comforting smell, I would untangle myself from the sheets and stumble into the warm kitchen flooded by yellow, dingy light. The light fixture hanging from the ceiling was dusty with cobwebs and bore two naked bulbs, although it could have held four. That was my mother's contribution to conserving electricity. All it did was give the kitchen a sickly gloom.

My father would methodically count through his cards: one ... two ... three, flip. I would watch with my chin resting on the edge of the table as he built neat columns of seven, slowly thumbing through his deck, only to slap the last of his cards down and mix it up again like a game of "Go, fish."

"Aah, I got dog luck, today," he would say as he picked me up and sat me on the bench beside him. "You be my good luck today, yes?" With a chuckle he would hoist me up to his neck and scratch his stubbly chin against my cheek, making me laugh. We would make our way to the door and Pig-Slop Day would begin.

On those mornings, my father carefully wrapped me up in the Army blanket, government green and itchy, and placed me into the front cab of the truck. I was little then, not able to look out at the road without having to stand on the seat. This was always a struggle with the blanket snug around me. From my perch, I gazed up and out at the sky, still dark and faintly lit by stars, fearful of the mesquite trees the Hawaiians called kiawe.

The trees scared me. Bald and dried with age, their branches clawed at the night air. They beckoned me, gnarled fingers ready to pluck me out of the truck to be swallowed into their rough trunks. I squeezed my eyes shut, venturing an occasional sneak, bracing for the feel of their rough limbs around my neck. At the creak of the driver's door opening, my fear dissolved as my father heaved his large frame into the truck, punctuating the night silence with a reassuring slam of the door. My father crossed himself in the dark as he always did before leaving home, whispering his short prayer to the Father, Son and Holy Ghost. I was glad they would be coming too.

With a haughty glance back, I stuck out my tongue at the silent trees that were powerless now with my father next to me. I saw them cower in fear of the Holy Trinity who were surely hovering above us, wrapping their protective arms around our truck. Sorry! Not this time! The trees stood frozen and mute, eventually blending into the night sky as we drove away.

In the back of the old Ford, two empty oil drums crowded the truck bed, still reeking from last Saturday's haul. Slowly weaving along the rutted, dirt roads of the plantation, we made our way along the rows of lower camp where we lived near most of my father's friends from his old hometown in the Philippines. The houses, dark and quiet with sleep, waited expectantly for my father, the Pig-Slop Man, who arrived early every Saturday, long before the morning sun brought the loud crows of the roosters ready to meet their fate at the day's chicken fights.

At each stop along the road, my father cranked up the hand brake, wiggled the stick shift into neutral and left the truck, motor running, parked alongside each house to retrieve the pail that would be left hanging from a large nail protruding from the outside wall. Each bucket would be overflowing with slop, bearing the week's leftover meals—fruit rinds, potato peels, vegetables gone bad—everything combined to make a load of precious stew which he carefully poured into the dark oil drums. The mixture splashed against the metal and gave off the familiar, sweet-sour, rotting smell of a brew that only those lucky pigs would love.

Most Saturdays, we made our way undisturbed. I sat dutifully in the front seat of the truck, wrapped in my blanket, steadfastly guarding the cargo. Confronted by the putter of the old Ford, I watched my father retrieve the buckets, his footsteps fading in the distance. I could smell the rich tobacco smoke coming from his pipe, growing faint as he walked toward each house.

I strained my ears in the darkness, waiting for my father's voice, sniffing the air for the distinct apple-scented tobacco, ready to scream for him if those old trees had somehow uprooted themselves and were coming after me. But, before long, his black rubber boots hitting the hard earth announced his return, and I would see him, heaving yet another load of juicy pig slop into the oil drum. The clang of the bucket against the barrel pierced the night air, and I slowly exhaled in relief. Just as quickly, he returned the bucket to its nail and we moved on to the next house.

One Saturday, we ran into Tata Harry, who lived at the end of our street, in the shadow of the wooden crates used to carry the pineapples during the week. Tata Harry was wide awake, sitting at his back door step, the red glow of his cigarette bouncing in the darkness.

"Kumusta! Hello, hello!" Tata Harry's voice was gruff, made hoarse by his endless screaming at his nine children, who ran wild without a mother to teach them civilized manners. Sometimes I would hear his exclamations from our house.

"Ay, Sus, Maria, Josep!" he would yell in his thick accent so that it sounded like one word. "You are so dirty," he would say to his children caught playing in the mud again. "Look at you, only your teeth and eyeballs are white."

Despite his many children, Tata Harry was lonely and liked to talk a lot, but my father was always in a hurry, eager to return before Saturday cockfights began. Still, we could not afford to miss Tata Harry's house because with all of his kids, he always had a lot of pig slop. Sometimes two buckets full.

"Hey Harry!" my father greeted him "Saturday today, go back to sleep."

"Plenty time for sleeping when you dead," Tata said."

My father laughed. "Harry, you gonna live forever."

"Nope. Too many kids, they gonna run to me into the grave," he said.

"Go back home Philippines," my father urged, "bring back a wife to keep you company, help you out. You gonna live longer that way."

"Yep. Maybe next time when I go home," he said.

Tata Harry came to Moloka'i from the Philippines when he was sixteen years old. Unlike many of the plantation workers, he had never returned to his homeland in the off-season to visit his parents, always promising, next time. Now that thirty years had gone by and his parents were dead, he had no reason to go back.

With a wave of his cigarette, Tata Harry retreated to his chair on the dark porch, as my father carefully made his way back to the truck.

"Daddy," I said, "how come Tata Harry sits in the dark like that? He looks like a black ghost with one evil, red eye."

"Tata Harry doesn't want to wake up the flies," my father explained. "The flies smell the slop, and pretty soon, the slop got plenty worms. That's not so good. Besides," he added, wrenching the truck into gear, "the flies get mad when you wake them up so early on Saturday."

"Oh." I nodded earnestly. My father was so smart. He always made perfect sense.

The thought of worms squirming in the pig slop made me think of my sister, Ella. She was being especially curious one morning, trying to peer into a barrel of slop that my father had placed under a big guava tree. Someone else was going to take it to feed their own pigs.

"Get away, Ella," my father said, scolding her. "You gonna tip that barrel over."

My sister, with her hands firmly grasping the top edge of the oil drum towering above her had been struggling to pull herself up over the barrel to get a peek inside. Failing that, she climbed the sturdy trunk of the guava tree until she found a branch that reached directly over the barrel. She shimmied across the branch and peered dangerously over until she could glimpse the mess of old fruit and rotting meat and to her horror, millions of fat maggots squirming in the soup.

11

"Ewwwwww," she cried in fascination, "look at all those worms. Look at that!"

My father, startled to find her stretched out on a thin, trembling branch screamed at her.

"Hey! Get down, right now!"

Too late. The tree branch snapped, dropping my sister like a bomb, straight down into the slop barrel with a dramatic, sickening splash. In a flash, my father had reached into the barrel, pulling my sister out by her waist-long hair, now completely coated with maggot-strewn slop. She howled in disgust, her mouth a perfect O, her eyes round with terror and her arms, jutting straight out from her body to keep from squishing the worms crawling at her sides. I cringed at the sight of poor Ella, who was soaked to the bone in slop and worms.

"Better close your mouth," my father said, laughing while he hosed her off. "You don't wanna eat the stuff."

At that, my sister wailed even louder, to the delight of my two brothers, who were now taunting her with shouts of "maggot breath," a name that makes everyone shiver to this day.

"Nope," I told my father as we continued down the road in the old Ford. "We don't like worms or flies."

Before long, the oil drums were full, and my father and I in the rusty truck, followed by a procession of stray dogs, drove slowly down to the main highway to make the twenty mile pilgrimage to my grandfather's place where my father kept his pigs. At the start of open road, the truck accelerated, leaving behind the plantation and the pack of hungry dogs.

After decades of working for the plantation, my grandfather, Apo Tinong, had saved enough money to buy land near the ocean and retire far away from the plantation. His house was a short walk to the beach where he spent most of his time, casting his net near the reef or plucking crabs from the walls of the fishpond when the tides was very low.

Apo's house was heaven compared to the dusty plantation with its miles of pineapple fields surrounding the town and the smell of chemicals permeating the air. Apo's yard was rich with the sweet scent of plumeria trees that lined the front yard, mixed in with the salt-sea air and laced with the unquestionable stench of pig manure. The smell hung in the air on hot, still afternoons and woke me up with a start as the truck crunched down the gravel driveway of Apo Tinong's house.

My father's pigs squealed in unison as if they knew we were coming. I could barely see them through the thick banana trees concealing them from view. Maybe the smell of pig slop was too much. Or maybe they caught a glimpse of those 55-gallon oil drums which were also used on pig-slaughter day. Maybe they knew that after they were killed, my father and Apo Tinong would lift their dead bodies from the table and dip them into a cauldron filled with boiling water to free the coarse hair from their skins.

I feared for those pigs, wanting to comfort them, to pat their white faces and cluck my tongue in the soothing way my mother did when I rubbed my eyes after pulling red chili peppers from her tree. I wanted to tell them it was not slaughter day, it was pig-slop day and they would get their long-awaited Saturday treat. But at the sound of their screaming, I was frozen to my seat. I slapped my hands to both ears, imagining them running around the cement floor of their pens, sick with fear of my father and his shiny knife.

"Make them stop screaming," I begged my father.

"The pigs are happy," my father said, prying my hands from my ears. Listen good, you can hear them laughing."

I closed my eyes and listened hard for sounds of laughter, but all I heard was high-pitched, panic-stricken screeching of pigs.

"Don't kill them, Daddy," I cried. "It hurts them when you slice their necks."

"Ay-yah, balasang ko," my father sighed, "my poor-thing, little girl. Okay, no killing today," he promised as he picked me up out of the truck. "Today, they get a good meal, a good hose-down and then can sleep all day."

I wrapped my arms around his neck, wanting to believe

that the pigs would be saved, but knowing someday when they were big and fat, they would go the way of all pigs. Straight to Piggy Heaven, where according to my sister Ella, pig slop fell in an endless rain.

"You know," Ella once explained to me as I cried behind the banana trees one Saturday when the pigs were being slaughtered, "they live for raining pig slop. Everybody knows that."

"And then," she said, "they run around laughing and singing like Gene Kelly in *Singing in the Rain*."

I could almost see those pigs stomping in the puddles of slop. I wondered if they could swing around the lampposts, too.

\*

In my rental car, I laughed at the memory of the Pig-Slop Man, my father, undoubtedly the first to introduce recycling to our small community. I cried for those times when a single morning with my father was everything I wished for. Funny how life makes you forget.

The pavement gave way to gravel as I turned into my parents' driveway. We had left the plantation long ago, building a new house on Apo Tinong's land after he died. I was greeted by the familiar scent of plumeria, the fresh salt-sea air, and occasionally the smell of pig manure, waiting in from the backyard.

The slam of the car door brought my father out from the house. He was old and stooped now, much smaller than I remembered. The ever-present smoke pipe jutted from his mouth. I ran to meet him, his arms outstretched. The Pig-Slop Man's daughter came home.

**Bio:** *Mila Faraon Heubeck was born and raised on Moloka'i, Hawaii, along with her two sisters and two brothers. The quiet, simple lifestyle of the island, overshadowed by the presence of the pineapple plantations where her parents worked, provides much of the background* *for her story "Pig-Slop Man." She is presently an attorney in Los Angeles, California, where she makes her home with her husband, John and their two Chow Chows, Ipo and Manchu.*

# NEGROS

Eileen Tabios

"*DAAAAA-deeeeeeeee! Daddy, daddy, Daaaaa-deeeeeeeee!*"
My mother did not look dignified yelling down the mountain. Her hands flapped like wings of chickens we chased for dinner, her blouse escaped from the waistband of her skirt, her hair streamed in all directions from her loosened bun and her mouth thinned around a circle of prominent teeth. She screeched from the balcony of our house which stood on top of Mount Asawa. She, most assuredly, would have been dismayed if she realized that her voice topped that of Auntie Feling's whose water broke when she was visiting the previous month. Clutching her belly, Auntie Feling's exhortations to call the doctor had been audible even to the traffic on the road circling the bottom of the mountain.

Mount Asawa was actually a hill, but everyone was accustomed to calling it a mountain because of its name. The other thing about its name was that "Asawa" could have meant "wife" in Tagalog. Thus, my father's friends always enjoyed a rollicking good time discussing the many ways to "Mount Wife" when they first heard of it.

Anyway, there was my father's asawa ordering me and my father as we were half-way up the mountain to hurry in a voice loud enough to carry to Manila. We broke into a run, wondering what disaster had befallen the household. My father had gained weight over the years but he easily ran ahead of me-his quivering backside, encased tightly in brown polyester, looked like the rump of fat water buffalo.

As we burst into the house, the servants were running through the living room, much like the time Mama stood barefoot on the sofa and screamed with regard to the unexpected visit of a neighbor's pet monkey who slipped in through an open window. "Ayyyyyyyyy-sussss! Everyone get that lice-ridden creature before he tracks his diseases through the house!"

This time, my mother was instructing all servants, "Black, black, as much black as you can find!" before dashing off towards the servants' quarters.

"What's going on here?" my father demanded as we followed my mother. We entered Manang Inday's bedroom where we found the maid lying on her bed, clutching her knees to her chest, mumbling and shivering despite the heat.

"Ayyyyy-sussss!" we finally deciphered some of Manang Inday's mutterings. "I am freezing!"

My mother started layering the clothes bundled in her arms over Manang Inday as was my father and I watched, open-mouthed with amazement. I reached for my father's hand which returned my clasp firmly.

"Her body has been taken over by mamau," Mama explained, her perspiring face looking back at us and inviting us to share in the horror of the matter.

"Mamau -- a ghost?" I repeated, concerned and moving behind my father. My father closed the cavern of his mouth and snorted.

"Another ghost? Why did we move to this place?" my father complained, releasing my hand as he disgustedly flung both of his up in the air. "Ever since we arrived in this city, I've been haunted by floods, neighbors who eat the evidence of their depletion of my chickens, a roof that won't stop leaking and a different ghost showing its pathetic presence every month! Are these mamaus breeding behind the chicken coop?"

Then my father laughed at the ceiling, apparently thinking he inadvertently displayed some wit. I smirked, too, as his lack of fear made me unafraid.

"Well, and what does this ghost want this time?" my father asked after he stopped barking to himself at the sight of Mama's frown.

"Have you no respect? The body of Inday, who could never hurt a soul and undoubtedly was just minding her own business, has just been invaded by an unwelcome visitor from the other realm!" my mother, her hands on her hips, chastised my father.

"The other realm?" my father mocked in high-pitched tone.

As the warning look become murderous on Mama's face, he calmed himself, smoothing back the sparse strands over his glistening scalp. He sat in the lone chair of the room which, next to the servant's bed, allowed for a direct look into Manang Inday's grimacing face. He pulled me to his side and whispered, "We're in this together, buddy. Let's discover the surprise du jour!"

Du jour was French and meant "of the day." My father loved to teach pieces of trivia that he thought I would not learn otherwise from the nuns at my elementary school.

"All right, let's hear it," my father said, sinking his chin into his chest with demeanor of preparing for a long, tedious story. His profile was that of a multi-bellied Buddha in a yellow, short-sleeved golf shirt. "But first, why did you cover Inday with your slips? Isn't it better to cover her with a blanket then your underwear?"

My mother dropped her eyes and blushed before she responded, "My slips are black. Nana Sitang said that if ever a ghost takes over the body of someone in our household, we should cover the body with black material because black feels more comfortable to a mamau."

I remembered Nana Sitang's visit to our home and the conversation turning to the nature of ghosts. Nana Sitang could not explain, however, why black was more comfortable to mamaus or why the comfort of ghosts was significant, only that she had managed to pick up these gems of wisdom from her village's witch doctor when she was a teenager. Of course, she had cackled through tobacco-stained teeth, this was before Nana Sitang's parents discovered and put a stop to her visits to the witch doctor who also dabbled as the bookie at local cockfights. Before my father could remind Mama of these points, we heard a slight scuffling noise behind us.

"Oh, good, Neta, you found more black," my mother said to one of the servants who stood just beyond the doorway, her head tilted away from the room as if there was a disease she could catch by just looking. Manang Neta blindly held out a bundle of clothes. Sighing, Mama allowed Manang Neta to avoid entering the room and went over to take the pile from her hands.

"Hey, that's my jacket," I piped as I noticed one of the articles of clothing my mother was layering over Manang Inday from the results of Manang Neta's forage through the closets.

"Shusssh, boy," my father ordered. "Why do you need a jacket when you live in a tropical country?"

"But it's American and from Uncle Cosmos," I mumbled to myself ignoring his lesson that I lived in a "tropical country" and wishing only to retrieve the jacket my favorite uncle had sent me for my tenth birthday. My jacket was black with a picture of Captain Kirk, Mr. Spock and Dr. McCoy on the back.

"Okay, Gloria, what does this ghost want?" I could tell my father was losing patience by the way he emphasized his words. Since we moved from Manila to Baguio City three months ago, we had been visited by three ghosts, including the one who inhabited Manang Inday's body.

The first one was a dark shadow that hovered outside my parents' bedroom window and pleaded for old clothes that they could spare. The ghost made its request in what my father called a "whining, toadying tone that no self-respecting ghost would ever use because real ghosts should have no reason to behave towards humans in a servile manner!" In disgust, my father threw out his old bathrobe but refused to let my frightened mother empty the drawers for more clothes to dispense out the window.

"It's only a loko-loko from the neighborhood trying to stiff us," he said, waving at her to return to bed and slamming the shutters closed. However since my parents' bedroom overlooked the air over a steep-sided valley created by one side of Mount Asawa, we have never determined how a person could have managed to throw a shadow from right beyond my parents' bedroom window.

The second ghost appeared a month later and took the shape of my father's old bathrobe floating beyond the bathroom window when my mother had to exercise an act of nature in the middle of the night. With one frayed sleeve pointing at my mother, the mamau chastised my parents for their selfishness. The tunnel-like darkness of the empty sleeve reminded her, my mother later said, of the throat of a shark that had opened its jaws at her when she was a little girl swimming in the seashore by the fishing village where she was born. My mother decided to make a generous donation to the local orphanage the following day, much to my father's dismay.

"You weren't there!" Mama replied heatedly over breakfast after my father berated her for confusing dreams with reality. I sneaked a forgotten mango slice from my mother's plate as I waited for my father's response.

"Of course I wasn't there! Since when have I ever accompanied you to do your Number 2? It does not smell sweet, Madam!" my father roared back, stabbing his fork in the air and breaching one of my mother's rules of never pointing an eating utensil towards the direction of another. But my father's anger did not accomplish anything as my mother proceeded later that day with her gift to the orphanage.

"Susmaryosep! Don't use that tone of voice with me," Mama snapped back at my father as they discussed the third ghost. "You can listen, too, with your elephant-sized ears as I question the spirit."

By expressing "Susmaryosep" instead of the shortcut "Ayyyy-susss," I could tell my mother was really agitated. "Susmaryosep" is short for "Jesus, Mary, Joseph" whose names my relatives frequently invoked in moments of stress.

My mother bent over Manang Inday's quivering face. Poor Manang Inday, I thought as I always did whenever I happened to pay attention to her. Her face bore a distinct resemblance to Uncle Fillmore's bulldog: the same mournful brown eyes surrounded by drooping lids; the slack multi-layered folds below the chin; and a bulbous forehead. Uncle Fillmore also had noticed the resemblance upon acquiring the bulldog and so named it after Manang Inday, much to the distress of his wife, my Auntie Feling who sure must have busted one of Uncle Fillmore's eardrums with her views on the matter.

"Now, now. You should be warmer now," Mama crooned, her face about an inch away from the bump protruding from the tip of Manang Inday's nose. "Who are you and why are you visiting us through poor Inday's body?"

Manang Inday started to act like a fish, disconcerting my mother and causing her to move closer to us. The servant's lips kept shifting as she breathed through her mouth. Finally, the ghost discovered that one can breathe more easily through a nose and after a few times of becoming accustomed to this notion, used Manang Inday's mouth for speaking.

"Is that you, my little garbage can?" Manang Inday, or rather, the mamau, asked. It had to be the ghost because the voice did not sound like Manang Inday's voice. The voice was melodious instead of Manang Inday's that had reminded many listeners of the braying of a discontented goat.

"Is that you, my little garbage can?" the ghost repeated lovingly.

"Yes," Mama could manage only one word through the surprise, then prolonged wince contorting her features.

"Mama, why is she telling you a garbage can?" I asked the question as well on behalf of my father as, both wide-eyed, we looked at her.

The mamau laughed with Manang Inday's face: soft rolling peals that sounded like the hymn being outlined on air whenever the bells tolled from the church another hilltop away.

"My little garbage can, this must be your son, Matthew," the ghost said. "Well, I'll tell you why, my sweet boy."

I scowled at being called "sweet" but leaned closer with my parents toward Manang Inday's body. The mamau's voice was full of mischief, courting us with the manner of sharing confidences.

"When your mother was a little baby, I helped take care of her. We would spend many afternoons in the shade of the biggest star apple tree in your grandmother's yard. There we would sit, I rocking her back and forth while I feasted on little bags of sweets.

"Oooohhh, I had such sweet tooth," the ghost said with an air of self-congratulation. "I always carried around bags of churros, susporos de casuys, palitaos, polvorons, maja blancas, maruyas and bibingka. My favorite was puto maya; I loved to watch my mother make it with sweet rice, coconut milk, brown sugar and grated coconut meat. My, my, they were so delicious!"

Here, the mamau interrupted with a few choice smacks with Manang Inday's lips. My mouth also started to water.

"One day, your mother started crying and crying. I kept rolling her and patting her on the back but she would not stop bawling. Then I noticed her small chubby hands reaching into my bag of sweets. Your Mama wanted some, too.

"Well, she was just a baby and couldn't have eaten the snacks with her soft, little gums. So, after much thought, I chewed and chewed a tiny piece of my favorite puto maya and then fed the result to her. She loved that so much. And that's how she became my garbage can. Because I would chew sweets and feed them to her, directly from my mouth with a kiss."

"Eeeeeeuuuuuuuwwwwwwwhhhhh," my father cried out before we both burst in laughter and pointed our fingers at my mother who stood frozen, a pained look on her face. Mama tried to hide her embarrassment by starting to straighten her blouse and smooth her hair back into her bun.

"That's why you're a garbage can, because you ate her leftovers when you were a baby?" I wheezed between my laughter.

"Aaahhh, but Matthew, she was *my* little garbage can and so I loved my honey honey bun bun," the ghost noted, screwing up Manang Inday's lips into a grin wide enough to display the blackened fillings in all of Manang Inday's cavities.

My father elbowed me to look at him. Cross-eyed, he started whispering in a sing-song, "honey honey bun bun." Choking on my laughter, I bent and crossed my legs as I felt my bladder begin to expand.

My mother cleared her throat and asked in as business-like a demeanor as she could manage, "Auntie Lina, why are you there? What can we do for you?"

"I'll tell you, my darling, but before I do, could you bring me something to drink? I am so co o o o ld," the ghost replied and made Manang Inday's body shiver exaggeratedly.

Mama quickly called for Manang Neta. Manang Neta showed the back of her uncombed head again as she still refused to look into the room. "Yes, Ma'am," she squeaked.

"Heat up some Campbell's," Mama instructed.

"Yes, Ma'am," Manang Neta squeaked again and ran away to the kitchen.

"Campbell's soup? How kind of you to share such luxuries as American food," the ghost said gratefully. "But now, let me tell you why I'm here. Do you remember, my little garbage can, your distant cousin, Eliel?"

"Only vaguely, Auntie Lina. Doesn't he now live in Negros?" Mama asked, referring to Negros Occidental, the country's primary sugar-growing province.

"Yes, yes. Things are bad in Negros for your cousin's family. My heart breaks to see Eliel so skinny. He refuses to eat because his children do not receive full sustenance from the little that he can offer them. Yet he's the one who must remain strong to be able to feed his family," the ghost nodded Manang Inday's face up and down as she sighed.

"That is sad," Mama said. Solemnly, my father and I nodded our heads in agreement.

"Well, you and Andrew are doing so well here in Baguio City, two well-educated professionals that you are," the ghost continued. "Congratulations, Andrew, on your recent promotion to Senior Vice President at Banco Baguio! My goodness-you've become such a big-shot banker! And Gloria, to be principal of Baguio High School-what a coup!"

"You don't have to explain, Auntie Lina. We will be more than happy to help," my mother quickly interrupted. Mama later told me that hearing the mamau recite our family's good fortunes made her uneasy. "Never take blessings for granted, Matthew," my mother warned.

Unlike the situation with the other two ghosts, my father did not utter a single word of complaint over my mother's offer to provide assistance. He only pulled me closer and looked sadly at my mother.

After my mother agreed to assist Uncle Eliel, the mamau did not speak again, despite mother's questions and other attempts to engage her in conversation. She only indicated her presence by intermittently making Manang Inday's body relapse into a fit of shivers until Manang Neta brought the soup. The ghost still uttered no words as she finished a bowl of Campbell's noodles in chicken broth. After she emptied the bowl and emitted a loud burp, Manang Inday's body sat up on the bed with a startled look on her face, the layered clothes flung off disarray around her. When Manang Inday brayed at us familiarly like a goat, then we knew the ghost had departed.

\*

Before we immigrated to the United States three years later, Uncle Fillmore and Auntie Feling agreed to my father's request that they provide assistance to Uncle Eliel and his family. But until we left, Mama dispatched a servant with packages of food and money every six months to travel the hundreds of miles to Negros which was located on the Southern part of the Philippine Archipelago.

As I helped my mother the day after the incident to pack the first set of provisions to Negros, Mama mentioned that she doubted that the mamau was actually Auntie Lina because she inhaled and drank the soup loudly.

"Your Auntie Lina never would have slurped. She was a lady," my mother emphasized, her hands patting the bun on her head to ensure that it had trapped all the stray strands of her hair.

"Yes, Mama," I agreed dutifully and then asked, "But Mama, why did you consent to helping Uncle Eliel if you didn't believe that the ghost was Auntie Lina?"

"Because Negros is Negros, my son. And I had no doubt that Eliel's family needed help. The ghost was just reminding me, that's all," Mama replied before turning aside and bending down to look at something in the rug.

She would have been upset if she knew I saw the teardrop sliding down her nose, I thought as I allowed her to pretend to rub away at an invisible stain on the rug.

Later, as we were packing to leave the country, my mother stumbled across a shoebox of correspondence from Uncle Eliel. She read from some of them and gave me the first letter Uncle Eliel wrote to her. Mama said I should bring the letter with me to the United States so that I will remember those who are left behind. My letter said ...

*We are so grateful for your help. We ate meat that day, the first that we have had for over a year. We usually eat only rice and vegetables, sometimes with fruit, and, of course, we have our water and salt.*

*The last time we ate meat, we found some frogs in the fields. We put on pieces of old clothes—of course all of our clothes are old, heh-heh— and kerosene in a bottle to make a light. Then we went frog-hunting at night. But, more often than not, we are too tired to hunt at night. When we get back to our barracks, it is late and we are so tired that all we can do is sleep.*

My Uncle Eliel's letter mentioned other things but I usually thought about how his family did not have much to eat. Many years later, I conducted some research as an aide to a United States Senator who was being lobbied by Amnesty International regarding certain labor incidents in Negros.

I learned that about seventy percent of the province's sugar growing land was located in haciendas, a remnant from the Spanish colonial days which has been compared to American Southern plantations before the United States' Civil War. The workers' houses were typically rough-hewn wooden shacks with no more than twenty-five square yards of floor space. Most families possessed only sparse furnishings such as thin straw sleeping mats and a few utensils. Many haciendas also contained barracks that were partitioned by cardboard walls to house sacadas, seasonal farm workers, from the poor of neighboring provinces. The sacadas were treated the worst among all workers, usually assigned the most menial and hardest jobs such as cutting cane. I remember my mother telling me that Uncle Eliel originally moved to Negros as a sacada and never managed to earn sufficient money to leave what he thought would be a one-year posting.

I learned that most hacenderos belonged to a tight-knit political oligarchy. Some were absentee landlords, enjoying the fruits of their wealth in Manila, Hong Kong, London, New York and elsewhere outside of Negros. Some paternalistically defended the hacienda as the best way of life for the people of Negros, who, some hacenderos said, were unable to become self-proficient. At this notion, the representatives from Amnesty International scoffed before adding that in any event truly benign dictators would have been less inclined to ignore the widespread hunger and illiteracy surrounding them.

I learned that the landless comprised as much as ninety-eight percent of Negros' population and that the province's poverty rate exceeded eighty percent.

I learned that the land reform promised by Corazon Aquino when she overthrew Ferdinand Marcos never materialized and that the landless and impoverished continued to provide fertile ground for labor and political agitation, driven not only by communists but also local priests and nuns responding to the grinding poverty afflicting their flock.

I learned that Negros Occidental was a microcosm of the extreme economic and political inequities that affected the entire Republic of the Philippines. I grew to picture it vividly in my mind as a place where darkly-windowed luxury cars drove around malnourished children too hungry and deprived of energy to do anything but mimic puddles on the dirt.

Finally, to finish my research, I tried to live on water and salted rice for as long as I could. I did not last long -- a failed experiment that also made me recall the aftermath of the ghost's visit to my home in Baguio City. I remembered once more my consternation over how Uncle Eliel and his family would have hovered on the brink of starvation without my parents' aid. My childhood sense of security had been uninterrupted until my exposure to Uncle Eliel's dilemma as he worked the sugarcane fields of Negros. It was the first time in my life that I felt the ground shake beneath my feet. Uncle Eliel was not a stranger to my family; he was family. I never met him but for a long time after the mamau took over Manang Inday's body, I felt Uncle Eliel's presence every time I sat down at our dining table.

*Ahhhhhh. Delicious, isn't it, my little garbage can, my honey honey bun bun?* I would hear his voice behind me as I ate. When I turned around, there would be no one there or only one of the servants looking quizzically at my frightened expression. I came to imagine Uncle Eliel as a diaphanous, floating face with elongated chin exaggerating the size of his mouth, an open chasm trickling saliva from one corner as he coveted my food.

I lost weight that year. It was also the year when, with hunger as my teacher, I first learned how to faint.

*Bio: Eileen Tabios was born in Ilocos Sur and grew up in Baguio City before emigrating (at age ten) to the United States; she currently lives in New York. She became a full-time writer in 1995, leaving behind the corporate world where her last "day-job" was as an international project finance banker and Vice President of Union bank of Switzerland. She also has worked as a journalist, economist, country risk analyst and stock market analyst since obtaining her B.A. in Political Science from Barnard College and an M.B.A. in Economics and International Business from New York University. Since becoming a writer, she has received residency and fellowship support from the Virginia Center for the Creative Arts, the Helen Wurlitzer Foundation of New Mexico, Fundacion Valparaiso of Spain and The Witter Brynner Foundation. She has published her fiction and poetry in numerous journals and anthologies in the United States. In addition, she received Poet Magazine's 1996 Iva Mary Williams Poetry Award.*

*Currently, she is the editor of the* Asian Pacific American Journal *and a contributing editor to* Forkroads *(both publications are literary journals based in New York). In 1997, the Asian American Writers Workshop (New York) will publish* BLACK LIGHTNING, *her collection of essays/interviews with leading Asian American poets. Only two years into literary life, she says she "can't imagine doing anything else but writing, writing and writing."*

*She dedicates "Negros" (an excerpt from a novel-in-progress) to her parents, Filamore and Beatriz Tabios, with a heart-felt though long-forgotten word from the past: Agyamanak.*

# DOLLY RIVERA

## John L. Silva

MARIE AND I, in our pajamas, were playing Monopoly that December night.

It was close to Christmas and the game was one gift we were allowed to open before Christmas Eve. The doorbell rang and Mom and Dad, waiting for the ring, quickly stood up from the living room couch. Mom opened the door and there was Lolo, carrying huge colorfully wrapped boxes. My sister and I immediately looked at each other with big knowing smiles. Lolo was visiting us in San Francisco on his way home to Manila.

Marie was eight years old and I was seven, and our grandfather's gift-giving was legend among the older grandchildren. A visit from Lolo meant gifts no one could equal, not even my parents. Once, I got a radio-controlled ship, a replica of a passenger ship he owned. Another time, it was a bright red push-pedal car with battery-operated headlights. My sister, the first grandchild, would be lavished with not one, but ten dolls at a time with hundreds of custom-made dresses. Elaborate dollhouses crowded her bedroom; numerous cooking sets, jewelry and party dresses were flown in from New York bearing little gift cards with florid notes—mi muneca … little angel—all in Lolo's exquisite handwriting.

So when Lolo walked in with gift boxes towering above his head, Marie and I cheered in delight, jumping up trying to kiss his cheeks.

Following him into the doorway was a demure but elegant-looking woman and a smiling young man in a well-fitted sharkskin suit.

As we kissed Lolo, we couldn't keep our eyes from the lady wearing a knee-length white fur coat, emanating a subtle perfume scent as it softly swayed. She was younger than Lolo, probably as young as my mother. She looked like the movie star, Rita Hayworth, with her mestiza features and her smooth porcelain arms and legs, revealed when Dad helped remove her coat. Her dark brown hair was pulled up into a bun revealing a strand of pearls on her neck.

Lolo introduced Miss Dolores Rios as his secretary. I didn't believe it. In Manila, I remembered Lola, my grandmother, having a secretary. My uncles too had secretaries in their offices and I didn't recall them ever looking as elegant as Miss Rios. I looked at my mother to find an answer but she turned away, excused herself, and discreetly headed for the kitchen to fetch pastries and coffee. Miss Rios gently tugged and smoothed her skirt downward, raising her neck a little higher, like one being scrutinized.

The guests were ushered into the living room. Miss Rios sat on the edge of the sofa, fumbling with her cigarette case and her cigarette holder as Marie, with wrinkled brows, circled her. I was too young to think Miss Rios had any deeper relationship with my grandfather, but I did sense she was no secretary.

Lolo introduced us to the young gentleman, Dr. Hector Enriquez, a Cuban veterinarian. Lolo and Miss Rios had come from Cuba as guests of Don Emilio Bacardi. As old friends and sugar plantation owners, Lolo and Don Emilio visited each other's plantations to exchange the best grade of cane stalks to grow on their haciendas. On this trip, Don Emilio presented Lolo with a gift of two Arabian horses. To ensure proper care of the horses in Manila, Don Emilio sent his veterinarian, Dr. Enriquez, along with Lolo and Miss Rios.

Lolo was subdued that evening as he slowly drank his coffee. His double-breasted suit fit perfectly with his wide shoulders even as he sat on the sofa. Lolo was a dresser; years later, his tailor would recount the hours he spent kneeling beside Lolo who posed before a mirror until he was satisfied with the fall of his pants.

Lolo had drawn my mother to his side and they spoke almost in a whisper as Dad entertained Miss Rios and Dr. Enriquez. Mom was his eldest daughter, the rebellious one who decided to leave the comforts of plantation living and go with my father and us children to live in the United States. We had been away over two years and Lolo, missing his favorite daughter, made San Francisco a stopping point for his trips so he could see Mom.

From his weary eyes, I sensed Lolo was unhappy. His lips, pulled back and downward, affecting a slightly sour smile, was a Loreto family trademark indicating a discontent, a loathing for mundane matters. My granduncles and grandaunts have his smile. My great-grandmother had this smile. I never heard any of my relatives raise their voices at the servants; but when they displayed this peculiarly false smile accompanied by a slow heaving of the chest and an exasperated sigh, the servants knew to tread very lightly with their slippers around the house that day.

Lolo was sighing that night as he whispered to my Mom who bent over him. At moments, he would raise his voice just a bit for me to catch the phrase: "Ay, hija, that mother of yours ..."

After several hours of coffee and dessert, and with Lolo looking more relieved and unburdened, the visitors prepared to leave. Lolo secured the promises from my sister and me not to open his gifts till Christmas. Outside, in the thick fog, a limousine waited to drive them to the airport.

That was the last time I saw my grandfather. Eight months later, he died in an explosion in his steel mill on the day of its inauguration. On that day, there was a crowd of government officials, businessmen and the press, assembled early in the morning to witness the opening of the first steel plant in the country. From an old newspaper photo, a severe-looking Don Juan Loreto, in a white suit, is posed beside a priest in front of a ribbon waiting to be cut at the entrance of a huge plant.

The engineers operating the plant were late and couldn't be found. In his impatience, Lolo cut the ribbon, and with the priest in the crowd following, walked to the console room and pushed buttons to turn the plant on. The vats of molten steel creaked, shook violently, and there was an explosion. The crowd ran away except Lolo who stumbled and was showered with hot sparks. Lolo lived another week until he finally died of first degree burns.

Several months later, our family returned to Manila, Mom and Dad called to help run Lolo's business empire. We lived in a new sprawling ranch house in Forbes Park bought by Lolo before he died. Lola lived in another new house in the neighboring subdivision of San Lorenzo.

*

It was one of those very hot afternoons when the dangling tamarind fruits on the tree by the verandah were oozing with sap. There were occasional snores coming from some parts of the house as everyone took their siesta. Old Gorio and I were the only ones awake, seated on the verandah, catching a rare breeze. Gorio had been Lolo's personal driver for so many years and I asked him, very curiously, why Lolo and Lola had separate houses. Hesitatingly, he answered in a low voice that the house we were living in was originally for Dolly Rivera, Lolo's friend.

"I was with your Lolo when he met Dolly," Gorio recounted, "just before the war started. There was a nightclub at the boulevard called The Nile where you could meet the most beautiful women. Every night, private planes would arrive in Manila, carrying Hong Kong taipans, rajahs and Japanese tycoons. They came to see Dolly. She entertained them but she gave her heart to your Lolo, Don Juan."

Gorio paused, closed his eyes, tilted his face upward and, as if remembering a beatific vision, described how Dolly scandalized Manila with the slinky revealing dresses she wore. He boasted how she had no qualms seeking him outside the nightclub or at the bar, and while the drivers and sultans looked on, would softly ask: was he comfortable, did the bartender serve him, was Don Juan happy or sad that evening. He described the lascivious eyes of doormen and bodyguards when he opened the car door and Dolly would alight, her flawless translucent legs and thighs revealed for an instant. Gorio made a clucking sound as he bent lower and spoke in a whisper, telling me how hard it was to drive when you could see in the rear view mirror, Dolly's ravishing eyes gazing at Don Juan as they embraced in the back seat of the car. I remembered how a woman once looked at Lolo that way. I knew then that Dolly was the Miss Rios I had met in San Francisco.

"What made her fall in love with Lolo?" I asked.

"Among all the men that courted Dolly, your Lolo was a gentleman who gave her cariño. The others wanted Dolly so they could show her off. Not your Lolo; he treated her con mucho respeto. Dolly was also proud to be seen with your Lolo because he wore the most expensive Americanas. But in the end, it was his dancing that won her over. Everyone in Manila knew your Lolo, after President Quezon, was the best tango dancer. When he led Dolly on to the dance floor, everyone stopped and moved to the sides to give them the whole floor. Their cheeks were pressed to one another as their feet, in perfect precision, glided together. The crowd in turn stooped, eyeing their feet intently, hoping to catch a new step, a bend, a twirl that Don Juan Loreto picked up on his latest trip to Cuba. There was one tango hit, a hit then in Manila—"El Dia Que Me Quiero"—it was your Lolo's Favorite."

Gorio stood up and with one arm curved holding an imaginary partner and the other outstretched, he began to slowly pace the marble verandah as he hummed the song.

"When the tango came to the final refrain, everyone in The Nile would sing it:

*On the night that you love me,*
*the stars would look at us jealously from the sky.*

"Your Lolo and Dolly would make a final twirl, and with your grandfather's hand clutching her waist, Dolly's head and chest would snap backwards while Don Juan's face would stop inches away from her heaving breasts. They froze in that position for a long time as the crowd cheered and clapped."

Gorio, his body arched forward motionless in the same description as my grandfather, slowly came to life and he looked at me wistfully, hoping to see Lolo's soul appear out of my body.

"It was like that every night in The Nile. Don Juan would sit me at the bar, give me all the pesos in his pocket and I watched him dance with Dolly for hours. I knew it was morning when the Chinese vendors with their newly baked breakfast breads crept into the nightclub to watch Don Juan and Dolly still dancing. Yes, every night, it was like this. When your Lola would go gambling, your Lolo and I would be in The Nile. Your Lolo lived for Dolly and tango."

*

I grew up, with Lolo slowly, slowly turning into a diminished memory brought up only during Christmas or birthdays when my cousins and I would recall the bounty of gifts we once received. Our grandfather's empire was fast being dismantled as haciendas and companies were sold to sustain a family incapable of business. Lola continued to gamble and a sole male uncle enjoyed the company of businessmen. The three daughters, including my mother—never groomed for empire building—attended board meetings only to collect the requisite per diems, which they called "shopping money." If there was a lingering remembrance of Lolo's legacy, it was that the family sustained a comfortable existence, shorn of excesses, only because there was so much of Lolo's empire to squander.

Lola, despite her house being transformed daily into a casino, became the abiding widow and the only hint of any pining for lost romance were the tawdry novels stacked on a side table at the foot of her bed. That and the occasional trips to downtown Manila to watch racy movies with me, the oldest grandson, now in high school, as escort. One afternoon, after watching *From Here to Eternity* with Burt Lancaster and Deborah Kerr, we were being driven home to Makati, past wide stretches of grassy fields, when Lola let out a deep lament saying, "I wish I had more time to be with your Lolo."

This was the chance to ask her side of Lolo's affair.

"Lola," I gently started, "did it hurt you to know that Lolo had another woman?"

There was a long silence and then I heard the soft tinkling of her silver rosary as she slowly pulled it out of her purse and began rolling each bead between her fingers.

"Hijo, there was nothing I could do," her voice resigned. "Your Lolo was a man and I had to accept it. Just as I accepted having to marry him when our parents saw how much bigger joining their haciendas would be if we married. I had to learn to love your Lolo. When I began to love him, it was ten years later and by then, he had fallen in love with that woman. I gave him children, I gave him a son, but the affection, the cariño that I had to learn—since no one taught me that—came too late."

\*

Pulling her shawl tighter around her as the air conditioner turned the car into a little freezer on that evening drive, Lola continued: "Even in the most difficult times, your Lolo was already distant from me. We were living in Baguio during the war, when one day, leaflets rained down from the airplanes of the Americanos warning us to leave the city because they were going to bomb it. Your Lolo quickly hired Igorot mountain guides to lead us down the mountains to Lingayen where we heard the Americanos would be landing."

"Your Lolo hired two sets of guides, one for our family and the other for Dolly. When your Lolo and I, with the children and the maids, walked down the mountain trail, Dolly, with the other guide and her maids followed some distance away.

"These were frightening times, hiding from the Japanese soldiers who were desperate, shooting and bayoneting anyone they saw as they retreated from the lowlands and into the mountains. At some point, your Lolo would lag behind and I would plead with him not to go to her because we were afraid to be without him. But he calmed me, assuring me the guide was capable and careful. He would join Dolly to walk a few hours with her. At night, thinking I was asleep, he would softly creep away from our camp to join Dolly. We reached Lingayen after a week of walking and I knew then my bitter fate."

She gathered her rosary, kissed it, inserted it in her purse and sighed, I wonder if your Lolo ever learned to love me."

*

Every year, there was a gathering of relatives and family friends to remember the anniversary of Lolo's death. After a morning Mass, everyone congregated at Lola's house for breakfast. Around the long dining table, with Lola at the head, the visitors would outdo each other reminiscing about Lolo and assuring Lola:

"Yes, yes, absolutamente, Nena, Juanito revered you ..."

"It's true, Nena, he was devoted to the familia ..."

"A saint ... that's what he was, Nena, a saint ..."

The conversation on the patio by the garage where drivers congregated was more interesting. Each driver outdid the other by relaying the gossip their Dons and Doñas murmured to each other in their cars before arriving at the house. *The explosion was no accident*, everyone agreed. *It was suicide*, that sentence repeated over and over as the servants around the drivers made quick signs of the cross and groaned. *Dolly was leaving him and he did not care to live any more. He was not impatient that day the plant was open. He no longer had reason to live.*

Pidiong, our long-time gardener, would have the last say with the story he repeated to the drivers at every reunion. He was in the family mausoleum several days after Lolo's funeral, cleaning the grounds. Dolly appeared in black with a mantilla covering her face. She laid a bouquet of flowers and a note which Pidiong kept and showed, again and again, to his yearly audience. In edgy handwriting, it read, "Amor, lo siento."

No one would hear from Dolly again.

\*

My own life, like that of my rebellious mother, changed a decade later. I was in Berkeley in 1972, a new member of the Brigada Venceremos, the yearly group of North American radicals who travelled to Cuba to cut cane during the sugar harvest or build houses in a show of solidarity with their revolution.

I was a leftist, opposed to Martial Law declared that year in the Philippines, and searching for alternative political systems. Cuba intrigued me; it grew sugar, just like my home province of Negros. But the country provided free education to all the children of cane cutters, a superior health system to anything in Latin America, and job guarantees that the rich in

Negros would not have thought of nor considered.

I grew up knowing the family's wealth had much to do from taking so much from the cane cutters and their families with so little return. My cousin once reminded me of an accident that made me decide never to return for summer vacations to the family hacienda, San Vicente. I was ten years old, reading one afternoon on the patio, when I heard a voice wailing at the entrance gates. I walked to the gate and found a woman kneeling beside a cardboard box containing her dead baby. She was pleading with the plantation manager to lend her a jeep to take her and the box to a cemetery in town. The manager refused, demanding payment, which she didn't have. She cried louder and the manager had the guards force her to leave so as not to bother our family from our siesta. I remember the woman looking at me, hoping perhaps I would intervene but I stood there, paralyzed, wondering why one jeep, one we used for picnicking at the beach or hunting the mountains or driving to a fiesta couldn't be used for this woman who needed to bury her baby? That moment and a few other incidents made me disavow my privileged life, of which, by a fluke in history, I was on the receiving end.

There were 140 Brigaditas on this three-month long trip. We were to build one and two bedroom family houses for a new dairy cooperative located forty minutes from Havana. We worked every day, Mondays through Saturdays, waking early at dawn; then we were given breakfast with a shot of Cuban espresso, and, with hardhats on our heads, we were trucked to the site where we slowly fitted concrete slabs into sidings to form houses.

The Cubans working on my team and our jefe took a liking to me because I was Filipino. Drilled from childhood about U.S. Imperialist history, the Cubanos singled me out from the other Brigadista as a compañero, who, along with Puerto Ricans shared a common history of revolts against Spanish and U.S. colonialists.

On our free Sundays, we were loaded onto buses to enjoy a day at the beach or visit historical sites. One day, our camp interpreter, Juan Romero, who had lived most of his life in New York but returned after the revolution, came to me suggesting that on my next free weekend, I should go to Havana and look up his Filipina friend, a fellow interpreter working at the Havana Libre. Her name, he said, was Delia Enriquez.

The following weekend, I decided to visit Juan's friend. I looked forward to traveling to Havana on my own. On previous bus trips to that city along with the Brigadistas, I felt a special kinship to Havana. Parts of old downtown section where finely dressed residents strode about with inflated gestures and boisterous sounds, rekindled childhood memories of vivacious fair-skinned Filipinas chattering only in Spanish in old Manila's pasticerias.

I wanted to look good and blend in, like a Cuban dandy on a solitary furlough to Havana. I had been in grimy T-shirt and construction boots for the whole week. That day, I wore a white tropical suit and a pair of two-tone shoes. Wearing a Panama hat, I hitched a bus ride to Havana, dropped on the Malecon and walked the bayside toward the imposing skyscraper of the Hilton Hotel.

The hotel lobby still retained its opulent Miami-look with hanging chandeliers, 50's torch light sconces and bright pink lounging sofas slightly frayed but unchanged since the last American gangster sat on them. A sleepy-eyed receptionist directed me to the translator's office down the hallway where I would find Mrs. Enriquez.

Entering the office with empty desks still neatly flushed to one side of the row. I noticed a woman seated at her desk at the very end of the row. As I walked towards her, passing posters of Cuban beaches and Che Guevara, the woman slowly looked up at me, opened her mouth wide and began to gasp. She grabbed her eyeglasses hanging on a chain from her neck and squinted hard through it. With one hand to her mouth, she let out muffled scream. Shaking her head, as if in disbelief, she bolted up, backing away only to be stopped by the wall behind her.

"JOHNNY ... JOHNNY LORETO! Could that be you?" she cried hoarsely.

"No, I'm not Johnny," I reeled back, surprised by her words. "I am John. John Silva. John Loreto Silva. Johnny Loreto was my grandfather."

She looked me up and down, mouth agape, while it dawned on me that I had met this woman years back, as a little boy in San Francisco. Lines traced her forehead and under her eyes. The sheer porcelain face I remembered was now sheened with a layer of makeup. Her hair was stiffly teased. The perfume scent though, was unmistakable. She was Miss Rios. Dolly Rivera. Despite the years, she remained as beautiful as when I first saw her.

With her arms locked in mine, we walked aimlessly for hours in downtown Havana. She alternated in her astonishment, looking at me, renewing her amazement, murmuring "Como Johnny," and gazing at the top of palm trees, at the sky, trancelike, to a distant memory.

We wandered to the Malecon and found a long empty stretch of a concrete sea wall, which we clambered on to sit. It was close to sunset and she was at ease, expansive about her absent years.

Shortly after visiting us in San Francisco, Dolly returned to Manila and began a secret love affair with Dr. Enriquez. A servant of Dolly revealed the affair to Lolo but he didn't confront her. Instead, he thought it best that their relationship die a natural death so he could reassume the obligatory and respectable role of a family man. But Lola, busy with mahjong tiles and the monte cards, had long ago decided to give Lolo his freedom.

Lolo was despondent and, by the time his steel mill was ready for operation, had become suicidal.

"I was with Johnny that morning before he went to the steel mill," Dolly reflected as she gazed at the golden sea. "He was angry with me because I had been with Hector at The Nile night before. A friend of his had seen us dancing and told him. He was deeply hurt; I was bold enough to be seen cavorting and dancing with someone in his employ. If I have to have an affair, he wanted me to have some amor propio and not let all of Manila know. I told him I no longer wanted to be a querida. I was growing old waiting each night for his phone calls, wondering when I would see him. The gossip columns called me 'Madame X with expensive tastes.' No matter how well your grandfather treated me, no matter all the fine things he gave me, I was still the high-class puta from The Nile for as long as I was his querida. I told him Hector had proposed to marry me and I had accepted. When he left me that morning, I had a fearful sense he would hurt himself."

As I stared at the setting sun, I thought of the drivers meeting in the garage. They were right. My distraught Lolo, not caring much, had the temperature raised in the vats with molten steel, unmindful of the consequences.

Dolly received a sizeable insurance claim from Lolo's estate and with Hector, moved to Hong Kong and were married. A year later, they moved to Cuba, just months before the revolution. When Fidel Castro entered Havana, Hector, a Batista follower, was arrested and shot in El Morro, the fortress prison, at the end of the Malecon.

In the years that ensued, there were opportunities for Dolly to leave Cuba, but she stayed on. I looked at her face now tinted golden from the dying sun. She straightened her back and raised her neck.

"The Revolution said I was a New Woman under socialism. Here, I drove a tractor during sugar harvest. I joined the Literacy Brigade and walked up the mountains teaching English to the campesinos. Now I'm an interpreter. One time I even accompanied Fidel to Europe to interpret for him. What could there have been for me in Manila?" She shrugged and laughed. "Nothing but be an old puta."

Havana was illuminated with lights when I told Dolly that I had to return to camp. She persuaded me to stay in the city one night, promising me a room at the Libre. We agreed to meet for dinner that evening.

I almost didn't recognize Dolly at the hotel lobby when

we met again. She had changed into a clinging red cocktail dress and her hair was combed loose to one side, showing off a large pearl earring studded with diamonds, a gift from Lolo. Her face glistened with excitement as she took my arm and we walked to a nearby restaurant.

Over dinner I asked her everything she knew about Lolo. She regaled me with stories about how fastidious a dresser he was, how he charmed the women and how shrewd he was in business.

After dinner, Dolly took me to the Tropicana to watch a Las Vegas-like revue of skimpily-clad women, wearing feather headdresses and sequined suits. It was close to midnight when the show ended but Dolly continued to be radiant, ordering another round of drinks, eager to hear more stories about my family and how Manila had changed. Tango music came on and her eyes lit up and a sensuous smile appeared on her face.

"Ah," she sighed, her head leaning back. "Volver. Johnny and I used to dance to this. Come, dance with me."

"I don't know how to dance the tango."

"Just follow me; you carry yourself muy fino, like your grandfather. Therefore you can dance."

Holding her hand, she led me to the center of the outdoor dancing floor. Naked colored bulbs swaying from an evening breeze criss-crossed above us. Dolly pressed her body to mine and from the feel of her thighs, I followed her feet as we moved slowly on the dance floor. The movements, the turns, at first abrupt, began to flow as I understood each gesture from her body and her longing gaze.

"Oh, Johnny, dear Johnny, lo siento," she softly whispered as she clung to me. "Allow me my fantasia tonight, por favor. Let me pay my respetos to the man who taught me how to love and how to tango."

She gently rested her head on my shoulder and as our steps moved in unison, she sang the tango's lyrics:

*"I suppose the lights blinking in the distance*

*and marking my return are the ones that illuminated*
*my hours of deep despair.*
*Although I did not wish to come back,*
*One always returns to the first love."*

**Bio:** *The son of Ilonggo and Ilocano parents, John L. Silva migrated to the US in 1971. A vocal critic of the Marcos dictatorship, Silva was included in the infamous "black list" of eighty US-based Filipinos, preventing Silva from returning to the Philippines at the time. While in exile, Silva opposed the Marcos regime's human rights violations and wrote many articles denouncing Marcos and his policies.*

*Silva earned his MA in Philippine-American History at Goddard Cambridge. He has worked as the executive director of GCHP, a San Francisco-based organization that managed education and health care programs among Asians and Pacific Islanders infected with HIV. Silva has done advocacy work for increased AIDS funding. He was also former associate and advertising director of US-based* Filipinas Magazine. *In 1996, John Silva returned to the Philippines to manage the Geronimo Berenguer de los Reyes Foundation Museum.*

# OF MIDGETS AND
# BEAUTIFUL COUSINS

## Veronica Montes

"WHERE ARE we going, Beto?" my sister asks. She squeezes my arm with her small, pretty hand.

She is seventeen and beautiful. Our cousin Beto, with his dark eyes and smooth light brown skin is beautiful, too. I watch him bring a cigarette to his lips. His lips are always moist like peeled white grapes.

"Just this club I know," he says. His accent is gentle on my ear, not the kind that makes the people at home whisper and laugh. He has always lived here and keeps disappointing my sister by not being interested in her stories about our life in San Francisco or our trips to New York and Los Angeles. He likes Spain, he says, and travels there to watch soccer games and buy decent shoes. Beto is twenty years old, and he is angry with his mother, I know, for making him show us around.

Yesterday afternoon two of his friends came to the house and sat outside in the garden drinking cold San Miguel beer and waiting to catch a glimpse of my sister, who claimed she had a headache and refused to come downstairs. She sent me instead. They were skinny and well-dressed and smelled clean, like freshly bathed and powdered children. They were brothers, maybe.

After a polite introduction, I sat for fifteen minutes before anyone spoke to me again. "You're American?" they asked.

"Filipino," I had answered, confused by the question. They leaned back in their chairs and burst out laughing. Beto joined in, shaking his head. They elbowed each other in the ribs, releasing quick, unrecognizable words whenever they could stop laughing long enough to say something. I ran inside the house and up the stairs to my sister's room, one of the many guest rooms, where she sat in front of the mirror, arranging and re-arranging her perfection. She gave me a quick hug and told me to never mind, but I did. They didn't even try not to laugh.

My sister again. "Come on, Beto, what's it called?"

"Small World."

"Like the ride at Disneyland?"

*

I've never been to a nightclub. Earlier tonight my sister put blush on my cheeks and lined my eyes saying, "This is so much fun!" every few minutes. But before we left, Beto turned to me and wiped the back of his hand across each side of my face. He took his handkerchief, sweet and musky, and blotted my lips. Then he pushed me out the door without saying a word, the tips of his fingers tangled in the ends of my hair.

My sister talks without stopping, jumping from subject to subject without any response from Beto. He is rude, but in a courteous way. He finally shows some interest when she shares her favorite story about me. She does it really well this time, going into great detail about the exact expression on my face when I jumped from my seat and ran out of the movie theatre crying. "All he did was try to touch her, you know, down there," she says. She thinks that's why, but it isn't. It wasn't so much the touching part; it was that he stuck his tongue in my ear and whispered, "Do Filipino girls really taste like fish? *Do they?*"

Beto just smiles and throws his cigarette out the window, looking at me for a second and then fixing his eyes on the road. My sister laughs and gives me a quick hug. Sitting between them, I am very quiet.

*

I once read a travel brochure that described Manila as the "pearl of Southeast Asia," and cited its excellent shopping opportunities and "graceful, dark-eyed women with tapering limbs" as reasons. But it forgot to mention a lot of things. Like the whole army of little boys in bare feet who run between the cars on busy streets selling chewing gum and cigarettes by the stick. Or the old women trying to trade bunches of small white flowers for the change in your pocket. They tap their dirty fingers on the car windows and smile, flashing rotten teeth. My sister laughs when I get scared or when I roll down the window to hand them money.

There was a time, just a few years ago, when I was too scared to come here. My cousins huddled together and told stories about wicked nuns and family ghosts, but it was the ones about the marketplace that made me sick and sent me running to my father.

At the open market chickens had their heads chopped off and their bodies ran in circles, spraying blood like a fountain from their necks. Dark, skinny thieves sliced off your fingers to steal your pretty rings, and half-naked beggars clutched at your clothes until you handed them coins. My sister never listened to those stories. She only heard the ones about no drinking age, dancing all night, maids and drivers, clothes made-to-order.

That's why we're here.

It is starting to rain.

*

Beto pulls into an alley already filled with cars and opens our door. My sister hesitates, worried about the effect the rain will have on her hair. "Did you bring an umbrella, Beto?" she says. He doesn't answer, so I push her gently.

Everything smells like rain. My cousin and his navy blue linen blazer, this alley, even the heat, the kind that crawls along your skin and makes you itch. The drops are warm against my face, my bare arms, my tongue. Beto leads us quickly through the parked cars and up the street, stopping abruptly at a large door. Above it, the words "Small World" flash in a pink and green neon circle that's supposed to look like a globe. When I put my hand against the door, I feel the music vibrate right through. Beto waits for me to move away, and then he pulls it open.

My sister's brown-green eyes narrow as she looks around. Then she runs a hand through her hair and pretends, very hard, to look bored. Red, blue, yellow lights crisscross the ceiling, and the music thumps inside me like it's looking for a way out. Which is probably why my mouth is open. "Stop it," my sister says, pinching my arm. Cigarette smoke burns the corners of my eyes and gets trapped in my hair. It is crowded and sticky. I thought there would be more room.

"Three!" my cousin yells, but he sounds so far away. He grabs my hand and pulls me forward roughly. When he is certain that I'm following right behind him, he drops my hand, and I feel the way I did the first time I climbed a tree and was too scared to work my way back down. I reach under his blazer and grab one of his belt loops.

After a while, my eyes adjust. I see tiny people. Midgets. All over the place. There—near the door where we came in and cracking ice behind the bar. They must be standing on something behind there. Bringing drinks to the tables, sitting on stools and smoking in the dark corners, their faces sometimes hidden, sometimes brightly lit by the passing lights. Giant heads. They have giant heads. At the table next to ours, though, there are people who look like us. On the dance floor and up on the stage singing, too: *Come sail away, come sail away, come and sail away with me.* To my sister, this is a joke. She's laughing out loud at the tiny people with the gigantic heads. Beto is laughing on the inside.

I think I'm the only one who sees the midgets. Now that the surprise has worn off, my sister doesn't pay any more attention to them. She keeps looking over at one of the mestizos at the table across from us—the only one not staring at her—and bouncing her head softly to the music.

Beto hasn't said a word except to order drinks from our midget waiter, who wears black high top tennis shoes and speaks broken English in a voice so low it seems not to come from him. His buckteeth are yellow, and they hang neatly over his thick, black-cherry colored lower lip. Quick, blinking eyes and a carefully ironed Coca-Cola tee shirt give him an alert, eager look. I have been staring at him, and he stops listening to Beto for a moment and looks right at me. I should turn away, but I don't until my sister finally kicks me under the table. She raises one eyebrow and looks at me like I'm crazy. Before the midget goes, he whispers something in Beto's ear, and my cousin smiles and nods.

The girl on stage has long hair that swishes around her waist when she spins. Her dress is white and tight, cut low in front, covered with sequins. She sings corny Barry Manilow ballads and old Motown hits while the lights bounce off of her and right into my eyes. Some American army guys—four white, two black—sit at the table right in front of her yelling things like, "Sing for me, baby," and telling her she's beautiful, over and over again. She smiles and shakes a finger at them like they're naughty little boys.

My sister's conquest appears in front of us and asks Beto's permission to dance with her. She loves the ceremony, I can tell. She keeps her eyes lowered the whole time like a geisha girl in a lousy movie, and while I wonder where she learned to do that, I watch my cousin. He takes a long look at the guy: at his thick hair, his expensive watch, the pleats in his plants, and finally his shoes. Then he says, "Okay, sure." My sister winks at me and puts her purse on my lap. Then she disappears into the crowd and resurfaces on the dance floor.

Our waiter is returning, holding a tray with three glasses on it high above his large head. "Scoose me, scoose me." I can't hear him, but I know this is what he's saying as he professionally maneuvers his way to our table. Something pink for my sister, tequila with lime for Beto, and Coke with a cherry in it for me. Out of the corner of my eye, I see my cousin steal the cherry and pop it in his mouth, but it's okay. He tosses the stem to the floor.

A tap on my shoulder. It's Beto. I turn to him and lean in.

"Someone would like to meet you," he shouts above the music.

The midget waiter stands next to Beto with both hands behind his back. He is now wearing a red silk scarf around his neck. It is tied into a neat knot. I look from the midget to my cousin and then to the midget again. "This is Noel." He places a hand on Noel's shoulder and pushes him forward a little. "And Noel, this is my cousin. From the States."

Noel whips his right hand out from behind his back with a graceful flourish. I feel my face getting hot. I hold the Coke to my cheek and then I take a sip. I look around for my sister. Above Noel's head I can see my cousin's eyes, squinting encouragement. Finally, I grab Noel's small, fat hand in my own and shake it. I nod. I try to think of something to say, but I can't. Beto sends Noel away and looks at me. I drink my Coke and tear my cocktail napkin into little pieces.

He lights another cigarette.

My sister is back, cheeks flushed and lipstick faded. "Oh my God, that guy is so cute," she says, fanning herself with his handkerchief. "He told me to keep this," she says, holding it out to me. When I don't take it, she shrugs and presses it to her nose. She closes her eyes and takes a deep breath. "Can you believe it?" she says. When no one answers her she says extra loud, "Hello? Did I miss something?"

"We're leaving now," Beto says. He puts some money on the table. Way too much, I think.

"We practically just got here." My sister's whine makes him flinch. I'm embarrassed for her. He is putting out his cigarette, but stops mid-motion and simply stares at her. He offers his hand to help me out of my chair and after a second, I take it. He doesn't let go, even after I stand up. I look up at him, and he's about to say something, but doesn't.

Outside it's still raining and the insides of my ears throb. My sister is silent, pouting. Beto is a few steps ahead, his hands stuck deep in his pockets, staring at the ground as he walks. Then, from somewhere behind us, I hear a low-pitched scream that gets higher and higher as it continues. We spin around, all three of us, and Beto's hand grips my shoulder. My sister grabs my arm. Someone is running towards us, umbrella in hand. It's a child, maybe. No, a midget. One of those midgets. As it gets closer, I see the red scarf, now tied around his head. Noel the midget. I try to run, but Beto holds me steady.

"Mees! Mees!" Noel shrieks. His eyes bulge. He looks like a fish.

My sister is in hysterics. She's bent over laughing and says, "Oh my God," over and over again. She even stamps her feet.

Noel is in front of me now, jumping frantically, umbrella held high in an effort to keep me dry.

"Mees, don't get wet," he says, forming each word carefully. He is smiling as he jumps, all his yellow teeth showing. I try to accommodate him by bending down a little. He is walking with us to the car, jumping to keep the umbrella over my head, and running to keep up with my walking. Beto is behind us somewhere.

It feels like we'll never get there. I think this midget will follow me forever, like some kind of living souvenir. But finally we're at the car, and Beto unlocks the back door and tells my laughing sister to get in. He opens the front door for me, waits until I get settled, locks the door, and shuts it quietly. My sister is talking to me about something, but I don't hear her because I'm watching my cousin place some coins in Noel's hand. Coins for protecting me from the rain.

**Bio** *of Veronica Montes: I was born in San Francisco in 1967 to overly kind parents and two highly amusing older brothers. We lived down the block from my Lolo and Lola and on many weekends our entire clan gathered from various points around the Bay Area, moving back and forth between the two houses while they ate and gossiped and ate some more. It is their stories, voices and faces that inspire my fiction.*

*I am a graduate of San Francisco State University where, one memorable semester, author and teacher Jeffrey Paul Chan was nice enough to encourage my writing. He published my first story in the* Yellow Journal, *a publication of the Asian American Studies Department. Since then, my short fiction has appeared in* Prism International *and* Furious Fictions.

*After having lived in Vancouver, British Columbia and Washington D.C., my husband Andrew and I now split out time between Santa Barbara and San Francisco.*

# FLIP GOTHIC

Cecilia Manguerra Brainard

DEAR MAMA,

Thank you for agreeing to have Mindy. Jun and I just don't know what to do with her. I'm afraid if we don't intervene, matters will get worse. Mia, her Japanese American friend, had to be sent to a drug rehab place. You'd met her when you were here; she's the tiny girl who got into piercing; she had a nose ring, a belly ring—and something in her tongue. Her parents are distraught; they don't know what they've done, if they're to blame for Mia's problem. I talked to Mia's Mom yesterday and Mia's doing all right; she's writing angry poetry but is getting over the drug thing, thank God.

There's so much anger in these kids, I can't figure it out. They have everything—all the toys, clothes, computer games and whatever else they've wanted. I didn't have half the things these kids have; and Jun and I had to start from scratch in this country—you know that. That studio we had near the hospital was really tiny and I had to do secretarial work while Jun completed his residency. Everything we own—this house, our cars, our vacation house in Connecticut—we've had to slave for. I don't understand it; these kids have everything served to them in a silver platter and they're angry.

We're sure Mindy's not into drugs—she may have tried marijuana, but not the really bad stuff. We're worried though that she might eventually experiment with that sort of thing. If she continues running around with these kids, it's bound to happen. What made us decide to send her there was this business of not going to school. Despite everything, Mindy had always been a good student, but this school year, things went haywire. This was what alerted us, actually, when the principal told us she hadn't been to school for two weeks. We thought the worst but it turned out she and her friends had been hanging out at Barnes and Noble. It's just a bookstore; it's not a bad place, but obviously she should have gone to school. We had to do something. Sending her to the Philippines was all I could think of.

She'll be arriving Ubec on Wednesday, 10:45 a.m. on PAL flight 101. Ma, don't be shocked, but her hair is purple. Jun has been trying to convince her to dye her hair black, for your sake at least, but Mindy doesn't even listen. Jun has had a particularly difficult time dealing with the situation. It's not easy for him to watch his daughter "go down the drain," as he calls it. He feels he has failed not only as a father but as a doctor.

It's true that it's become impossible to reason with Mindy, but I've told him to let the hair go, to pick his battles so to speak. But he gets terribly frustrated. He can't stand the purple hair; he can't stand the black lipstick—yes, she uses black lipstick—and the black clothes and boots and metal. I've explained to him that it's just a fad. Gothic, they call it. I personally think it looks dreadful. I can't stand the spikes around her neck; but there are more important things, like school or her health. She's just gotten over not eating. That was another thing her friends got into—not eating. Why eat dead cows? Mindy would say. She was into tofu and other strange looking things. For months, she wasn't eating and had gotten very thin, we finally had to bring her to a doctor (very humbling for Jun). The doctor suggested a therapist. One hundred seventy-five dollars an hour. She had several sessions then Mindy got bored and started eating once again. She's back to her usual weight, but well, the hair and clothing might scare you, so I'm writing ahead of time to prepare you.

Thanks once again Ma, for everything, and I hope and pray that she doesn't give you the kind of trouble she's been giving us.

Your daughter,

Nelia

*

Dear Nelia,

She had blue hair, not purple. Arminda explained that she had gone out with her friends and found blue dye—obviously you were unaware of this. She brought several boxes of dye, including bottles of peroxide. Can you imagine—peroxide—what if the bottles broke in her suitcase? Apparently, she has to remove color from her hair before dying it blue. The whole process sounds terribly violent on the hair, but I didn't say anything; I didn't want to start off on the wrong foot.

Arminda arrived an hour late-PAL, you know how that airline is. She was not wearing boots; she had left them in New York, she explained, and was wearing white platform shoes instead. It's an understatement to say that operations at Ubec Airport came to a halt when people caught sight of her. People around here like to say Ubec is now cosmopolitan, with our five-star hotels, our discos and our share of Japanese tourists, but it will always retain its provincial qualities. When I saw

Arminda—blue hair, black clothes, sling bag, platform shoes—
I was not sure Ubec is ready for Arminda. I had to remind
myself that I survived World War Two and therefore will
survive Arminda.

Indeed she is rebellious. It does no good to tell her
what to do; in fact she goes out of her way to do exactly the
opposite of what you say. I have placed her in your old room
and have stopped entering the room because the disorder is
too much for me to take. Clothes all over the bed and dresser
chair, and scattered all over the floor as well. One cannot walk
a straight line in that room. There was also the business of blue
dye all over the bathroom. The maid Ising spent one whole
afternoon scrubbing the tiles with muriatic acid to remove the
stains.

Her language is foul, her behavior appalling. I will not
pretend that it's been easy having Arminda here. I try to give
her a lot of leeway because she is just fifteen and doesn't know
any better, but having her here has been purgatory.

Frankly, Nelia, I blame you and Jun for all this. If she
had been trained properly, if she had been taught right from
wrong, she would not be this incorrigible brat. Forgive me, but
I don't know what else to call this willful, mouthy, and arrogant
child. I have repeatedly called your attention: I have warned
you that that child will bring to your knees if you don't
discipline her. But all I heard from you and Jun was: Ma, don't
be old-fashioned; this is the American way. Here now is the
result of your American experiment. My words have proved
prophetic, have they not? There is some poetic justice in all
this: your daughter has finally shown you the pain parents
endure, as I have endured on account of you. I am still trying
to figure out why you left for America when you had a good
life here. You parroted all the clichés about America—
freedom, quality, human rights, opportunities—well, obviously
you have learned that clichés are just that.

I am not enjoying rubbing it in and pray she can still be
saved. And I also pray that you and Jun can alter your ways.
You two have become too American for your own good. This

has contributed to the problem. You have spoiled her. You yourself admit you have given her everything. Every material things, perhaps, but not a good sense of herself. It is clear this child is terribly insecure, that she does not like herself. Coloring her hair, this outrageous get-up—she is simply hiding behind all these.

Another thing, you do not even keep an altar in your home; and even though you go to church when I visit you in New York, I am well aware that you do not always go to Mass on Sundays. Despite all your wealth your family does not have a solid foundation, so there you are. But let us drop the matter for the moment. After all, you and Jun are paying for your mistakes, and I can only hope that it is not too late.

Let me resume my report on Arminda.

Arminda has been so disagreeable, the kids of Ricardo dislike her intensely. I hoped they would all get along and that therefore Arminda could spend time with her cousins. I am old, and my interests and hers are very different. Miriam and Oscar are close to her in age. Unfortunately things didn't work out. In her New York accent Arminda called her cousins backward and ignorant, and therefore they boycotted her. She has only me and the servants who barely speak English. She does not really talk to me but does extend standard cordialities: good morning, Lola, good evening, Lola, at least you have taught her that much.

She is restless; she does not know what to do with herself. She roams around the house and yard. She likes helping the gardener build bonfires in the afternoon; of course her playing with fire makes me nervous so we keep a close eye on her. There is no telling what will enter her mind. In the evening, she watches television. She is constantly flipping the channels, from "Marimar" to CNN, my head spins when I watch TV with her. The maids say she reads and writes when she is in her bedroom. I have suggested that she write you and Jun but she says she will never talk nor write to you.

Obviously, she cannot hang around here forever. I've visited schools around here so she can go to school soon. She will not do at St. Catherine's. The nuns there are as strict today as they had been half a century ago. Ricardo suggests enrolling her in American School. Your brother says American School is more liberal, less traditional; perhaps Arminda will not be so different there.

Oh, another thing, she insists on being called Arminda, not Mindy. She said she has always hated that name; that it reminds her of some dumb television show, "Mork and Mindy."

I will let you know how her schooling goes.

Love and kisses,

Mama

*

Dear Nelia,

Arminda is not in school. I had enrolled her at American School, but the night before she was supposed to go to school, she shaved off her head—the whole thing except for the blue bangs. Even the liberal Americans will not have her. She hated school in New York and will never go to school again, she insists.

I was very angry but have decided not to force her. At any rate, there is no school in Ubec that will take her. The Christmas holidays are almost here, then there's the Sinulog festival; nothing much will be happening in school any way. I have told her that she must spend a few hours reading in our library; your father had many history books and there's the entire collection of the *Encyclopedia Britannica* besides. For once she agreed to something.

Frankly I feel she is unhappy about having shaved her head. She has been wearing that black fedora hat of hers with the veil in front. When she is not in the library, she sulks in her bedroom. I have raised six children and have eleven grandchildren; I know better than to give her attention.

Mama

P.S. I forgot to mention that it had entered her head to dye the hair of my Santo Niño. Since you were an infant, that poor statue has been standing at the landing of our stairs, unmolested; we offer it flowers, we light candles in front of it; we take it out for the parade; the artist Policarpio Lozada carved it from hard yakal wood, which is now impossible to find, and here your daughter comes along and colors its hair bright blue. It looks ridiculous, Nelia—the Child Jesus in red robes with blue hair. When she saw how upset I was, she offered to dye the hair black, but I told her to leave it that way as a reminder to all of what she has done.

I am saying the novena to the Santo Niño, patron saint of lost causes, for your daughter.

*

Dear Nelia,

I don't know if the Santo Niño had something to do with it, but she has discovered the animals. I have three pigs, one enormous black female and two small males that I've earmarked for Christmas lechon. She releases the small ones from their pen in the morning and chases them around. Sometimes I catch her talking to them. The runt, the pink one with freckles down his back, cocks his head to one side and stares at Arminda, as if he is listening. She gets the water hose and hoses them down. The piglets root about and roll around the mud near the water tank, then afterwards, they march back to their pen.

She also plays with my two hens. Abraham had given these to me several months ago, but one day, they started laying eggs and I could not kill them. The chickens run around scot-free and they never learned to lay eggs in a regular place. I'd tried to make nests for them near the garage, but they prefer the many nooks and crannies around the yard. Arminda hunts for the eggs daily. She says the hen that lays brown eggs favors the place under the star apple tree, whereas the hen that lays white eggs lays under the grapefruit tree. She asked the cook to teach her how to prepare the eggs properly so Arminda now knows how to fry eggs, scramble them and make omelettes. This morning, she made me a cheese omelette and she arranged it on the plate with parsley garnish to make it look pretty. She was quite delighted at her creation.

She is really still just a child. I cannot help wondering if your lifestyle there has forced her to grow up too quickly. Your way of life is horrible; when I am there my blood pressure rises from all that hurly-burly. Life does not have to be such a rat race. One ought to "smell the flowers"—as your kitchen poster says.

Love and kisses,

Mama

*

Dear Nelia,

We did not have lechon for Christmas. I had seen it coming. Christmas Eve, when the man I contracted to slaughter and roast the pigs arrived, Arminda begged me not to have the pigs killed. She was in tears. She said she would grow out her hair once again; she promised to behave— anything to save the pigs. Like Solomon I weighed the matter: Christmas meal versus the pigs. I could see that the pigs meant a lot to her, that in fact, the pigs are partly responsible for her more mellow behaviour. In the end I decided to save the pigs. For the first time since her arrival, Arminda kissed me on the cheeks.

She was actually charming to her cousins. We joined

them for midnight Mass at Redemptorist church, then later we gathered at home for the Noche Buena meal. Even without the lechon, there was plenty of food. It's always that way every year, even when you were small, too many rellenos and embotidos; and Ricardo always makes his turkey with that wonderful stuffing. The desserts are another whole story: sans rival, tocino del cielo, meringue, mango chiffon cake, maja blanca, all way to the humble sab-a bananas rolled with sugar.

I don't know if it was a joke but Miriam and Oscar gave her a black wig. Arminda removed her hat, tried on the wig and kept it on the whole night. I was surprised to see that she looks a lot like you.

Arminda gave everyone poems written in calligraphy on parchment paper. I do not know what mine means but it says:

*I fled from you*
*A world away*
*I turn and*
*Find you*
*All around me.*

As usual, she wore black, but this time it was a dress sewn by Vering. It had a nice flowing skirt, and instead of a zipper, the dress had black ribbons that criss-crossed and tied together. She wore black net stockings and black chunky shoes. She continues to wear black lipstick but we have become used to it. Actually we have become used to Arminda and her drama; and I believe she is getting used to us.

I hope your Christmas has been as lovely as ours.

Love and kisses,

Mama

\*

Dear Nelia,

Arminda wanted to know more about the Sinulog festival. People are getting ready for the Sinulog and the Christmas decorations have given away to the banners with the image of the Child Jesus. I explained that even before Christmas days, Ubecans have always celebrated during harvest time. When Christianity was introduced, the statue of the Child Jesus, called the Santo Niño, became the focal point of the festivities. People dance to honor the Child Jesus. In parades, people dance to the beat of the drums. Some people blacken their faces and they wear costumes and dance through the streets of Ubec. People do get drunk and it can get wild sometimes, so one must know where to go; I told her this because I could see her eyes sparkling with interest.

We visited the Child Jesus at the Santo Niño church. I could not help myself -- I pointed out to her that this original statue does *not* have blue hair. Embarrassed, she looked down at her shoes and mumbled that she had offered to dye my statue's hair black. I explained that if we dye the statue's hair from blue to black to God-knows-what-other-color, it will lose all its hair. She apologized once again for having touched my statue. She said this sincerely and I decided to let the matter go.

I related stories instead about the Santo Niño: how the Child gives food to his friends. And I told Arminda of how you were born with beriberi and how I danced to the Child Jesus so that you would be saved.

The last item fascinated her.

"What is beriberi, Lola?" she asked.

"A disease caused by lack of Vitamin B," I said.

"What happened to my Mom?

"She was born near the tail-end of the war, and I had not eaten properly when I carried her. Your mother had edema and nervous disorder. Her eyes were rolled up; she was dying."

"I didn't know my Mom almost died."

"I prayed to the Santo Niño for her life."

"She never told me she was sick when she was a baby."

"Perhaps she did and you didn't listen."

She furrowed her brows and thought for a while before asking, "How did you pray?"

"I danced my prayer."

"Show me," Arminda said.

And so outside the Santo Niño Church, we held candles in our hands we shuffled our dance to the Child Jesus. It was midday and quite hot and sweat rolled down our faces as we swayed to the right, then to left. People gathered to watch us. I am usually shy about this matters, but this time I did not mind. Both of us were laughing when we finished.

She also wanted to see the old Spanish fort, so we drove to Fort San Pedro and later we stopped by the kiosk with Ferdinand Magellan's cross. This got her interested and she scoured the library for information on Philippine history. She was pumping me full questions; then this morning, she expressed interest in going back to school. After the Sinulog, I will meet with the principal of the American School.

I think, Nelia, that Arminda's problem has been basically a question of identity. I know Jun has talked to Arminda, telling her she has Filipino blood but that she's American citizen. I am not sure that is enough for that child. At the hospital where he works, Jun is treated like a god; he is a doctor and is not subjected to the "looks" and the questions: where do you come from? Or worse—what are you? He doesn't feel the discrimination, not as much as Arminda may, in your American world.

These past months, she has immersed herself in our world—granted it is not her world because one day she will return to America—but in the meantime, she has a better understanding of what it means to be Filipino. It is important for one to know where one comes from, in order to know where one is headed.

Love and kisses,

Mama

*

Dear Mom and Dad,

I need six packages of blue dye and three bottles of peroxide. If you call Mia, she can tell you where to buy them. Tell Mia, I'm glad she's well and that I wish she were here with me. She'd like this place; it's cool. Tito Ric has brought us to the beaches here, and he's promised to take us to the rice terraces this summer. He said the place is very old, and there are mummies there, and there are fireflies at night. He also said some of the people there, especially the older ones, have tattoos on their bodies. (He's already told me I can't have a tattoo, so you don't have to worry.) I can't wait for summer.

Last week we had the Sinulog. It wasn't as fancy as the Rose Parade nor Mardi Gras, but there were numerous parades all over the city. Day and night for a week you could hear the drums beating. People from other towns came to the city and many of them slept along sidewalks. The city was crammed with people, celebrating and eating and dancing. I went around with Miriam and Oscar. They were such dorks before, but they're not that bad any more.

For the main parade, we wore costumes—Lola lent Miriam and me some of her old sayas; Oscar blackened his face and wore a huge feathered hat. The three of us had blue hair. People stopped us in the streets to ask about our hair. They fingered our hair and wondered how we turned it blue. We just laughed. We did not tell them we used dye from New York. It was like a secret—our secret.

But I've ran out and need more. Be sure and send it; but don't rush because the school does not allow blue hair. I'll have to wait until summer vacation before I can dye my hair blue again.

Love,

Arminda

***Bio*** *of Cecilia Manguerra Brainard: It all began with the little pink lock-and-key diary that my sister gave me when I was in grade school. I started writing and never stopped. The writing grew from girlish diary to short stories, essays, novels, and it's branched out into other activities such as teaching, editing, book publishing and distribution, and pulling women together to empower themselves under the name of Philippine American Women Writers and Artists (PAWWA). I'm not sure where it'll stop, if it'll stop, but even now I continue to write in my journal, if not every night, during the nights when I feel the need to jot down what could be dismissed as one person's life except that it happens to be my life and therefore cannot be dismissed by me.*

*Born in Cebu, Philippines, I attended St. Theresa's College in Cebu and San Marcelino. I also attended Maryknoll College and UCLA. I am married to a former Peace Corps volunteer to Leyte, Lauren R. Brainard; we have three sons: Christopher, Alexander and Andrew. (more of her in the Editor's biography)*

# OUR FAMILY/MY GANG

Lilia V. Villanueva

IT BEGAN with my name. *Onofria.*

Who gives a child that name in 1980? Well, they did. My Ma, she says, *What you ashamed of, ha? Your Mama's name not good enough for you, ha?* I don't say anything when she gets in that mood. We just end up fighting. We've been fighting for five years, since I was eleven. It's a little better with Papa. But not much. They just don't understand. They *look* young but they don't understand what it's *like* to be young-in America.

They bring us all the way here to America *So you kids can have a future like we never had.* That's what they told us every day we're growing up—I mean *every day.* My sister and I, we're the ones who hear the chant. My brothers pick up and leave when they start up. But we can't 'cause we're girls, you see, until I joined my other family. Then I left the house with my brothers when the folks started up with their *You're so ungrateful after all we've done for you* shit. *We should have left you in the Philippines and you'd grow up right.* Yeah, right. They're not home all day so

65

no way they knew how we're growing up.

**How It Started**

Like I said, it started with my name. I moved to this new school when I'm in the sixth grade. My parents, they worked so hard, both of them, that finally they could afford a house in the suburbs and they're so proud of this. More Pinoy in this 'burb, including auntie this and uncle that. Yeah, more Pinoy kids, too, and gangs.

One day, this black girl in my class came up to me at recess and started yelling, *Give me that, give me that comb. Give it to me right now.* I stood there frozen. I was scared 'cause she was so big. And she was yelling. I've never heard anyone yell that loud to me before. Even when Mama gets angry she didn't yell as loud as that girl. Spit was coming out of her mouth. I was scared shit but I had nowhere to go so I stood there and get rained on by her spit. Then she says *O-no-rea. O-no-rea. Rhyme with go-no-rea, go-no-rea.* I didn't know what it meant but I knew she was making fun of my name, and she was making fun of Lola, my grandmother. So I stuck my head in her open mouth and pulled her tongue out. That was my first fight. And that's how my sisters met me. My gang sisters.

When the girls jumped on me to rescue their friend's tongue from my gripping fingers, I didn't feel anything—the blows, the ripping of my clothes. All I heard was a crowd crying out *Go-no-rea, shit, go-no-rea, let 'er go, let 'er go, shit.* Next thing I knew there were other Pinays on the ground, yelling and kicking at the black girls. Somebody squeezed my wrist so hard that's when I let go of the girl's tongue. They dragged me out of the yard and into the alley before the teacher came.

**The Sisters**

All of them, Pinay, like me. The tallest one, Nina says, *Not bad, girl, for someone so skinny.* They were laughing at how I got the girl's tongue pulled out so hard her hands were flailing at her sides like a chicken. *You still have an ugly name,* Nina says and I lunge for a collar. Pura—she's the one who rescued the girl's tongue—caught my hand and told everyone to shut up. Pura's quick with her hands. *Who give you that name, anyway?* It's a funny name, someone else says. I screamed back at all of them: *It's my Lola's name and I didn't ask for it!* I didn't say I hated the name, too, even though I love Lola a lot. That day they started calling me Beauty.

Chrysta is the prettiest and the baddest. She's got a boyfriend since she was thirteen and she's always cheating on him. She says he cheats on her too, so it's o.k. She's always beating up on the girl she thinks her man's cheating her on. And the others have warned her to stop because she's not always right about the girls.

Jewellynn has gone in and out of the group for four years. She's never out more than two months so no one cares. The only time it mattered was when she started hitching up with a boy from a gang in the next suburb. We warned her she was gonna have her ass kicked if she didn't quit seeing him. It was enough trouble keeping our noses clean with the Brotherhood.

Pinky is one of the originals. She was a girlfriend of a Brotherhood and it was her idea to call the group Truly Yours, meaning truly yours for the Brotherhood. Pinky's people are from Batangas and she's not scared of anyone. She showed us how to work the switchblades and butterfly knives that her brothers collect.

Blue's our color. Every year the shade gets lighter. Don't know why but we like it that way. You know, playing with the different shades of blue.

### Initiation

At first there was no initiation. Getting a boyfriend who's with the Brotherhood was kind of it, really. But as the Brotherhood got bigger in number, all of a sudden a lot of girls, Pinays and Latinas, started to hang out with us. We felt protective. So Pinky and Pura suggest we gotta test who's a real TY, you know.

We do real mild initiations, not like the other gangs.

Just enough to prove that you're one of us, that's all we're looking for. You gotta be willing to fence for the guys, like carry and hide weapons, drugs or stolen goods. Me, they asked me to dog this girl in the mall. They knew she belonged to a gang but I didn't know. I went up to her and stared in her face. We get into a screaming match, then we were punching away. I drew blood from her chest before we were chased out of the mall by security guards. Yeah, it felt good to draw blood. I admit that. That same girl spotted me a few months later at the Filipino fiesta weekend celebration in the city and she had her entire gang come down on me. I was browsing in this book stall and before I know it all hell broke loose. Luckily the TY girls were nearby and I wasn't hurt too bad. The security guards kicked us all out and chased us out of the parking lot. It was kinda messy.

Pinky did her own initiation. She gave herself to several guys in the Brotherhood. I wouldn't do that but several guys thought it was a good idea. No way. I told them I'm out of there if they tried to rape me. I wouldn't let them and they wouldn't dare either. They know I'm good with a knife. I can't come down on Pinky for doing it though. She says she's watching out for disease and stuff like that but I don't believe her.

**Our Life -- Then**

I just turned twelve when I joined TY. That day I yanked the girl's tongue out was a happy one for me. I felt powerful and the sisters made me feel even more powerful. Going to the mall with them after school was fun. We'd chill at the bus stop right outside of Macy's and drink Coke. We'd hang out there until the Brotherhood showed up. First it was Pinky's boyfriend. Then he started to bring a friend who hooked up with Chrysta. Before long, the Brotherhood gang was protecting us. They were also taking us all over the place—the mall, movies, fast food places.

I didn't want to have sex in the beginning. I was too scared my Mom would find out and I'd get kicked out of the house. My brothers threatened me, too. They saw me with Brotherhood guys so they didn't want to mess with me. But I knew they'd do something if they found out I was having sex. I held off for almost two years.

It wasn't a good experience, I don't think. I liked him a lot but I don't think he felt the same way about me. We were at his friend's house and he jumped me when we were alone. I let him because I liked him, you know. But he wasn't very gentle and when I told him that he got on my case—yeah, like I'm not supposed to notice. Putang Ina. I didn't let on how much I cared for him, though. When I found out he was making it with other girls I pretended not to care. But it hurt. Sure I wanted to talk to somebody about it. But not anyone in the family. They'd kill me. I was still going to church with Mom and Dad every Sunday. Most of us did, except for Jewellynn whose folks were Protestants or something.

School was a place to meet, that's all. My heart was not into studying or anything like that. The teachers were o.k. but they couldn't control the kids and they didn't know how, anyway. The gang was everything to me. It was a reason to live. At home everyone was either fighting or lecturing or yelling. Mom was getting down on me for everything. She didn't want me to wear dangling earrings because I looked like a prostitute and not like a good decent girl. I wasn't setting a good example for my kid sis, she said. My kid sister was throwing up every meal and no one wants to talk about it. She was too nervous to join TY so she turned bulimic instead. She said she was used to Mom yelling at everybody—my brothers, even my aunt, her younger sister who lived with us. She yelled at Dad, too, but she'd stop when he raised his fist at her—like she was going crazy or something. So I started staying out of the house and spending more time with TY.

The only time I had a run-in with cops was the time I agreed to drive with the Brotherhood when they did this job on a small mom-and-pop store in the east part of town. They said they wouldn't use a piece but Pinky's boyfriend pulls a big one out of his pocket when they got out of the car. I was scared shit when I saw that piece. When they ran to the car he gives the piece to me and says *Hide it, I'll take it later.* It was very warm. I didn't ask questions. Later, when we were parked at the drive-in, this cop car pulls up next to us and two big cops get out. They start asking questions and the guys tell us girls not to talk. The cops quickly throw three of them against the car and tell them to spread their legs as they searched them roughly. I was pissing in my pants I was so scared. But then I saw how brave the guys were—no one showed any fright. So I stopped being scared. When Pura put up a stink with the cops they slapped her around and told her to stay out of it. Then this cop comes around the car and starts asking me questions. I said I knew nothing, just acted dumb and then he went back to rough up the guys again. I kept seeing the piece in my mind and hope it wouldn't start beeping or something like that.

**Our Life -- Now**

Jewellynn got pregnant last year and she dropped out of sight. Her family sent her back to the islands, to another city other than where folks are from, until she had her baby. Last week she showed up in the mall with her mother and she was pushing a stroller. She looked uncomfortable with us and her mom wasn't excited about seeing us, either. Jewellynn looked fat and she said she'd talk to us real soon. She wouldn't let us call her at home though and we said o.k. It's usual. When a girl gets pregnant, she quits the gang and goes home to mama. I know the father of her kid. He's cute and speaks with a thick accent like everyone in his family. He got in trouble with a gang member and the Brotherhood rescued him. So he joined. He's cute but real short.

Nina graduated from high school but Pura didn't—she quit after 10th grade. Nina's talking a lot about working someplace that serves Pinoy youths. She must be seeing that counselor in the youth clinic. He's kinda cute but too goody-two-shoes for me. I saw him once to talk about college. He was interested; I wasn't. But I went because we got an extra free period if we signed up to have a session with him. Nina saw him many times after his first visit at school.

I suggest that TY should free from the Brotherhood. Pura's not interested. But Chrysta and the new member, Isa, are. I'm getting tired of being treated like their personal slave. We go to movies they wanna see, to malls they wanna hang out; and dress baggy like they do. I remember the guys came down real heavy on Isa for wearing a tight skirt. Pura's still not listening. Lori and Devonne, who joined two years ago, they're listening. They're sisters, both mestiza itim, whose father was a black G.I. Lori and Devonne call him Army, short for Armstrong, just the way their mothers call him. Not Dad or anything like that. Lori and Devonne are both the same age, almost like twins. They had different moms, one from each bar on the main street off Clark Air Force Base. Army stayed on in the islands after the Vietnam War. When the girls were little, their grandma in Oakland took them both back with her after she buried her son in a remote barrio in Pangasinan. Yeah, Army died there and the girls' moms wanted the grandma to take them with her to America. When the grandma died a couple of years later, Lori and Devonne were taken in by some Filipino aunt and uncle. Now Devonne is seeing this guy from another gang and she wants the Brotherhood off her back. It's not a rival gang but like they own us so we're not supposed to be with anyone except them. Fuck that, I say. I've had two boyfriends with them and they were nothing to brag about. And I say we've saved their ass as many times they've saved ours in fights. Everyone agrees except Pura.

**Our Life -- Ahead**

Everything's changing fast. Papa says he won't support me after high school unless I go to college. Shit, I don't wanna go to college. Last summer I tried working at McDonald's and that sucked. So I don't know. Maybe I'll think about college next year when I'm a senior. All I know now is I don't want to be a mama yet. I've been taking precautions but I feel guilty. Like I don't care about children or something but I do. I keep thinking, *What if I can't get pregnant in the future when I'm married and settled down?* You know, like a punishment from God for taking birth control pills now. I don't know. Sometimes it doesn't make sense and sometimes it makes a lot of sense. Nobody in the family knows this. Oh God, Mama would die if she knew I was on the pill. I pray for God's forgiveness all the time. I know He understands why I don't want to be a mother yet. I hope so.

TY still means a lot to me. I love my sisters a lot. More than my own sister, you know. I know they can protect me and they do. We all protect each other. And we don't stab each other on the back. At least not anymore since Jewellyn left. There are more girl gangs in the gangs in the neighborhood nowadays but we we're one of the oldest so we get a lot of respect. And that's real important. I wonder if Jewellyn will tell her kid about us someday.

Who knows what's going to happen in a year or two? I've been with TY six years and I have lots of photos to prove the good times. And the bad times? No one remembers to take pictures during those times. So we don't remember them.

**Bio** *of Lilia V. Villanueva: I credit my older sister, Nena, who was never without a book, for my love of books. I wore eyeglasses to emulate her bookish demeanor, only mine had no glasses in them. My brothers said I looked silly; I thought I looked right for a literary career; my mother tolerated the play-acting as long as I continued practising the piano.*

*I was born and raised in Bacolod City, Philippines and vowed to go to college in the land of Nancy Drew. When serious negotiations began, my parents ruled out the East Coast (no relatives to look after me) and San Francisco was the compromise. In 1970, I received a Bachelor's degree from the University of California, Berkeley where I learned both from the classrooms and the streets in protest over the Vietnam War.*

*My first job as a journalist in Manila was the incubation period of my interest in writing short stories. "She knows what to do during a riot; she came from Berkeley," my boss said in defense of sending me, a rookie, to cover the student protests at the University of the Philippines, Diliman. I learned to write fast while running for cover from tear gas.*

*My return to the U.S. with a husband was unplanned but turned out to be the best. I have been married to the same man for twenty-five years, evolved my career from journalist to editor to broadcast producer to public relations to marketing in the arts. My short stories and other articles have been published both in the Philippines and in the U.S. I co-authored a book on the life of Philip Vera Cruz with my husband, and a couple of years ago, I began a scary journey to writing a novel.*

*I live in Berkeley, California with my husband Craig Scharlin, and our son Ben.*

# VALENTINUS

Mar V. Puatu

MY CONGESTED world begins to unscramble before my sixteen-year-old eyes this fourteenth day of February.

It is nine o'clock at night.

The burning smells of dried moonfish, sapsap and rice gruel assault my nose. The kitchen odor comes from downstairs. My mother must be cooking the evening meal.

In the second floor of a roach-infested dwelling owned by the Laperals, I lie in a three-cornered, 8 x 10 room. My family will have to content itself in the two-bedroom multi-layered apartment to grant me a slice of privacy. I have fought for my own room. Finally, I have my own!

The heat has not subsided with the night. The energy still seethes, squeezing sweat from my body. A 10-watt bulb barely lights my cramped space.

Wiping my forehead, I scribble some lines. I hope these will become immortal. My countrymen will hail me as the next Poet Laureate. Ha! You ask what's a heaven for, Robert

Browning? Well, a young Filipino boy can inspire to write poetry—or lines that pass for verse—even though I may borrow your language and Keat's and Shelley's. I should write in my native tongue, but what can I do? English has seduced me! Anyway, it's only a dream, my attempt at poetry.

My pen scratches my fingers on the newsprint that I have saved.

> *here i drum my fingers on the sill*
> *looking out the rear window*
> *of my crowded one room:*
> *seeing nothing but what stares back,*
> *clash of kins*
> *and blares of stomachs growling,*
> *tasting foul the shirtless air:*
> *discovering, discovering.*

I wish Nita would hear these lines! She doesn't know I exist although Eufemio, her younger brother, is a classmate of mine. Nita will soon be on the rooftop, waiting for her man-friend. He is older than she. I have seen them hold hands, surreptitiously. With envy in my heart—no, jealousy, though I have no right to—I have seen them kiss. I have seen their shadows coupling in the dark ... Oh, I could gore to death that man-friend!

A knock on my door dissipates my anger.

Nonino ... my mother calls.

Quickly, I cover my writings with the *Manila Sunday Times*. I borrowed it from Eufemio's father.

"What is it, Mother?" Perspiration makes my body sticky.

"Dinner's ready."

"I'll be right down." A break in my voice betrays me as a teenager.

"Stop writing," my mother says. "You can't make money by your writing. Nobody can understand what you refer to in your fancy talk anyway. What can you get with big words?

You'll only catch TB, like your father."

With these bitter words, she tramps away. Her receding voice leaves me rebellious and confused.

The pencil burns in my hand. I lay it aside, and pick up Richard Burton's *Arabian Nights*. Next to the Filipino version of *A Thousand and One Nights* and Norman Mailer's *The Naked and the Dead*, lie Daphne du Maurier's *Kiss Me Again, Stranger*, and Morton Thompson's *Not As A Stranger*. I must return them to the library soon.

I eat my precious pocket-books. I digest them to my fancy. All the money I earned selling pesticide from door to door, I spend on these jewels. I scan the ads in the Times. Will Durant's *History of Civilization* are on sale! Still, how can I afford these books? They cost so much.

The distant sounds of Manila's traffic fill my ears. The pedestrians hurry. The motorcars add to cacophony.

I take off my shirt. The tiny laceration that is my window invites my eyes. Across the sky, the moon sails with an ache in its heart, like a galleon flown by a haunted Dutchman. It casts shadows against the neon lights. From my confined quarters, I see the neighbor's windows overlooking the galvanized roofs. Their radios blare.

"Leave me alone!" A gruff voice from a soap opera, *Wheel of Fortune*, bellows. A female character cries, "But, I love you."

A phonograph hisses from another apartment, "Soft o'er the fountains ..." The melody catches my whimsy ... "lingering falls o'er southern moon."

Inwardly, I sing:

> *Nita, O my Juanita,*
> *ask thy soul, if we should part.*
> *Nita, O my Juanita,*
> *lean thou on my heart.*

In one of the many windows, I see a neighbor, blind old Mang Miguel. He plucks his guitar. He accompanies a *kundiman*, a sad song about unrequited love. Pilita Corrales sings the ballad of a captive dove over the radio. In another apartment, Annie Gonzales laments her loneliness in America, *Ten Thousand Miles Away From Home*. Still in another, Nat King Cole regrets that we are *Too Young*. Finally, Frank Sinatra wonders what to do during *The Wee Hours of the Morning*.

The wretched sight turns into a melodious canvas. Music feeds my imagination. What does Shakespeare say? "If music be the food of love, play on."

Among the clotheslines, a young girl climbs up and sits on the galvanized roof. She endures the torrid fever, the white heat of the sun long gone. Her long hair is braided with a matronly bun to make her look older. She wrings her white chemise. The semi-light exposes her figure. It is full now, not budding, as I remember it. I know her! She is Nita ... Juanita who comes softly o'er the fountain and lingers o'er the southern moon. Even Wordsworth will agree, "She is a phantom of delight!"

After a few minutes, the man-friend climbs onto the roof. Nita springs up and hugs him. He unclasps himself from her embrace. His head shakes. He looks stern. He jabs his finger to Nita's face. Abruptly, he turns his back. He distances himself from her.

Nita is confused. She holds on to the man. He takes off her hand. His finger jabs, this time at her body. I can't hear what he says, but I can feel the anger in the man's voice. I can picture Nita's shock. She slaps him. Immediately, she cups her mouth. The man leaves.

Nita's hands fall to her belly. She rubs it tenderly ... tenderly. Then she balls her fists. She hits her stomach. Once, twice, over and over and over again! She sobs. Where she would hold hands with him and whisper sweet nothings, she is alone. Her body is spent, I feel.

She looks up and rolls her eyes up to heaven. Her eyes scan the apartments. No one pays attention to her. Except me. She catches me at my open window.

"What are you looking at?" she shouts.

Quickly, I jumped in the shadows. I hear her rant on the roof. Then, she is gone.

How I wish I could go to her! I long to comfort her and hold her hand and tell her that, like her, I am all alone, too. Solitary, forsaken, alienated -- all, all alone -- this Valentine's Day.

I dip my pencil into my tongue. I continue writing my poem.

*how charged the evening is*
*with pregnant electrons ...*
*how lives with glowing coals*
*the howling sun has set the roof ...*
*but, still, a nascent maid stands*
*barefoot, akimbo at the moon:*
*fear not, o pretty maid,*
*I'll rescue you on my winged hoof!*

*tinkle, tinkle brittle fish*
*on my dented plate of tin,*
*i want to shout, o if i could,*
*water would not have to force it in.*

*sticky, hot the night,*
*then, framed against the light*
*the lonely silhouettes i spot*
*of eager faces,*

*fingers drum on the window sills*
*in misery, in misery ...*
*within the walls of poverty*
*like me, like me.*

The kundiman echoes itself. Frustrated, old blind Mang Miguel smashes his guitar. Once, twice, over and over and over again!

My heart goes out to the old man. He cannot burst

from his cage. Can my writing liberate me?

> *i dwell in this unreal world*
> *for now*
> *the only world real enough;*
> *I'll dream of worlds beyond the seas*
> *somehow,*
> *and dreams will make me tough.*

The next morning, Eufemio does not attend class. I drop by his apartment in the afternoon to return the *Sunday Times* to his father. I jostle my friend for being absent. He blows his top when I needle him to tell me why. Finally, he breaks down. He tells me that his sister has hanged herself in her room.

**Bio**: *Born in Manila, Philippines, Mar V. Puatu immigrated to the U.S. in 1977, and he now resides in Sun Valley, California.*

*After graduating from the University of the East, he worked for J. W. Thompson and other international advertising companies. He wrote, acted produced, and directed for Philippine radio, television, stage, and cinema. He was a six-time winner of the prestigious Don Carlos Palanca Award for Literature. He also won the Arena Playwriting Contest. In 1995, his story, "A Love Lost," won in the PALM (Philippine Arts, Letters and Media Council's short story contest.*

*An active member of the California Writers Club San Fernando Valley Branch, he is editor of its monthly publication,* The Valley Scribe. *He is publisher of* The Center Voice, *a quarterly put out by West Valley Jewish Community Center, and* Sojourn, *an anthology of short stories and poems.*

*His stories have been anthologized in A Class Act by Bernard Selling, given public readings by the Wednesday Writers a Joslyn Center, Burbank, and included in* American Poetry Anthology of 1985. *A Hollywood producer has optioned "The Death Angel", a legend of the half-woman/half-devil called manananggal. In 1996, he came out with* The Girl With One Eye and Other Stories. The Enchanted Land, *a collection of mystical short stories, will be released in 1998, together with his semi-autobiographical novel,* The Quest.

# RETURNING FIRE

### Vince Gotera

THE HEAT and humidity blasted Bogey Reyes in the face as he stepped off the C-130. It was déjà vu—like 187 days ago, when he'd stepped off a Braniff airliner into a wall of heat that took his breath away, hoisted his OD duffle bag up onto his right shoulder, then double-timed off the runway at Tan Son Nhut Airport. Vietnam. The 'Nam. In country. Three fucking hundred sixty-five virgin slots left on his short-timer's calendar. A damn FNG. A *fuckin' new guy*—a red, white and blue target painted on his back. And now, walking off another plane at Clark Field in the Philippines, the customary black AWOL bag bumping his leg rhythmically he paused to look around: the wide spaces of concrete and tarmac, waves of tropical heat shimmering over the macadam apron where the C-130 sat like some hulking dead albatross. "Jesus H. Christ. Just another 'Nam," he said, slipping his Zippo out his pants pocket. "Land of my forefathers, Land of the Morning -- just another Viet-fucking-Nam." Bogey lit up a Salem and stood there for a moment, idly fondling the lighter's chrome surfaces. Hell of a place for a week of R and R. Though he didn't know those grunts he'd flown here with, he'd bet his last RPC that they would be soon on a search-and-clear mission on the streets of Manila, hunting round-eye prostitutes. Bogey planned to be on a train to his father's village, a little farming and fishing hamlet near the Lingayen Gulf. He was on a pilgrimage, like any good Pinoy. Bogey flipped the Zippo into the air, where it flashed in the noon sun for a shining moment, and then plucked it out of the sky. He turned and walked into the Clark Field terminal.

*

The train to San Fernando smelled like pigshit and bagoong. Bogey's mother -- a nurse who'd been raised on a dairy farm a few miles from Cedar Rapids, Iowa -- loved all things Filipino except for bagoong -- a salty fermented fish paste which his father had dearly loved. At least so he'd been told: Bogey's father, Raymundo Reyes, had died when he was a mere toddler. In 1939, Bogey's mother, a dewey-eyed eighteen-year-old farm girl named Margaret Fisher, had become intolerably weary and bored with her parents' acres of corn and pasture; so she had taken the unprecedented step of attending nursing school in Des Moines and shipping off to the Philippines to work at a leper's hospital run by Presbyterian missionaries. The religious connection was really only to mollify the folks; what Maggie was really seeking was high adventure in the South Seas. She had subsisted as a young girl on romantic novels about places like Sumatra and Fiji; her favorite was *The Hurricane*, and Maggie would have wanted nothing more than to be lashed to a tree by a clear-eyed, handsome and muscled Samoan boy while monsoon winds whipped the ocean into gigantic waves that threatened to engulf the island of their tryst in paradise. Instead, all she got was World War II, long hard hours at a military hospital just outside Manila, a hospital that was first the U.S. Army's and then later taken over by the Japanese (she had refused to leave her patients when the other American nurses were evacuated). Maggie miraculously avoided harm during the Japanese occupation, and when the hospital had been reclaimed by the Americans, she had tended a brown-eyed Filipino infantryman named R. Reyes, or Rey-Rey as his friends called him.

Raymundo Reyes had been a college student who became a Philippine Scout during World War II. Reyes and his unit had fought valiantly and with honor, as they say, under General King until his surrender of Bataan on 9 April 1942 and the infamous Death March which followed it. Rey-Rey, a corporal, contracted some rare jungle disease in the concentration *camp*—a disease that manifested itself in occasional but chronic bouts of malaria-like symptoms. It was because of one of these attacks that he had ended up as Maggie's patient. The rest is, as they also say, history: a whirlwind romance, rendezvous after secret rendezvous in the moonlight of Intramuros—the old Spanish presidio—and morning strolls at Quiapo market, a sparkly Catholic wedding with a few friends at the Church of Our Lady of Antipolo, and then they honeymooned Stateside, as the expression goes. Rey-Rey had become a naturalized American citizen as a result of his wartime service, and he and Maggie settled finally in San Francisco in 1947.

On All Saints' Day, 1949, Maggie gave birth to an eight-pound-five-ounce baby boy, whom they christened Humphrey Bogart Reyes. When Bogey was three, Rey-Rey had another one of his chronic attacks and died. Humphrey being no name to grow up with in San Francisco—his classmates began calling him "Humpty-Dumpty" in the third grade— "Bogey" became the boy's name of choice. He had a fairly uneventful childhood, except that he remembered he saw his mother rather seldom, since she never remarried and had to work long hours at General Hospital. So Bogey knew next to nothing about his father's background and life. All he knew was that at Polytechnic High—the toughest, rowdiest school in the city—he had to fight every single day. Whites and blacks both were continually hassling Bogey because he wasn't white and wasn't black. "Hey, Hirohito!" a blond-haired boy had called him one morning at the basketball courts; switchblades swiftly sliced into open air, and Bogey had ended up flat on his back for a week at his mother's hospital with a punctured lung. The Filipino kids—the Flips—they didn't consider him one of their own, either. His nose was just not flat enough, his lips a bit too thin, his hair just a shade too fair. So for Bogey, "Flip" became a nasty word. Just some more people he had to fight.

Nevertheless, Bogey couldn't help but wonder about his father and the Philippines. Perhaps he never really connected the Flips who called him undecipherable Tagalog names in the hallowed halls of Poly with the postcards of outrigger boats and emerald-green volcanoes that would occasionally come to his mother from her old friends in the Philippines. After Bogey graduated from high school, his Uncle Sam sent him a congratulations card that started out "Greetings" -- he was instructed to report to the Oakland Induction Center at the end of the summer. Bogey gladly signed up and found himself a few months later in 'Nam. He was only a hop, a skip, and a jump—as they say—from his father's homeland.

*

So now Bogey found himself on a Philippine train, and it smelled like pigshit and bagoong. There were other smells too: under the passenger seats all around him were chickens being transported in large domed baskets, people eating their lunches of bagoong and rice or their snacks of suman—sweet sticky rice steamed in a wrapping of banana leaf—all melting with the pungence of fertilizer from the fields swooping by beyond the train's windows. The air was filled with a strange cacophony of noises: the staccato gobbledygook that was, to Bogey, how Tagalog and Ilocano sounded, mixed with the strident squawks of chickens, and piercing squeals and bleats of pigs, and high-pitched screams of children running up and down the central aisle of the passenger car.

In the middle of this vortex of sensation, Bogey could only marvel at how much these Filipinos seemed, to him, Vietnamese. The green rice fields outside with their paddy berms punctuated by an occasional nipa hut seemed just like the boonies he had been humping for the last six months. He found himself expecting incoming from the tree line—— rockets, maybe, or mortars—and kept having sudden panic attacks when he would alternately realize that he didn't have his flak jacket and then that he didn't need it here. Every time he would drift off to sleep, he felt like he was walking through some ville in Vietnam, the mama-sans and their kids all in black pajamas, peeking out of their sorry hootches ... the same smells, the same smells. Lock and load one magazine. Then pivot in place, trigger finger jamming, rocking and rolling, bullets spraying everywhere and every which way, the Vietnamese pigs like miniature rhinos running and falling over, mama-sans huddling over their screaming children—blood, blood, blood.

"What the fuck!" Bogey screamed, jumping to his feet ... somebody had touched his arm.

The man who'd been sitting next to him had also bolted, jumped up, and was now staring at him, wide-eyed, his voice quivering, "Sorry, Mister. You ... you were moaning, and I thought ... I thought ..." The man trailed off, then looked abruptly away.

Bogey looked around the passenger car. Everyone was staring at him; even the kids, the pigs, the chickens had all quieted down. As if by signal or conspiracy, they all averted their eyes. "You're all gooks, you know that?!" he yelled. "Just gooks. The things that happen when you don't have your weapon!" Bogey reached for the Zippo and shook out a Salem, his hands trembling just a little. "Just motherfucking gooks."

\*

"Here, you will sleep here, "Uncle Mariano pointed out

Bogey's room, a nipa-walled cubicle equipped with a sleeping mat or banig, and a mosquito net. In the corner, a small wicker table held an ancient kerosene lamp. When Bogey had stepped off the train a half hour earlier at this small whistlestop called *Batong Ginto* partway between cities of Bauang and San Fernando, his uncle (not actually a relative rather his grandfather's grandson, nevertheless an uncle by Filipino reckoning) Tio Mariano had been waiting. Mariano Jacinto was a small man, not even five feet; his eyes looked almost Chinese, and on his chin, he had a few wisps of white beard. His shoulders were rounded, and he walked with a stoop. In fact, he limped and leaned visibly on a gnarled walking stick he held in his left hand. "An old war wound," Tio Mariano explained, "I stepped on a Japanese mine, but it did not have much powder. I was lucky. Your Papa carried me on his back, along with both our rifles and ammunition, gas mask, five miles through the jungle to get me to a doctor. Very strong man, your Papa." Bogey, however, could not shake an anxious, nagging feeling that, if they had been standing in Vietnam that very moment, this man -- his father's buddy -- would have been Vietcong. He imagined Tio Mariano in black pajamas rather than white cotton shirt and bright red neckerchief, rough serge pants; Bogey could almost see him bent over a work table deep in some Vietnamese tunnel, arming booby traps with stolen G.I. material or sharpening bamboo sticks to be smeared with human shit. Bogey shook his head sharply, as if to clear the image from his brain.

"And here, this is your pinsan, my daughter Carmelita ... Mely." The woman standing at the bottom of the bamboo stair was lovely—soft clear skin and straight white teeth, blue-black hair cascading past her slim shoulders, bright almond-shaped eyes like Tio Mariano. *Slant-eye*, Bogey thought. He looked past Mely to the house: a large house on stout six-foot bamboo stilts, the walls made of intricately woven nipa, certainly large enough to contain several rooms, unlike the smaller one-room nipa huts they had walked past. A split-bamboo stairway where Mely was waiting. A thought flickered at the edge of Bogey's consciousness: *Just another hooch, another goddam hootch.* Mely smiled and dropped her eyes.

*

Over the next two or three days, Bogey began to feel more and more relaxed. His taut nerves were loosening up, their knots untying. Evenings, he and Mely would stroll down the beach, watch the village boys climb coconut trees and hack coconuts loose with their bolos and machetes. They would look out across the Lingayen Gulf, the sun floating like a purple salted egg over the South China Sea, the sky streaked with vermillion and pink clouds, and Bogey could hardly believe that he was looking towards Vietnam. That at that moment, grunts in his company were checking their stuff -- Claymore mines, flares, tracer rounds. That they were preparing to set up listening posts, guard the perimeter of Fire Base Jezebel. And here he was with a beautiful woman, talking of the horrors of Vietnam, of how the fog rolls in nights in San Francisco. She giggled a tinkly laugh when he described the flower children in the Haight-Asbury, patchoulli oil and giant daisies, the Grateful Dead and the Charlatans putting on free concerts in the Panhandle. He smiled as she recounted to him stories of religious festivals, of candlelight processions through the streets of Bauang City, of the blue-and-silver statue of the Blessed Virgin carried by the strongest men of this village whose name meant *rock of gold.* Then they would walk along the waterline, their hands touching briefly in the indigo air just after sunset. Once, they came upon some beached fishing boats and laughed together at the name painted on one: *Bogart.*

On the fourth night, Bogey dreamt of 'Nam. As squad leader, he was collecting his grunts. The platoon had been ordered to hump to a remote ville to check on rumors of Vietcong activity. *Fucking commie sympathizers, all of them*, he thought. The platoon sergeants had brought all the residents and lined them up at the edge of a rice field: not one able-bodied man among them ... all wizened grandfathers and old women, or young wives with filthy babies. Where were the young men? Vietcong, each and every one. Then Smitty discovered a tunnel under one of the hootches. A dull boom sounded and then another as they slung frags into the tunnel. "Get yer Zippos out!" Bogey yelled, and as the Vietnamese begged, "Please, G.I." or screamed "You number 10, dien cai dau," he flicked the Zippo's small wheel and a yellow sheet of flame engulfed the first hooch. Bogey was stoked to the max, he had been made for this. He was King of the Mountain. He was headman of the Zippo squad. The Vietcong scared their children with stories about him: the Bogey Man. Then he felt a funny tingle in the hand which held the Zippo. Bogey looked down. The skin on his right wrist, his forearm, was mottling, writhing, tightening -- it was turning gray and purple, a reptilian, knobby carapace. As he watched, fascinated -- thinking *acid flash* -- his skin burst painfully into flame, crackled and burst, oozing some vile-smiling liquid -- Bogey began to scream -- the lizard skin and the flames were traveling up his arm, engulfing his shoulder -- his fatigues, his boots were burning off with an oily smoke -- around him, no one paid attention, his men setting fire to hootch after hootch as the villagers wailed -- Bogey was almost afraid to look down at his body -- the skin of his legs was hardening and then exploding in fire -- he looked down and screamed -- still no one noticed -- the burning skin triangulating on his cock and balls -- a thousand cicadas were buzzing in his head -- someone was screaming, "Stop! Stop it! For God's sake, Stop" -- his shrivelled penis scrotum were turning green and barky like an alligator's back -- it felt like a hundred bees were stinging his crotch -- the heat of an imploding sun centered on his groin, ground zero --

"Bogey? Bogey? Are you okay?" It was Mely, her cool fingers caressing his temples. Bogey shuddered and came out of the dream, sobbing. She lay down next to him and held him in a tender but firm embrace. Bogey turned his eyes towards her and saw gold flecks glittering in her dark eyes. He hid his face between her breasts.

\*

At breakfast Tio Mariano handed Bogey a small, slim notebook. Its leather cover was moth-eaten in places, but the paper inside was in good condition, "This was your Papa's, Bogey. It is his journal. He kept it during the war. I want you should have it. I think you need it now." Bogey went to his room and began immediately to decipher his father's scrawled script, dipping in and out, reading here and there in the journal.

*Today we found a Jap cache of food. We took a case of condensed milk. What a luxury! We ate about two or three cans each of the milk. And then we got pinned down in a crossfire. Retreat, Retreat! ordered Lieutenant Gutierrez. So we ran through the jungle, and the bullets were singing like little wasps over our heads. And as we ran, we all began to have diarrhea. My stomach was boiling. Ay, naku! No time to stop. We just ran and ran. Literally. Later, we all had a big laugh about it as we washed out our uniform pants in a river.* Bogey recalled the sapper they had shot at Jezebel a couple of months back, how they had found a pack of Marlboros and two Pepsi's in his little back pack. But then he also remembered burning barrels of shit, the stench and the smoke. He had always given his stinky uniforms to the Vietnamese washwomen, and now Bogey wished he could have washed them himself with his buddies in the river. A smile broke out like sun streaming through clouds as he imagined the incredible event of dodging a hard rain of bullets, shitting sweet milk all the way.

*After General King's surrender last week, we burned our uniforms and began pretending to be farmers and fishermen. God help us, we can be shot now as spies: Mariano and I, Pabling, Francisco, Lieutenant Guttierez, Charlie, and Duling-duling. It's becoming too dangerous. On 13 April, a farmer told us the Japs were setting up roadblocks and checking the right index finger of all able-bodied men. And if you had a callus over there, they would bend you over right in the road and cut off your head with a samurai sword. No trial, no bullshit. So that morning, all seven of us decided to hide out in the wagon. And none of the cans would fit through the bars. And the wood was very tough. We had been on half-rations for months even before the surrender, so we were too weak to cut through the wood. But you never know what a hungry man can do. Mariano reached through the bars and picked a can of evaporated milk, and he squeezed it and squeezed it until it could fit through the bars.* Bogey remembered how he had set fire once to a hootch filled with rice, probably an entire harvest. He began to cry silently.

Tio Mariano was standing at the door. He smiled gently. Then he opened his right hand to show Bogey the scars like gnarly vines in his palm, on the insides of the fingers. For the first time, Bogey noticed that the hands was slightly deformed, misshapen, spatulate fingers hooked ever-so-slightly like small scythe handles. "We were in a bunker far back in the jungle, maybe two weeks after the surrender of Bataan. A Japanese grenade came in through the fire window. We had nowhere to run. Everyone just froze. I reached down and held that grenade tight as I could, and it went off in my hand, but I kept in the blast. Maybe like that mine that crippled my leg, it had too little powder. I don't know. But after that, we knew we must give up. Your Papa and I both ended up in the Death March. I don't know how, but Rey-Rey was able to keep that book. The whole time in the concentration camp. Wait here, I have something else to give you." Tio Mariano went back out of the room and Bogey flipped to another page near the end of the journal.

*Our prisoner-of-war camp is a horrible place. There is very little food. Sanitation is terrible. Everyone has dysentery and beriberi. It might almost be better for your head to have been chopped off for lagging behind when the Japs marched us to this camp. But this morning I gained hope again. I do not know what today is, but I know we have been here for several months. This morning, a guard at the fence beckoned to me. I thought, oh no, what foolishness will I have to face now? But he only wanted to give me a cigarette. It was a Camel. I wonder where they get Camels? He gave me the cigarette and smiled. I realized he is only a boy. Probably no more than eighteen or nineteen. And he is lonely. As we are too. Friend, he said to me in English but with a thick accent. Friend. Hai, I answered, arigato.*

"I have one other gift for you," Tio Mariano came back

with a long bundle wrapped in cloth. "This is also was your Papa's." He unwrapped an old but meticulously clean rifle -- twenty years old if it's a day. "This was your Papa's hunting rifle. He bought it on the black market after the war. 1946, maybe. It's a converted military rifle, a Garand. We don't know whose it was originally. Your Papa liked to think that it had been the rifle of one of our dead comrades, Lt. Guttierez or Francisco or maybe even Duling-duling—"Old Cross-Eye" we called him in English sometimes. Your Papa gave me this rifle when he married your Mama. He said, Mariano my brother, you keep it for me, but he never come back. Now it is yours. Tomorrow you will have to leave for Clark Field so you will not be AWOL, ha?" Tio Mariano left, and Bogey sat there until dark, his legs folded in lotus position, the rifle nestled in his lap, and read his father's journal from the beginning to end.

*

Bogey's last R-and-R morning dawned magnificently. The eastern sky was a pale mauve, shading to a deep purple at the western horizon; the silhouette of mountains and pine forests stood crisply against the dawn like a serrated blade. The air was sharp and cool. Bogey was still sitting in lotus, book and rifle carefully arranged on the floor in front of him like two precisely placed stones in a Japanese garden. He got up and began to pack his stuff in a rucksack he had purchased in Bauang City two days before, when he and Mely had gone on a little shopping junket.

Mely came out of her room to prepare breakfast, and they met, held hands at arm's length. Then he kissed her gently, first on the forehead, then on the lips. She closed her eyes. "I love you," he whispered. "Please wake up Tio Mariano, okay?" She roused her father, and they both went outside. There was Bogey: rucksack and rifle, hiking outfit of heavy broadcloth, hiking boots. His class A's were folded neatly on the veranda next to his spit-shined low quarters.

"Thank you, Tio Mariano. You're one hell of a wise

man. So you must know, and Mely, you know too, that I can't go back to Vietnam. It would shame my father's ghost—his memory. I feel as if evil now runs in my veins like poison. But I'll be back someday. Mely, I love you. Please understand." Mely slipped down the stairway in her bare feet and gave Bogey a last kiss. Tears slid down her cheeks. Tio Mariano nodded his head slowly his own eyes glistening.

Bogey held her hand for a brief moment, then turned to walk east toward the mountains, toward the peak of Mt. Pulog. After a few steps, he stopped and looked back. Then he fished the Zippo out of his pocket and pitched it in a low arc towards the beach. As it spun through the morning air, it lit up briefly like a miniature comet, then disappeared. Bogey turned back towards the rising sun.

*Bio:* *Vince Gotera was born and raised in San Francisco but also lived in the Philippines for some years as a young child. He now lives in Cedar Falls, Iowa-in the midwestern United States-with his wife Mary Ann and their school-age daughters, Amanda, Amelia, and Melina. Vince also has a twenty-four-year-old son, Martin from a previous marriage.*

*Since 1995, Gotera has been an English professor at the University of Northern Iowa, where he teaches poetry writing and poetics. Before moving to Iowa he was a professor for six years at Humboldt State University in California, teaching ethnic American literature and creative writing as well as directing the creative-writing program.*

*Gotera has a bachelor's degree in English from Stanford University, a master's in American literature from San Francisco State University, a master of fine arts degree in poetry writing as well as a PhD in English and in American Studies from Indiana University.*

*In 1994, Gotera's book of literary criticism,* Radical Visions: Poetry by Vietnam Veterans, *was published by the University of Georgia Press. He also published in 1994 a book of poems entitled* Dragonfly *with Pecan Groove Press in San Antonio, Texas.*

*Gotera won a Creative Writing Fellowship in 1993 from the National Endowment for the Arts, an Academy of American Poets Prize, the 1988 Mary Roberts Rinehart Award in Poetry, and the Felix*

*Pollak Poetry Prize.*

*In those rare moments when he has spare time, Vince plays electric bass—blues, rock, jazz.*

# SEBASTIANA'S FIRE

Oscar Peñaranda

*MY UNCLE Tio Ulóng was telling me this ... under the Golden State Bridge in San Francisco, by the low, wave-smoothed rock cliffs where we often went fishing, he was saying to me ...*

Now all this happened before I was born. But I know it's the truth. Most of it anyway. They're true to me, that is. Even though I knew I wasn't there, I am a witness to it because I was born *into* it. The countryside was soaked with legends and songs before I ever came to be, and their telling and singing shed light to my becoming.

None of this truth I talk about would show up in laboratories and formulas, however, 'cause you just can't prove it that way. So, if you're the type of person who believes that the truth can only be found in schools and country courts, church records, facts and datas and computers, then you just better get on with that chore you were thinking about doing this, 'cause this ain't for you. You ain't gonna like none of it.

*My uncle, Tio Ulóng, I have heard was a very lucky man. He would know nothing of a business, yet he would plunge into it and become very successful. They said it was because of his wife, Tia Sayong. But as one can see from this story, Tio Ulóng had probably been lucky all his life, starting with day one. Tia Sayong and Tio Ulóng were my Ninang and Ninong, godparents. That's a pretty big thing to us. In the late 70's, they immigrated to San Francisco and they've been there ever since. My uncle Tio Ulóng was telling this story ... Now it is being told to you ... I am telling you ...*

When he was being born under the house where all the animals stayed, Japanese soldiers were marching outside parading their prisoners and gathering all the males of the barrios in their wake. The Filipinos were told that all sharp objects must be accounted for. It was a well-known fact that any sharp object was either confiscated (by the Japanese), or concealed and probably taken to the hills by the guerillas, the Filipino resistance. For the owner, a blade of any sort was at once very precious and incriminating.

His father, midwife Antonio (the bayut), his older brother Bong (a boy of two), and Sebastiana were all huddled around his mother. The midwife Antonio was trying to decide whether he should cut off the umbilical cord to let the new-born breathe, because it had wound tightly around its neck and the slithering lump of flesh was turning blue, or wait a bit longer for the passing unaware Japanese soldiers to be at a safe hearing distance from the infant's anticipated cry, and therefore avoid the risk of being taken prisoners and probably killed one and all. The pair of sewing scissors by the big aluminium pan beside the banig his mother was laying on was what midwife Antonio finally decided to use to cut off the cord that for so long, an eternity it seemed, had choked the massive bluish-pink infant. Rumors had it from eyewitnesses that enemy soldiers were throwing babies up in the air and catching them with bayonets.

Suddenly Sebastiana darted out laughing into the

streets, chickens cackling and pigs squealing along her path, her skirt flapping against her strong bare legs. The Filipino soldiers working for the Japanese chased after her, trying to explain to the Japanese that she was just the village loony, that she was crazy that way. But it was too late for any explanations. They had seen Sebastiana. And though still in her teens, she knew that look in men's eyes.

Maybe it was the heat, the sun's dull haze, and though she was in plain view of her pursuers, everyone stopped the chase simultaneously -- momentarily, but simultaneously.

She was making little circles on the red dirt with her left toes. When the Japanese officer looked in that direction, she lifted up her foot, its sole crawling up the bark of the avocado tree behind her, her knee slowly jutting forward. She stayed that way for a while, at rest yet in motion, not looking at anything in particular. The river was in her again, swelling and heaving and silent.

The officer cracked the silence when he shouted disciplinary commands at his men who scattered like cockroaches in wildfire. He jumped over fences as he screamed the orders, drew his sword, hacking vines and branches to keep up with his helter-skeltering men. His buckle got caught in one of the half-open gates as he sped through backyards and gardens and by the time he caught up with his men, the sheath for his samurai sword had fallen into the earth and broken cement path-way, about ten feet from where the mother was giving birth.

Meanwhile, the soldiers marching their prisoners almost disappeared into the bend of the street up the road, half of them already wading in the river. Sebastiana was nowhere to be seen, only her intermittent laughter pierced the noonday sun, as the fiasco subsided.

Antonio, the bayut midwife, sensing and fearing that there was no more time to stall, took the mother's sewing scissors. With a seemingly resolute will, he cut the cord firmly with one stroke and eased the coil around the new-born's fat blue face.

"It's got to be at least twelve pounds! This baby waited too long."

But the baby made no sound. Antonio the bayut slapped it a little to jolt it into reality, this new reality it had woken into, spewn into its strange brightness. But the baby still made no sound. It was not until the Japanese soldier completely disappeared into the river that a burst of crying rang far and clear, and fear gripped the nativity cast under the old house, Sebastiana's ubiquitous laughter, now conspicuously absent. They were safe now. All his grown days he would hear Antonio tell people of his timely silence that crucial morning, that first morning of his life. The soldiers were already far away when the baby's wailing now took the foreground of noises until a scurry of pebbles thrashing and metal clanging emerged from the broken cement path.

It was the Japanese officer who had tried to discipline his rowdy men minutes before. He had come back to look for his sheath and he picked it up and buckled it around his waist, he saw directly in front of him, cowering and huddled in a corner of a makeshift shelter, two men, one boy of about two years, one woman lying limp but face glowing, and a new-born infant being washed over a pan of steaming water. He stared at the nativity scene for a long time, taking off his cap and wiping his brow and hair, squinting and once shaking the beads of perspiration from his eyes and face.

The two men and the boy in the corner, equally in shock, gradually softened their tense stance into resignation.

With a cap still in hand, the Japanese officer bowed slightly to the group and quickly turned to go. And when he did, he almost bumped into Sebastiana leaning against a tree with one bare leg up and a smile that many people since have seen on her but no one ever came to know.

Her stance was neither soft nor tense, nor cowering nor defiant. She stood there as natural as she always was, as the officer bowed to her, offered her his cap, a red sun embroidered upon the front. There was no word nor gesture of response. Her left hand kept playing with her hair, her right hand completely hidden behind her back against a tree. The officer bowed to her again, and again tried to hand her his cap. But with her eyes, she let him drop it on the ground in front of her and watched him scamper away squinting. Her eyes did not follow his leave. She kept staring at the people now washing the baby as she picked up the cap with her toes and raised it in front of her, impaling it softly with the pair of scissor she held in her once-hidden right hand.

*"And so I was born," Tio Ulóng told me. And he continued ...*

Some said she was crazy, demented, retarded. Others said she was bewitched, voodooed, spellbound. Still others insisted she was divine, touched by the hand of God, pure, and so much like a child. And still others were convinced that she was just playing a game, a sort of trick on the whole community merely because she enjoyed that sole feeling of superiority left her by the town and probably the only one she ever knew. But the one thing that struck people instantly was her posture and everything that went with it: her countenance, her bearing, her doomed defiance, which were windows to her being. She was not really beautiful, she just reminded people of beauty, or what beauty usually brought with it -- tragedy. Sebastiana was not a handsome maid; but her essence awed onlookers. And it was not only in the way she moved, but the very was she was at rest or in motion. There was a river in her. It was in her bones, in her soul. So everybody had their stories on why and how she burned the new movie house, the first movie house in Santander. At first everyone was just shocked. But when she burned it again right after they rebuilt it, well, like they say, theories started being formulated.

I remember vividly and beautifully the time Sebastiana burned the town's only movie house. I can still see clearly the flames dancing under her voice laughing publicly, yet it seemed I was the only audience at some bizarre re-enactment of a play. For me she always had a public and at the same time a private face. She knew it, of course. For a crazy loon, she knew many things.

"Let me in," she pleaded with the man at the ticket window.

"Sorry ma'am, I can't do it," was the curt reply.

"I just don't have any money now, but I'll pay you later. Please don't shame me in front of the boy." She wriggled forward a bit and as she got closer to the man, "you know I'm a Vilyasin, too," she whispered quite angrily. "I'm a relative of the family who owns this movie house." She started the sentence even-headedly enough but almost blurted out the last part. Sebastiana pleaded, even though she and everybody else in town knew that she was an "outside" member of the family, the illegitimate side.

"We can't do it," the man looked up and said again, much more coolly this time. "Even for 'outside' members of the family." And then he started to laugh, but was able to keep it in. But it was too late because whatever it was the Sebastiana was carrying swung into the man's face and as the crowd held back and carried Sebastiana away, she kept shouting, "I'm a Vilyasin! I'm a Vilyasin, too!"

*Between baits in our fishing, under the Golden Gate Bridge where Alfred Hitchcock filmed Vertigo, Tio Ulóng continued, his eyes glistening a bit as when he had been drinking ...*

For a simple young woman, she felt many things. She loved me so, yet I gave her nothing in return. She was filled with giving, yet she found no one to give it to, so maybe by my talking of her, I may repay her, a deed I could not accomplish while I was still there in the Philippines with her, while she was still alive.

"Come," she would say to me at times. "Come and let me see my man, how he has grown. Oh, look at him, my beautiful man." And everyone who might be present laugh benignly at me, and sometimes I would feel their soft stare. Once I caught a glimpse of Sebastiana's face under the armpit of one of the women. I caught a glimpse of Sebastiana looking at me, staring at me strangely, and I got that feeling that at that moment she knew more than I. She did, of course. Because immediately after that she hugged me with her hands around the back of my small head.

And then she would say with a sudden shift of tone, "If it were up to me, I wouldn't live in a place where people have to constantly make painful choices," and look at me, "would you?"

What could I say? All I knew was that when I was born there was a fire in the village fiesta where a year before my mother danced, as she always had in every fiesta, being the partner most sought after by the dancing men of the towns and villages and barrios. And that my mother had taught Sebastiana to dance, or at least was in the same family of Sebastiana's and that's how my mother and Sebastiana were quite close about the time I was born.

*My uncle spoke with that famous or infamous, Waray passion, with alacritous animation, when he spoke of his mother's dancing.*

My mother danced. She did not dance the way a wavelet would upon the ocean's crest, nor the way a palm stalk would in the breezes, no. She danced without comparison. She danced her self and the movements took her back and captured her and spun her into the dance until she disappeared in the dance, and she was swallowed up by the dance, and she became the dance herself, herself, no more no less; she danced her self away. She danced without comparison and the clouds gathered in the skies. Yet, she did not dance the way a crescent moon would sail slippery through the tamarind trees, nor the way the gull would glide across the bay after a storm, nor the way the notes would dance hovering around the rondallas, no; she danced without comparison, she danced without reference, she danced first and last time like a moment in eternity, inimicable and irrevocable; she danced herself and the mayas held their silence and hid themselves, their voices in shame, and right there and then the people of Santander and the surrounding barrios, the people gawked open-mouthed and swaying and singing and clapping, right there and then, they knew without question, knew without even asking or thinking about it, knew just as they, the townspeople, the community, the barangay, profound in their simplicity, knew how Pedong the town smith was born for the hammer and anvil, knew just as they knew that birds were born for the singing and eyes for seeing, and flowers for blooming, knew just as they knew that Pen-Pen was born to be legend and Totoy born for the remembrances of things past even centuries before his becoming, they knew, the common and humble folk knew that night, they knew without ever doubting it again, they knew what my mother's solace would be in her time of solitude and sorrow and old age. They knew that my mother was born to dance and all the dances of the world were waiting for her becoming, and that night at the Fiesta all waiting was over.

But all this happened before I found out that Sebastiana was carrying my father's child. That's why now, I tell you, I must talk of her.

*My uncle Tio Ulóng was telling me all this in San Francisco underneath the Great Bridge whose enormous strands of cables, like the hair of some sleeping giant, rose beyond and fell from fast-moving clouds, stretching its long, crimson neck across the Bay where shimmering Sausalito lay with its restaurants and quaint expense shops. My uncle and I fished all day and caught nothing so that on our way back, he had to stop by the fish market and tell relatives that that was his catch for the day so he would not have to come home empty-handed.*

*My Uncle was born during the Second World War, near the end of it, "liberation time" they call it. And every time we go fishing here under the Great Bridge, I imagine the hard time our family, especially my Uncle's mother must have gone through, and the painful times Sebastiana must have had ahead of her. My Uncle told me all this. Now I am telling you.*

**Bio**: *Oscar Peñaranda is a writer, educator, and community events coordinator and networker. Born August 21, 1944 in Barugo, Leyte, he moved to Manila at the age of four or five. He immigrated to*

*Vancouver, B.C. in 1956, then in 1961 moved to San Francisco, which has been his home ever since.*

*A writer from age fourteen or so, his works are short stories, poems, plays, scripts, novels-in-progress and essays. He received his M.A. in Creative Writing and his California Teaching Credential from San Francisco State University. An educator since 1969, he was one of the founders of Pilipino American Studies at S.F. State University, the first in the western hemisphere. He taught in the Creative Writing, English and Pilipino American Studies Departments at S.F. State from 1969 to 1980.*

*Currently, he is teaching Tagalog and Filipino Heritage classes at Logan High School in Union City and at DeAnza Community College in Cupertino. He assists the History and Language Arts Departments by giving presentations on Filipino American History, culture, literature and contributions. One of his expertise is incorporating and integrating Filipino Heritage materials in the existing curricula of schools.*

*He is the founding president of the San Francisco Chapter of the Filipino American National Historical Society, 1982-92. He is also the founding chair of the Filipino American Humanities Council.*

*His story "Sebastiana's Fire" is part of a larger work consisting of inter-related stories set in his fictitious place of Santander, Leyte.*

# THE FOG

### Luis Cabalquinto

THE YEAR I turned twenty-three I was boarding with a well-to-do couple in the country who lived in a big house next door to their married young (he was twenty) son's smaller house.

Although I could afford to pay for living accommodations in the poblacion (as the central area of a town is called in the Philippines), I was required by the government office I worked for as a "community development officer" to live "among the people" and be part of their community's daily life. It had been proven that a government rural worker was most effective in encouraging the people to initiate and carry out "self-help" development projects when the worker was seen by the people as a trusted member of their community.

The well-to-do couple's son's name was Arturo, but everyone called him "Atoy." Atoy and his wife, Isabel, whom he married after he had decided he did not want to go to high school, had two children: a boy who was two years old, and a girl age eleven and a half months old. Isabel stayed mostly at home, taking care of the house and children. A shy but beauteous woman, of the same age as her husband, she roused forbidden desires in me the moment I first laid eyes on her, desires I immediately suppressed and, in days following, had to make a big effort to control each time I got close to her.

From the day I moved in with his parents, Atoy became very helpful to me, acting, during his off hours, as my unofficial guide to the village. He introduced me to the local residents and their respected leaders. To his friends, especially when I joined them in their frequent drinking sessions, Atoy introduced me as his "long-lost only brother." It was all done in the spirit of friendship and fun and I was pleased at being so readily accepted.

Atoy supported his family from his daily earnings at the town's public market where he helped his parents with their business. They butchered buffalo and cattle, and sold the meat (with the help of hired vendors) at three retail stalls rented from the municipal government.

The income was good, and every afternoon, around three or four o'clock, they (father, mother, son and occasionally, a married daughter, Elena, who lived in the next village) would come home in high spirits (indeed, sometimes full of spirits imbibed earlier from a bottle) and carrying the choice parts of the day's killed animals: brains, livers, hearts, or -- most prized of all -- bull's testicles.

There were afternoons when I would be home going over my reports by the window and Atoy, upon spotting me, would dash red-faced and laughing towards my window and yelling, "Catch!" Deftly, I would catch the packages of meat and deposit them in the kitchen.

The family, which now included me, had a nightly ritual. The three unmarried younger (younger than Atoy) daughters (Magda, Lourdes, Regina) who lived in the big house with us, prepared supper under the supervision of their mother, whom I fondly called "Tia Marta." Their father, Tio Julio, and Atoy prepared the tuba for that night's family consumption. Everyone in the family drank tuba: the older ones considerably more, the younger ones proportionately less.

Each morning, Tio Julio's paid tuba gatherer, Miguel, would come and, bare-footed, climb up the palm trees to their crowns. He would cut a portion of the trees' sheathed penis-shaped flower buds to induce a steady flow of their sweet milky sap into aged bamboo tubes. The collected sap would be removed the following day for that evening's or (if any was left over) for subsequent evening's use.

Tangal, the dry powdered bark of a mangrove tree called bakawan was added to the sap to dilute its sweetness and to prevent souring. The longer the sap was kept, the more potent it became. Bahal was what aged tuba was called. It had a cool, dry, winey flavor with just a hint of bitter tartness to its taste. I loved the stuff and drank it as heartily as everyone else.

As each meat dish (pulutan, as we called it) was cooked, a heaping plateful was passed around for everybody to share. In addition to the family members, the night's company might include visiting relatives, neighbors, friends, or sometimes even co-workers of mine who were assigned to nearby villages. Distributed with meat dishes were platefuls of steamed rice and vegetables, which we ate as we continued to soak up gallons of the fermenting tuba.

The bull's testicles (there was much teasing about their alleged aphrodisiac qualities), sautéed in coconut oil, garlic, onions, tomatoes with a generous dash of vinegar and hot peppers, went only to the men, although some of the women, on a dare, would gingerly fork and swallow a tidbit. And the men would continue teasing the women: "Isa pa! Dagdagan mo pa!" (Once more! Take another bite!)

These were nights of joyous bonding, occasions of many calls to linked-arms "Bottoms up!" drinking among us, especially between Atoy and me to see who, at the moment, could drain his glass the quickest, as the others cheered.

Much later in the evening (the eating and the drinking often lasted well past midnight), with our bellies distended from the pulutan, heads slightly pickled from the tuba -- and our feelings getting more intense -- our inhibitions, together with our tongues, would be set free. We would talk shamelessly about sex (how often one could do it even at a late age), spin tales of the supernatural (claimed encounters with witches who lived in a huddle of huts up the hill), gossip (the blind girl in the next village, someone reported, had been made pregnant by her half-brother), and -- sometimes -- blossom forth with statements of surprising profundity.

One evening we were talking about why some people succeed and made more money than others. Tio Julio, his rice-pale skin flushed with the potent tuba and his squinty eyes (his immigrant great-grandfather came from Shanghai) wet and glittery from laughing, suddenly remarked: "In all my sixty-nine years I have learned many things, but when it comes to people there is one thing I can say without hesitation. Many people succeed because they are driven by envy. Inggit. Ambitious people cannot stand having less than what their neighbors have."

I asked Tio Julio if he were ambitious. "No," he replied quickly. "I'm happy with what I have, what God has given me. He has been kind to me and my family."

I never saw Tio Julio go to church, not even during the feast day of the village or town patron saint. As a matter of fact, none of us in the house, including Atoy, did, except for the women who sometimes went to church on Sundays and always on the religious feast days. They would go as a group, often with other women from the neighborhood.

Occasionally, the night-long drinking and eating sessions would open the door to family revelations. Tia Marta, I learned at one of the sessions, was twenty years younger than Tio Julio. They met after his first wife had died during the Japanese occupation. It was a brief courtship as she and her parents liked him from the beginning, despite his being a widower with two small daughters: (the eldest daughter, Carmen, who had finished high school, now married to an engineer and they lived in Davao where the husband worked for a big foreign company that grew and exported bananas to Japan and Europe. Elena was Carmen's full sister.) Atoy was the first child from Tio Julio's second marriage, followed by three girls. All the children got their physical features from Tia Marta, who had a Spanish friar swinging from her family tree: smooth fair skin, prominent nose, almond-shaped eyes framed by thick eyelashes. Tia Marta had many suitors, but she chose Tio Julio for his good looks and maturity. A few days before the wedding, she was molested by the old parish priest when she went to him for confession. The priest suddenly reached for her breasts and tried to pull her into the confessional. She had fled from him but had never told anybody about the incident until long after the priest was dead. But she never went to confession again after that unpleasant encounter.

There were times when the ritual supper would be at somebody else's house: at Elena's, the married daughter in the next village; at the neighbors'; at the barrio captain's, who headed the barangay council entrusted with looking after the government's interests at the village level.

One night Mang Andong, the barrio captain, hosted a big supper and invited our family, together with the barangay council members and their families, his neighbors, in fact almost everyone in the village who would come. Such generosity was expected of him, being the headman of the community. He had one of his aging water buffaloes butchered, in addition to two pigs and a dozen or more chickens. Mang Andong had a big house on a promontory with a wonderful view of the river. He had a large family, having also been widowed and remarried and -- it was rumoured -- fathered his wife's sister's three children. All of them lived together happily in that big house.

At this supper at Mang Andong's, which my family -- except for Atoy -- attended, we also celebrated the approval by my national office in Manila of the projects proposed by the barangay council: a piped spring water system, a suspension footbridge across the river, a village community center. Construction of the projects could start immediately as the village people were now ready with their counterpart volunteer labor and locally-available materials like sand and gravel. The hardware materials for the projects (cement, steel rods, pipes, cables, etc.) provided by my development office were also ready.

The celebration reached a summit when some village musicians arrived with string instruments and people began singing and dancing. In the midst of this revelry, I felt sick and stole away from the party and went home, walking on the mud dikes that cut across the rice fields. The moon was full and the light was caught by the fog sweeping across the fields and coconut groves. It was a haunting scene that I would witness many times during my stay in the village. That night, just watching it and breathing the cool tree-scented air made me feel better.

Back in the big house I saw Atoy drinking by himself in the kitchen. He was crying with anger. Very drunk, his tongue slurring the words like a hurt child, he was complaining that we had not waited for him before we went to Mang Andong's house. I sat down. "But you could have come after us. You were gone too long at the poblacion that we couldn't wait any longer."

"I no longer felt like going after ... after I came home and found you all gone. You are now like a brother to me. A brother waits for his brother."

I didn't know how to respond to this unexpected outburst.

Atoy reached into his pocket and pulled out his knife and a cigarette lighter. He exposed the blade to the lighter's blue flame. Several minutes passed. I watched transfixed, saying nothing.

"I want us to become real blood brothers," he said in a changed voice, his words now coming out slow and clear. "Here, cut my wrist." He reached for my hand and placed the knife's handle in it.

"Are you sure?" I said, my voice catching in my throat. Carefully, I made a quick clean slit across his arm, well above the wrist. A thin line of blood emerged growing slowly.

"It's my turn," he said, taking the knife from my hand.

"Give me your arm." he made an identical cut on my right arm. When the blood appeared, he brought my arm over his, joining the two fresh wounds. They remained joined for several minutes, while we drank-from the same cup that he was holding with his free hand. When our right arms finally separated, he sucked the blood, first from his wound, then from mine. He held my shoulders with both hands and kissed me long and deeply -- in the mouth. I smelled the blood in his breath.

"Now we are true blood brothers," he said. He looked at me and I could fathom the deep loneliness in his eyes.

We drank some more until we heard voices, distant but approaching. The others were coming back from Mang Andong's party. Before Atoy left he said, "I am now your blood brother and this brother will share with you everything he has. Anytime you feel for a woman, I'll share Isabel with you."

In the days that followed (especially after the superficial arm wounds had healed), we seemed to (or pretended to) have forgotten about that night. I got so busy with the village development projects and my meetings with the barrio captain and the barangay council often lasted late into the night, causing me to miss many of the ritual suppers in the big house. And when I managed to rejoin our family, Atoy and I avoided any indication to each other that we ever had that intimate exchange. More than before, I steered away from having to have any close contact with Isabel.

After the completion of the village projects, I was promoted and re-assigned to our main office in Manila. I was stunned by how the villagers received the news of my impending departure. I was visited almost daily by neighbors, friends, and acquaintances who brought farewell gifts. I was invited to so many suppers during the last month of my village stay that I lost count of them: supper at Mang Andong's, at three of the village councilors' homes, at several neighbors', at numerous friends', at the house of the widow Rosing who washed and ironed my clothes for a monthly fee and who -- on several occasions when we found ourselves alone in the big house -- had shared my bed.

On my last night at the big house my family gave a party in my honor and invited everyone in the village. The crowd was so large that we held the party in the backyard. When all the guests had left, and Tio Julio and Tia Marta and the girls had cried themselves to sleep, Atoy and I brought a full pitcher of tuba to drink in the veranda of his house. I was heartsick with the thought of leaving.

It was still night but the moon was full and bright. A mist was moving slowly across the fields and slipping through the many stands of coconut trees. We drank and watched the fog in the moonlight a long time before Atoy spoke.

"The night was like this when we confirmed our brotherhood with a blood compact, remember?"

"Yes," I answered.

"Remember what I said before I left you?"

"Yes," I said.

"I want to prove to you that I meant what I said."

"What about Isabel? Shouldn't she have a say in this?"

"We have talked the matter over. She's all for it. She likes you. In fact she has a crush on you. Just like all these women who carry a torch for you. Just like Rosing, whom I know you've been sleeping with."

"Let's not rush it. We have a pitcher of tuba to finish."

"Take your time. But it must be tonight, your last night with us."

"What if I get her pregnant?"

"It will be our joy, our child."

As I looked at the moving fog again, still sweeping over the blossoming rice and reaching out to the flowing sap of the sheathed buds deep in the crowns of the coconut trees, I remembered once, during my first year in the village, coming home from a late meeting with my co-workers in the poblacion. That night, too, was full of moonlight and mist. I was passing by a house that stood close to the road. It was the house of Isabel's grandparents, with whom she had grown up.

The house had a narrow front yard planted thickly with bushes of jasmine, now blooming profusely, the white flowers throwing their rich sweet fragrance into the night. The scent blended with the light and the fog, enveloping everything, and transforming the world into an ethereal realm of stunning beauty. Paradise! I felt light-headed from this overwhelming display of nature's perfections. Everything is possible in this world, I thought. I felt happy, needful, forlorn.

Across from where Atoy and I sat in the veranda, the fog seemed to have suddenly appeared at the door. It was Isabel, the great curves of her body pushing the long silk white gown she wore to form into sensuous mounds. Her lush hair was a waterfall cascading darkly over the smooth rocks of her breasts. I sucked my breath. She was smiling sweetly, impatiently.

Inside the bedroom, I could smell that remembered night's fragrance of my first year in the village. The scent of jasmine! Isabel had picked the flowers from her grandmother's yard and brought them into his room. The needful, forlorn feelings returned. As I moved my body closer to Isabel's body, now naked between us, Atoy whispered softly, "My farewell gift, brother!" he had the pocket knife in his hand.

**Bio:** *Luis Cabalquinto writes fiction, non-fiction and poetry in English as well as in Pilipino and Bikolano. He has also done translations from Spanish into English and Pilipino. He has three books of poetry published:* The Dog-Eater and Other Poems *(1989),* The Ibalon Collection *(1991) and* Dreamwanderer *(1992). Recently, his poem "Hometown" was included in three American college textbooks:* New Worlds of Literature *(W.W. Norton & CO.);* Literature: Reading and Responding to Fiction, Poetry, Drama, and the Essay *(Harper/Collins); and* Literature and Ourselves *(Harper/Collins College Division).*

*He is the recipient of the Dylan Thomas Poetry Award from the New School for Social Research, an Academy of American Poets poetry prize from New York University, a Fellowship Award in Poetry from the New York Foundation of Arts, and a Fulbright-Hays travel grant from the U.S. State Department. "The Fog" won a fiction prize from the Philippine Graphic.*

*Luis Cabalquinto has given lectures and readings at the American Museum of Natural History, PEN American Center, Dalton School, Writer's Community, Hunter College, Queens College, Sarah Lawrence College, University of Maryland, St. Mark's Poetry Project, and others.*

*He has a journalism degree from the University of the Philippines and did graduate work in creative writing at Cornell University and New York University. He divides his writing time between his Bikol hometown, Magarao in the Philippines, and New York City, where he has been a resident for twenty-six years.*

# GRANDMA AND SPANISH WOMEN

F. Delor Angeles

I WAS YOUNG when I lost my grandmother, that is, the mother of my mother.

The kids in our clan called her Lola Andeng, lola for grandmother and Andeng, a variant for Andrea. Her nickname was de cariño (very special). To all grandchildren, it meant, "Grandmother, I love you."

Everyone including cunning little devils she lectured to, loved her. I did. Once I fought with a boy who insulted my ancestry, and he pushed me, my behind landing smack on a cake of buffalo dung. Afterwards, as I stood pantless with diminished machismo before her, she mended clean shorts and restored my pride. "Villanuevas do not play with street boys."

Even cousin Rosita, who grew up with full breasts and a passion for men, adored her. You couldn't tell that when you saw her listening poutily to one of Lola's sermons. One evening, when the children of the clan were gathered in the ancestral abode, Rosita laughed raucously, but stopped short.

"Ladies," Lola warned her sternly, "do not laugh that way." Blunders of that sort usually led to snappy lecture on Spanish women.

You see, Grandma was placed in a convent school in Zamboanga by her parents, where she was brought up by Spanish nuns. When she returned to Antipolo, the Spanish woman had become her ideal—"proper, modest, and chaste"— a truth which she urged on her friends and relatives, then to the children who were born later into the clan, to Rosita, my three sisters who became spinsters, and two grandsons—"they're going to look for wives someday."

Gradually, after her death, I stopped reminiscing about the beloved old woman who mended my shorts. I went through primary school, then high school in another town, where I made new friends and discovered an interest in older girls.

A stage in my life, however, brought Grandma's memory back to me. This was when I was old enough to shake off provincial loyalties and to hunger after new lands and other races. A year-long journey through Hong Kong, Bangkok, Karachi and Beirut landed me ultimately in Frankfurt.

A youth hostel at the edge of town offered cheap but clean lodgings. Its food supervisor, a rather pleasant surprise, was a young española. "Me llamo Marites," she said.

"In other words, Maria Teresa."

The face brightened. She had stayed in Frankfurt two or three years and no one, till a Filipino came, had told how her name was coined.

Marites fit into a Filipino's archetypical image of a pretty Spanish woman, chin cut like a heart, small lips, a carefully chiseled nose and long dark hair reaching the waist. Her eyes were the gems of her face, distant stars that emitted winkling lights in the deep black of night.

I'd be a fool to ignore her, I thought, and so when we met downtown near a konditorei, I invited her to a cup of coffee.

"Accept it," her companion urged. A scolding in well-stressed Castilian cut the matchmaker short.

"Sorry," Marites begged off, "but we have to go somewhere." Her black eyes admitted however, "I'm lying."

The next encounter was on the stairs in the hostel. She had just finished bathing in the apartment of Erika, and her long black hair, glistening with water, connived with an olive skin and the sweet scent of her body to fuddle me.

Marites sensed the trapped animal, but moved away, shooting off in German, "Good night."

There are unexpected moves in chess, and in this game, a German girl was a surprise piece. Greta had tiny Oriental eyes which shut with laughter, and the way she said, "Gut, gut," sent tingles ripping around my nape, spine, and the little valleys of my ribs. We dined in a Chinese restaurant, chased each other in the snow, then settled down to tinned mangoes from the Philippines.

Perhaps it was the mangoes, or perhaps, it was the bare trees and the silent snow outside. Whatever it was, her eyes and my eyes kept closing and closing, we were trying to catch our breath, our heads leaning and moving at every rush of air towards soft collision. When Marites saw us, she complained to Erika, "I'm not college educated ..."

"He invited you to a cup of coffee, but you refused."

When Christmas came, Greta prepared to join her folks in Hamburg while I made ready a trip to Maryland to see my sisters. She saw me off at the railway station, puckering her lips to say kuss, then auf wiedersehen.

Erika wrote me in Maryland, "Marites has transferred to Cologne." But I remembered what Carmelo taught me about women: "Never court women by letters."

At any rate, I met Lourdes. I rode this commuters' bus to Washington D.C. from Montgomery County now and then, and one afternoon a young woman with Spanish eyes sat beside me.

"Pardon me, señorita, but are you an española, is it not the truth?"

Tiny fires of sapphires danced through aureoles before

she affirmed, "Si, si, si!"

Lourdes was taking English in Washington D.C., but speaking the languages only "a little bit," and was relieved to meet someone who knew her native tongue. She lived a few blocks from my sisters' home, and so did her girl friend, an American named Mary Ann.

"You know, Lourdes and I hardly talked to each other until you came along," Mary Ann imparted.

"Hombre," Lourdes pleaded, "you must help me translate Spanish recipes for Mary Ann.

That was what I was good at, translating, and as I interpreted for the Latin and Anglo-Saxon worlds, my eyes darted between the two women until they fell on Mary Ann's thighs. They were robust, rounded, like the trunk of the birch tree in my sisters' backyard.

But finally Iberian eyes won.

Winter passed into spring, and between these seasons, Lourdes and I went around Washington D.C. drinking of American culture and the happiness of a man and woman doing things together. We never met in the county, except on the bus; always, it was in the capitol.

Then, in summer, she said goodbye; she had to go back to Barcelona. At the airport, she introduced a young and dark Spaniard.

"This is Antonio, my husband."

We shook hands.

I left for Madrid a week later. In summer, the university there offered package programs in Hispanic studies, which included the Spanish language and arts with paella, wine, bullfight, and a session with flamenco thrown in.

My landlords in Madrid were Don Pedro Ibarramendia and his wife, Doña Juana; three daughters and a toddler two years of age completed their family. Don Pedro was a huge man, well built, but he seemed to shrink whenever he came home from the fondas. Before I had taken my early cup of coffee, he would be off into the streets, walking from tavern to tavern where he would consume his daily rations of snails, frog legs, and sherry and joust in song with the bar habitués. On nightfall, he swayed home, slurring, face puffy and red like the bottle of Pedro Domecq.

Doña Juana retained the beauty of her youth, but she was now heavy with flesh. Like Marites and Lourdes, her eyes gave out tiny dancing fires, and when she sat on the sofa, skirt receding, her thighs spoke, taunting and teasing. (Ah, Mary Ann!)

The Ibarramendias had a lovely patio where the sun fell friendly and caressing, and stayed. Pedrito, the toddler, and I both discovered this place and laid claim to it, and soon, his mother became bold enough to ask, "Will you take Pedrito to the park, por favor?"

Por favor. This was quickly followed by: "Please help me gather the clothes from the clothesline." "There is a German in the patio. He speaks English. Can you translate for me?"

Then Pedrito got sick: Doña Juana must take him to the doctor. "Carry Pedrito for me, will you?" The queen walked with grace and dignity while the page trudged along, the crown prince in his arms. The doctor had Doña Juana and Pedrito in his office for a long time; the poor boy sniffed and drooped, like a young chicken weighed by a cold. While waiting for my landlady, I scanned the diplomas on the office wall and saw visions of college dons in medieval shirts serenading the señoritas of Madrid.

On the way home, Doña Juana clutched me away from the calle real to a series of dark alleys. "This is a shortcut." Massive stone walls towards above us. It was like lying down in bed for hours with the lights off, not moving or making a sound, and feeling the contours of the walls in an effort to distinguish between shadows and the surfaces of the room.

Light from a house fell on us in a brief instant. Was the señora smiling? But why? Pedrito got heavier with each meeting of foot and cobblestone.

Dim light from another house fell again on us, then dropped behind. She was smiling!

But we reached the pension at last; that's what mattered most. Relief rose in my arms as Pedrito was deposited in his crib. I went to my room and, without undressing, sought the bed for a badly needed rest.

A slight noise restored me to the world. Doña Juana entered the room, closing the door after her. She went to the bed and sat on the pillow where my head was resting a moment ago. Her eyes, desperate, threatening, hurling the challenge of a street fighter, fastened upon mine and bored deep.

"Ppppaco! ... Paco!"

I left her, went to the kitchen, washed my face, and then shut myself up in the toilet. I was gone for a long time, and when I returned, my room was empty.

The bed was wet. My arms brushed against the spot, triggering message after message, as an excited reaction races through a computer.

I lifted the blanket and dropped it on the floor. There was a funny smell from the sheets. I brought my nose close to the cloth. It was urine.

I replaced the bedclothes and went out into the callejon. Don Pablo, his wife, his mother-in-law, and a strange woman were in the alley shouting at one another.

"Ven conmigo," the strange woman begged.

"Loca," Don Pablo yelled, "you are a fool!"

I fled back to my room and packed my clothes. In the morning, I informed Don Pedro and Doña Juana that I was leaving.

"Mama," the oldest girl was surprised, "you are crying."

"He is a good man."

The custom was to take her hand and kiss it. But I stepped without another word into the sunlit alley and walked towards the railway station.

When the train started, I felt sleepy. I forgot that agile hands snatched luggage in Spanish trains and slept all the way to Saragoza. But my luggage was safe, and two days later, in Barcelona, I boarded a Turkish boat for Marseilles.

The sea was calm and peaceful and the sun was out. A bunch of French boy scouts pressed round a guitar and sang a ballad.

When the Arabs heard the French boys, they looked at one another knowingly. "Hep, hep, ah, ah ah!" In macho voices they sang and danced in a circle.

Ethnic war. I moved away. At the stern, I watched the water swirling, leaving a trail in the sea.

And then I saw Lola Andeng. She was in her rocking chair, swaying gently back and forth on the Mediterranean. At her feet were cousin Rosita and my three sisters.

"Remember, girls," Grandma admonished. "When you grow old, walk like Spanish women. They are proper modest, and chaste.

*Bio of F. Delor Angeles: I grew up an impoverished preacher's son in Navotas, a fishing town near Manila. The best thing about my childhood was the smell of the sea.*

*And in my high school days? My teachers loved me, and Miss Soriano, the English teacher, encouraged me to write.*

*In college, I studied journalism under Armando Malay, but a wind yanked me to South Dakota where George McGovern gave us a love for history.*

*Now a historian, I taught, made pals with Teodoro Agoncillo and H. de la Costa, S.J., and was knighted in Fort Santiago by my old professor, Malay. My contributions to historiography include studies on the Spanish Inquisition and the Moro Wars.*

*"Typhoons" forced me out, however, and I roamed all over Asia, Latin America, Europe, etc. I worked as a teacher, dishwasher, clerk, casino porter, etc. Boy! These look like the path to full-time writing.*

*Except that now I have cancer; only God knows if I'll live long enough to see my grandchildren bloom. The "garden" is about the deer and rabbits in our yard; the children of America who'll never be mine: a Davanueña who gave me an apple at Silliman, a Zamboangueña whose message I didn't fathom, a Swedish redhead who made me write poetry on Lövånger, and an Algerian girl froom Mostaganem with hazel eyes.*

*Hemingway, Joyce, Rulfo, Lorca and Joaquin are my favorites*

*and Ric Demetillo and Migs Enriquez are my friends. As a "gardener,"*
*I hope to sign the wall in Mig's study someday.*

# THE BALIKBAYAN

Melissa R. Aranzamendez

MYRNA MOUNTED the wooden escalator step and began reading the half-page note she held in her left hand.

"Dear Ate," it read, in small unruly handwriting, "I can't wait until you get back home. When you do, please get me a pair of Doc Martens, size 6 ½. Raul's uncle from California bought him one, and I want one too. I miss you so much. Love, Tetchie."

As the escalator step reached the top floor, Myrna walked over to the shoe department and received some direction from an impassive salesperson. "High or low tops?" the girl asked her, to which Myrna replied, "What's cheaper?" The clerk rolled her eyes and disappeared into the stock room, and Myrna tried to remember all other items she had to pick up as pasalubongs for the folks back home. What would they want from America? she thought. It's been three years since she left the Philippines, and she was not quite sure what was in demand there at the moment. She had been to the discount shop to pick up some knick-knacks for anyone she might have failed to put on her list, but almost everything there was made in Taiwan, or made in Korea, and Myrna was sure that only American products would be appreciated. Some were even made back home! She also worried that her two bags would go over the seventy-pound weight limit required by the airline. She had already purchased a bag each of M&M's, Milky Way, and Hershey's Kisses, not to mention the dozen cans of Hormel's Spam, Libby's Corned Beef, and the family pack of Ivory Soap that she bought on sale at Shoprite. Furthermore, she had to buy linens and towels for her mother, shirts for her father, designer jeans for her older brother, sports caps for her cousins, and now, Techie and her Doc Martens.

The sales clerk finally reemerged with four shoe boxes. Myrna stuck her hand in her pocketbook and, within a worn-out air mail envelope, found a pair of folded paper cut-outs that out-lined the soles of a pair of shoes. She looked at the label on the first box and her jaw dropped. The price was $134.99. She examined its contents, anxious to find out what could possibly be contained within the box that was worth thirteen-and-a-half hours of her own hard work. They looked like any other pair of shoes, and Myrna tried to determine what was so special about the shoe that caught her sister's fancy. The least expensive pair was on sale for $99.95!

After fifteen minutes of contemplation, Myrna resigned herself to indulging her sister's whim, despite the fact that this purchase was going to cost her two days' worth of overtime. This might be the only opportunity she'd have in a long time to do something for her little sister, so Myrna picked up the cheapest pair and matched the paper soles to the real thing. "No, there are no other sizes, not even in the back," the sales girl informed her. Myrna settled for the size seven low tops, hoping that a pair of socks would fill the void between the leather and Tetchie's toes. Heck, maybe her feet were still growing. The shoes were, after all, on sale.

Her watch told her there were three more hours before the train would take her from Manhattan to Douglaston,

Queens. Her employer specifically requested that she return by two in the afternoon, since the family was throwing a party that evening and her help was needed in preparing and serving the food as well as cleaning up after all the guests leave. Although she usually took Saturdays and Sundays off, Myrna had not protested. She just hoped that the guests would not stay too late. Her balikbayan trip was coming up in two weeks and she would get all the rest she needed in a month's leave. Mrs. Benson was nice and charitable to her and had no problem with her extended, albeit unpaid, absence. "Just as long as you come back within a month," Mrs. Benson said, "you know we can't do without you." Mrs. Benson even offered some sample cosmetics and hand-me-down clothes (which Myrna graciously accepted but delivered to the nearest Salvation Army branch instead) for her to bring home.

While making her purchase, Myrna subconsciously picked at her nails, a habit she had formed after she was assigned her first task in the Benson household which was to scrub the kitchen floor. Prior to this job, when she was still in the Philippines, Myrna had not performed any hard physical labor. She was a college graduate, the first one in the family who actually used her mind to earn a living. It was her mother who washed other people's clothes, who worked with her hands. That was back in the Philippines; in America it was another story. Mrs. Benson had provided her with a cleanser that was too harsh for her sensitive skin and her fingertips began to peel. She learned her lesson and started using gloves, but she never stopped pulling on her cuticles since then.

"Oh, they make great household help," she heard Mrs. Benson mention on the phone once. "They never complain and they always do their job. The two girls before her, ugh, I couldn't stand them. First I tried a Black girl, you know how they are. Then the agency got me a Spanish woman who could barely speak English. None of them worked out. You tell them to do a little thing, and they're always reminding you, 'That's not my job.' But this one, she'll even offer to do extra work for you, that's how good she is. There was one time when the landscaper didn't show up, and of course I would not have my lawn looking a mess, I mean, what would the neighbors say? So I asked this one if she could do a little trimming on the hedges, and she mowed the entire lawn! The kids love her. And she cooks delicious. Of course I don't pay cheap, but let me know if ever you need one, maybe she's got sisters. I highly recommend them!"

Myrna took the elevator two flights up to the Bedding Department and walked to the clearance section. She was pleased to find a pile of queen-size irregulars, 200 thread count. Near the shelf was displayed a bed with a gauzy canopy hung over it, which suddenly reminded her of the comfort of her mother's bed, how as a child she used to fall asleep under the mosquito net in her parents' bedroom while her mother scratched her itchy back with her long, pointy nails. Her parents' room was the site for the nightly family rosary, since her mother believed that the family that prays together, stays together, even though only women were obligated to participate. She tried to picture them at this moment, a half day ahead of her, Techie falling asleep as always, while her mother led the litany, eyes closed, sacred words spewing from her mouth, and rosary beads in her firm grasp. It would just be the two of them now, and she wondered if they missed her. She so longed for the warmth and consolation offered by the area under the mosquito net. The bedroom that the Bensons offered her was air-conditioned, and her window rendered a pleasant view of the autumn leaves. It didn't matter, though, for despite the firm, innerspring coils of the Sealy posturepedic twin mattress she now used, she still would have preferred the colorful woven banig that her mother rolled out on the hardwood floor for her, each night under the watchful eye of Our Lady of Perpetual Help.

The sheet set proved to be within her budget, so Myrna bought them without hesitation. She decided she would not demand payment for this afternoon's services although she would accept if Mrs. Benson offered to pay her. After all, the Bensons did provide free food and lodging, and in spite of the fact that she had never been sick, she did have medical insurance paid for by the Bensons. She would simply ask if she could work next week-end, since she could make good use of the money, at least send most of it back home, just as she did every month. They always had something for her to do anyway: some drapes that needed laundering, or tiles that needed scouring, or toenails that needed painting. Her old job as an elementary school teacher for a private school in Manila paid less than half the Bensons wages; and this job, hard and unpredictable as it was, allowed her to help her family live comfortably and with dignity.

Myrna proceeded to the Men's Department to pick out some shirts for the men of the house. She tried to visualize her father in the forty-five dollar Polo shirt and decided against buying it. Such a simple-minded man would surely not appreciate the handiwork that went into the one hundred percent pima cotton shirt which Myrna stroked with her free hand. He had barely appreciated her contributions back home, not the groceries, not the paid utility bills, not the rent that drained her teacher's wages. Instead of soliciting passengers for his jeepney service, he went out cavorting with his drinking buddies and he brought no money home. He even demanded part of his wife's earnings as a lavandera to five different families. Yet nothing was ever enough for him, not the food that Techie made sure was hot and ready when he got home, nor extra effort that his wife contributed in order to be both mother and father to the children. It was he who had insisted that Myrna come to America to earn more money, money which afforded the brother's big resplendent wedding. She questioned why she even bothered to bring them anything; but then she reminded herself that it would be her mother who would be the target of her father's disdain. She ended up buying a plaid cotton shirt with the department store label for her father, and some underwear and socks for her brother. They may not have been what they asked for, but they were definitely more than what they deserved.

Pleased that she was done with her list, she walked

outside the department store and continued on to Pennsylvania Station. She sat and waited for the 12:45 train. She imagined herself being greeted by three carloads of relatives at the Manila International Airport, all eager to welcome her, all impressed by her new American ways. You've gained weight, Tetchie would say, must be all that stateside food! She would tell them all about her life in New York, how she had her own bedroom with wall-to-wall carpeting and remote-control color TV with cable, how her bathroom was equipped with a bathtub, how hot water came out of the tap. They would ask her if she had been to the top of the Empire State Building, or if she had climbed inside the Statue of Liberty, and she would say yes, what a wonderful sight it was! She would tell them how she bought all their pasalubongs at Macy's, the largest department store in the world. And she would speak to them in her heavily accented English, as if she were no longer accustomed to her native tongue.

The loud rumble of the train broke her reverie. Myrna boarded an almost-empty car and settled her purchases on a vacant seat. She started picking at her nails again, then looked out the window; and, as with each morning when she awoke, she tried to persuade herself to go to work.

*Bio: Melissa R. Aranzamendez was born in Manila in 1966. The second of four children, she grew up in an affluent subdivision in Parañaque. Her childhood took a turn in 1979 when her mother accepted a position with the United Nations in New York. She and her siblings followed a year later, and the family settled in Jersey City, New Jersey.*

*Melissa received a Bachelor of Science degree from the New Jersey Institute of Technology and earns a living managing technical publications in New York City. In 1993, a visit back to the Philippines reawakened childhood memories of her native land, and Melissa has since felt compelled to write about her experiences as an immigrant and the trauma of leaving loved ones behind. In addition to several short stories, Melissa has also written a full-featured screenplay and was assistant stage manager for the 1992 MA-YI production of* Kuti-Kutitap *at the Henry Street Settlement Theater in New York. She currently lives in New Jersey with her mother and her ten-year old son, Adam.*

# PAPERBACK DREAMS
# AND OTHER REALITIES

Eulalio Yerro Ibarra

I'M GLAD you came.

Nobody has really visited except my brother who asked me to sign some papers yesterday. Para sa insurance daw. He's selling my life insurance to some company. Fucking ghouls. But it's for the better, enjoy my money while I can, my brother said. This last episode was really bad, kaya I consented to autograph each page of the document that he presented to me. It's like tempting fate, but I need the money to visit the Philippines. As soon as I am well enough.

I never hid my sexuality you know. Even back home in Manila, I was already flaming. Bakla na ko since nineteen kopong-kopong pa. Unlike many of our countrysisters here. Only after they had landed in America did they unfurl their capes and adorn their heads with glittering tiaras. Sometimes they even have the audacity to order me not to tell anybody about them in the Philippines. Naku ha, putik-putik na and mga kapa nila, tiklup-tiklop pa rin. I mean, who do they think they are? They've been dirtying their capes here in the U.S. for years, but they still would like to think that they're innocent in the Philippines? Manigas sila.

That's why I like it here in America. It is so easy to come out here. But being Filipino and being gay, it's doubly hard, not only because we have to fight for our place in the American dream, but also in the gay American dream. It's as if we are invisible and can only exist in comfort on the fringes, in our own narrow subculture and its admirers. Buwa ng ina, kaya, well, we just create our own space, our own color in the rainbow. Many of the Flip gays I know here don't have anything to do with the White gay community. And it's not their choice either, it's just there isn't much interaction between the two. Except for rice queens. But rice queens are so diri! If you don't fit in the mold of what they think Filipinos or Asians are, you are not in their picture. Sometimes though, it's better that way.

Back home, my being bakla was not an issue at all. Fooey to all those scholarly studies that advance the idea that it is easy to be gay in the Philippines. They're all a sham. Sure, male-to-male sex is everywhere, but like anywhere else, gays are also ostracized by our families, by society. Filipino gays are often brutalized by our macho male figures, by strangers posing to sell sex, especially by policemen who want to extort money.

I was lucky, I did not have to suffer the family rejection that many baklas are enduring back home. My father was always championing the causes of the oppressed. My being gay was not a problem. There were more serious human rights issues he had to fight during the Marcos regime when human life did not amount to anything much. My father was always out there, demonstrating in the streets until his incarceration in the stockades where he died a mysterious death. Pero, my other relatives, even those here in the States, they'd rather that I keep my cape, my beautiful ermine cape, folded and tucked away in my closet. My being homosexual is a shame to the family name daw. As if the family has a name, no? Who are they trying to protect? Dito sa Amerika, we are nothing naman, e. That's why I never told any of them that I have HIV. They're one less problem I have to take care of.

My Filipino friends here in Chicago? My so-called. Mga buwa ng ina nila. Nobody really cares. To them, I might as well be dead already. Except of course I am the latest fodder for their vicious gossip. The first time I was hospitalized last year, chismis got around, kesyo, I got this and I got that. And what was left was the wait for the grim reaper to come. Hey, guys! I'm still here and I intended to stay as long as I can. Some even said that they expected me to get AIDS because I was so upfront with my life. As if I am the one to blame. Suddenly, everybody I know became the Virgin Mary.

And to think I was *Mother Lily* to them all when they were starting out here in Chicago. My life and my house were always open to them, to anybody who needed a respite, being strangers in a strange land. My house in Skokie used to be the party central for the Filipino gay community in Chicago, indeed the whole of the Midwest. Be it all night mahjong tournaments or fashion shows for closeted drag queens, everybody was always welcome. Naku, this is why I have closets full of bed sheets and curtains. Basta there is a gathering of Filipino gays, expected na those haute couture fashion shows or beauty contests to happen. The sheets and curtains were very handy for instant gowns created by the budding mujeristas. You can't imagine how much money I had spent on pins and staples and Scotch tape! It was so magical. My sheets and curtains, even though they were just bought from K-Mart, were transformed into elegant creations; Jose Natori, that Filipina fashion czar in New York, would have been envious.

Those were the days. But when I got diagnosed, only a few visited. Many sent their regards and flowers, some, even money, but they were afraid to see me! They might get Tita Aida from visiting me daw. A few became hysterical because they'd been to my house so many times. Well, at least something good came out of their hysteria. Many went to Howard Brown to get tested. But God, they're fucking hypocrites. And they're supposed to be highly educated.

Coño! This hospital bed is so uncomfortable and the nurses aren't always here to help. They are very good though, considering they're overworked. But really, with this disease, one needs a full-time attendant. There are even times when I can't lift my arm to reach for a glass of water because I am just so weak! This is one of those times that I wish I were home. Because in the Philippines, I could easily afford to hire a nurse, maybe two, to take care of me twenty-four hours a day. But I can't complain. I am not really that helpless yet naman.

Pero, some of the Filipino nurses here, especially those on the night shift, parang they're so ashamed tending to me. Because I am a Filipino and I got IT. As if I am insulto to them. They can't even look me in the eye, much less mention AIDS and HIV. Mga mare, it's AIDS and the virus doesn't choose the race it infects! You shouldn't carry my shame because you are Filipinos like me! I could have been a leprechaun, the virus wouldn't know! I understand them though. It is a burden for them, because I, being a Filipino infected with AIDS, tarnished their image. Because they're new immigrants and would like to project an image of propriety. Amor propio is such a heavy thing for Filipinos.

That's why I called you. I have got a lot of stories to tell. And I need to tell them, parang my life was not lived in vain naman. I never wanted to be a waling-waling that blossomed in the jungles of Mindanao, only to wither and never appreciated. I need to tell my stories now, before my memory completely falters. Putang inang virus kasi. It infects the brain and steals your memories. I know that they are there in my brain, but when I try to remember them, my mind just goes blank. Or the details become patchy. It's like when you lose a file in the computer. You know that you stored it but when you try to retrieve it, you can't. I shudder to think what will happen to my mind when my disease gets to an advanced stage. What's a person without memories? They are all I have.

My friends, my real friends, they've long gone to the disease too.

Except Neil. My dear old friend. We go back, way back since our high school days. He is one of the lucky ones. He went to New Zealand kasi, brought over by a Kano too. He wrote that cases are relatively few in New Zealand and most of them are imported. New Zealanders who came home from the States to die. Just like in the Philippines. Most of the gay AIDS cases there are also imported or gotten from foreigners. It's only now that they're seeing cases in the gay community that have been contracted locally. And the community is in denial. How do I know? Another good friend is leading the AIDS education effort there. He's such a saint.

Diyos ko. I should have gone to New Zealand, you know. I met Paul, a Kiwi, I was still back in Manila then. He wanted me to go live with him in New Zealand. Pero, I didn't go. I wanted to go to the Steyts. Brian, my Kano friend who was an officer at the US Embassy, had already arranged for me to go to the U.S. with him when Paul invited me down under. So I told Paul, next time na lang. Siyempre, for sale to the highest bidder, di ba?

Oy, legal ako! That's what the Filipino rumor mill says. I will be deported daw because I am an illegal alien and I have AIDS. Hah, I am legal, but I can't get residency. This is how I learned I got the disease in the first place. Because I had to have the test to apply for my green card. When the results came, I was HIV-positive. Na por nada. I should have applied for my residency a long time ago, when they only had to test for TB. But I just didn't see the point to it before. So now I am in limbo. But let the courts decide this for me. It is not my most pressing problem right now.

I came to the States on a business visa. Brian and I set up an import-export company, named Filipino-American Imports, Co., baduy ano? I managed to arrange some financial backing for me, at least on paper, from a cousin who was a corporate lawyer of the Benedictos, one of Marcos's cronies. So the documents to pave the way for my entry to the United

States were pretty much in order. I was blessed because I had connections.

After Brian's retirement from the diplomatic corps, we came directly to Chicago to set up shop. The first two years were hectic, Brian and I frequently visited Asia to purchase merchandise to build up our inventory. Now, we just get our supplies mainly from the West Coast. The company prospered and we now employ more than twenty people. The business is still pretty strong and has diversified. Thank God for Brian who had the vision to expand. We are now the largest operator of door-to-door shipments between the Midwest and the Philippines! I wouldn't have thought of it all. Sad to say, Brian and I ended our relationship. Putang inang, Narciso! My so-called friend. Snatched Brian right under my nose. I didn't even realize it.

You're new here, right? Just be careful, hane. Especially if you have a lover. Before you know it, your friends will be stealing your lover. Filipinos are like that, you know. No delicadeza at all. But Brian and I are still much in the business together. The company is my primary source of bread and butter, though we did not get started with bakery or dairy products. If I may say so.

Would you believe it was bagoong which sailed us through? For years, we had the monopoly of the bagoong business in North America, until many Fil-Am entrepreneurs, doctors with excess disposable incomes really, realized that selling bagoong was lucrative. So now everybody seems to be owning bagoong distributorships. Fucking copy cats. If you must know, bagoong is that horrible smelling fermented shrimp or fish paste. It's like caviar to Filipinos.

I really wanted to go to the States. Since I was small, I had dreamt of America -- the snow, Disneyland, Hollywood, New York. Ever since the time I learned English from Mr. Sean Marvin, the American Peace Corps Volunteer, in our town. How I loved to learn English from him. Mr. Marvin was so articulate, so tall, so handsome, he looked like the prince in Snow White and the Seven Dwarfs. He always talked about his home in Indiana, his family's red brick house surrounded by a white picket fence, and his mom's apple pie. Just like in the Dick and Jane primer that Mr. Marvin used to teach English to us. I always wondered how would it be like to have an American friend like Dick with eyes as blue as the November sky and hair so yellow like corn during harvest time. Someday, I vowed to myself, I will experience white Christmas too, and not just dream and sing about it.

My dreams of the United States were even made stronger after I read those cheap paperbacks written by big-time American hookers and hustlers, like the *Happy Hooker* and the *Happy Hustler*. They had such wonderful lives! I imagined that I could be like them too. That some blue-eyed Kano will take an interest in me. Clothe me with stateside shirts, feed me apples and grapes, and bring me to America to be in his arms forever. As if life is as simple as that.

Where should I start? Oh yeah, my first Kano. Short for Amerikano. Mostly decrepit old men, mind you. But rich. We called everyone Kano, even if they were from Europe, Australia, New Zealand or Patagonia. As long as they were white. Sometimes they were also known by their badaf name— afam, Kano, afam, white guy, they meant the same thing. And civam, shaolin, call-boy, hustler—they were us, the youthful Filipino bodies that the Kanos lusted after. Filipino youths in their prime, all yours for the taking, declared *Spartacus*, the gay guide published out of Amsterdam.

I wasn't really a hustler. I was an afamista, a Filipino who only wants whites. But I had no choice. It was only in the streets of Ermita where I could find an afam. So I hung out there, together with the boys. Until I became one of them. Might as well, because I really wanted to be like Grant Tracy Saxon, the Happy Hustler.

I met my first Kano at Shakey's restaurant in Malate. I was with friends from school, eating pizza. I didn't know then that Shakey's was a tambayan for boys. But I knew that there were many Kanos eating there. That was why I invited my friends to eat there in the first place. Maybe, I thought, I would meet someone like Mr. Marvin there. Shakey's was located right smack in the middle of the sex tourist district of Manila, near honky-tonk bars catering to foreign patrons of all persuasions.

A Kano with an American accent at the table next to ours asked us to help him order; he wasn't familiar with the flavors of Philippine pizza, he said. I had already noticed him because he had been looking at me the moment he sat down. I entertained the idea of acting out my dreams with him. *Those eyes, they're so blue!* I knew he was bluffing, of course. Shakey's is an American chain and the pizza they serve are the same as those in America. It said so in their menu, and they were very proud to advertise it on the radio, in magazines and on TV. This was why Shakey's was very popular in Manila when it opened. It gave ordinary Filipinos a piece of heaven, a taste of America.

My friends and I were not dumb, we were all from the University of the Philippines, the premier school back home, but, hey, Filipinos are supposed to be warm and hospitable, right? Even the Ministry of Tourism during Marcos's time insisted on calling the sex tourist industry that brought millions of dollars to the family's coffers with a tamer name, 'hospitality industry', and the women working in bars, 'hospitality girls'. Manila Loves You! said the promotional T-shirts given to every 100th tourist that came into the international airport. So we obliged to assist the Kano, to live up to our friendly and hospitable image. In high school during the first years of martial law, we were instructed in our civics class to always smile and be hospitable to tourists. So in Shakey's that evening, being the martial law babies that we were, we wanted very much to be the paradigm of the Philippines' legendary hospitality. But hospitality and graciousness aside, I thought helping the Kano would be my best opportunity to act out my fantasies. I wanted to be a Happy Hustler, Filipino style.

We invited the Kano to join us at our table, which he did without hesitation. He really looked lonely in his table. He thanked us with a round of San Miguel beer. After the usual introductions (he said he was from Chicago Al Capone Bang Bang), he started to talk to me, asking all kinds of questions, speaking slowly, clearly, loudly enunciating, each word, as he spoke. Have, I, been, with, a, man, before? Were, any, of, my, friends, and, I, lovers? What, did, I, want, to, drink, besides, beer? Did, I, want, more, drinks, and, get, cozy?

I was petrified. In front of my friends? What did he think of me? A pick up? Inside though, I was happy, for like in my dreams, a Kano took interest in me! I hoped my friends didn't notice the enthusiasm. I was all agog to accommodate the Kano. My friends thought him weird though. Here he was, a big brawny Amerikano, so handsome, so rugged-looking like a Hollywood movie star, trying to pick up a lowly Filipino? It just didn't fit. He continued on with his innuendos, so my friends started to disappear one by one. They said they weren't comfortable with the Kano's banter. I told my friends I'd follow them later. I didn't want to be rude to the Kano and just leave him there. I did want to follow my friends, I was afraid that the Kano would do harm to me. But back in my mind, a voice kept saying, stay, for your dreams, here they come. Boogie Woogie!

But why the hell was the Kano speaking to me in pidgin? And very loud? Just because I had thick Visayan accent didn't mean that I didn't understand him or heard him. I wasn't deaf, and I definitely also knew how to speak *de epol en Menhetten is red* diction that I learned from Mr. Marvin.

The Kano kept on proffering beer to my face, which I kept gulping down to hide my anxiety. I didn't know what to expect, I didn't know how to act in front of him. I had never been with a man before, much less with a Kano. Despite everything I knew from my paperbacks, I was very nervous. What if he got turned off by anything I said?

I didn't need much prodding on what to do, it turned out. The Kano was a smooth talker. "You're nice, I like you, you're alright. God, you're fabulous. You're the reason I like boys," he kept on saying. With superlatives like these, who wouldn't want to go with him when he invited me to his hotel for more drinks? Aber?

Pieces. Tattered pieces of reminiscences. A slow ride in a taxi. A shabby bar with naked macho dancers. More beers, then gin tonics. And more macho dancers appearing on stage, sporting nothing but construction worker gear, hard hats, tool belts and leather work books. And fully erect dicks. "The erector set!" announced the DJ with a fake American accent. The boys were gyrating their lean muscular brown bodies in front of the Kano, dancing to some sexy disco tune, their turgid genitals flopping in the air.

Another taxi ride, a hotel on the boulevard by the sea, plush red carpeting, a glass elevator over-looking Manila Bay. Dizziness. More gin tonics from small bottles from a small refrigerator. Mirrors. Gentle hands pushing me to a firm bed. Extreme dizziness. I wanted to puke. And wanted to go home.

When I was small, I went for the first time to Manila where my father lived. I lived with my mother in the province when I was young, and during summers, we all went to live in my father's big house in Manila. I was fascinated with the artificial rain in my father's bathroom, the sya-wir, one of my father's maid called it. We did not have anything like it back in my mother's house. So I played under the rain until the bathroom got flooded. I was having fun! But my father, without any warning, came to the shower stall and gave me a severe belting. I didn't understand why he did it, and I couldn't do anything but cry in one corner of the bathroom, wishing to go home ... to my mother's house.

As corny as it may sound, my world turned upside down that first night with the Kano. A gentle touch. *God, you've got a beautiful body.* A fiery kiss, seducing refreshing. *Tastes like whiskey!* Wet tongue on my armpit. *No, no, not there, I'm ticklish!* Wetter tongue everywhere else. One intense explosion of emotions, one tight hug, an overpowering groan, pain, severe pain, and then a one sided quivering pleasure. Then two. And blood! Crimson blood all over the white satin sheets. *It's okay Richie, it's okay.*

I just wanted to go home. To my mother's house.

And when it was over, I just lay there on the hotel bed feeling overwhelmed and relieved. I felt a whole gamut of experiences rolling into one, passing through me. Those strong obsessive feelings pent up inside me were spent to the hilt, just like a cigarette passionately smoked to its filter. The Kano reached out for a cigarette.

"So, what's happening next? You gonna kick me out after this?" I asked.

"Well, let's wait for tomorrow. Meanwhile, let's get some sleep here, eh?" said a tired but soothing reply.

Sleep. One deep, satisfying sleep. For the Kano that is. Because I wasn't able to. I tried, but I wasn't used to sleeping with someone beside me. I stayed on the bed with the Kano, but away from him, lying as still as possible so as to not to disturb him. Most of the night, I was awake looking at him, trying to mold him into the fantasies I had been creating. At last, here was Dick, now grown up, who would nurture me and bring me back with him to wherever he came from!

I was startled from my thoughts when I felt the Kano's hand reaching for me. In his sleep, he extended his hand to search for me on my side of the bed. And when he found me, he pulled my body toward him, turned me around and held me tight to him, my back toward his stirring front, as if we were two spoons stacked sideways, together. I felt as though I really had hit home. It felt good inside his embrace. I never felt like it before.

Just as I was about to go to sleep in his arms, I heard him murmur something to me, as if he were calling me, needing me to his side. But it wasn't my name that he distinctly uttered. I felt cold. I felt rejected. I felt silly, lying there with him. I wanted to go home. What was I doing there when it was someone else that he wanted?

"Do you have a lover, Mitchell?" I asked the Kano in the morning the next day while we were waiting for room service to bring in the breakfast that he ordered on the telephone -- cereal, toasted bread, butter and orange marmalade, scrambled eggs, bacon, crispy done, hash browns on the side, and fresh milk for me and coffee for him. It was very American, just like in the movies. I felt so special.

"Why do you ask that?"

"Just curious. I'm sure you have. Last night, you called me Dennis."

"Actually, yes, Ritchie," he answered without reluctance. "As a matter of fact, yes, his name is Dennis. He's a famous jeweler back in Chicago. Your First Lady bought an original diamond-studded butterfly brooch from his shop when she last visited. Dennis is about your size and build, rather, the lack of it."

"Puta ..."

"Are you Jewish, Mitchell?"

"Hey, you're asking so many questions, do you work for the Filipino FBI or what?"

Silence.

"And why did you think I was Jewish?"

"I don't know. It's just that I have some Jewish friends in school and you remind me of them. And I guess Filipinos and Jews have a lot in common -- the suffering, the oppression and discrimination -- I don't want to get into the politics of this, but we had our holocaust too. It was a little known fact, but when the Americans invaded the Philippines back in the 1900s, they massacred towns and annihilated villages." I paused, catching myself. Shit. Why did I always have to parrot my paperbacks? This guy was an American, I should not have said anything about American atrocities at all. I should have said things about the Japanese instead. "What a story to tell early in the morning, huh?"

Silence.

I felt ashamed. Did I insult him for being an American? It was unbecoming for a Happy Hustler to be impudent. A Filipino hospitality Happy Hustler, especially.

"And I heard that your mothers are a lot like screaming Filipino mothers too," I said meekly, just to break the silence.

The Kano just looked at me with a bemused expression on his face. I blew it. I should have just shut the fuck up.

"Besides, you're cut," I whispered, very disappointed at myself for offending the Kano's American sensibilities.

"Hey, you know a lot, don't you?" the Kano said, grinning and reaching out tussling my hair. "Are you sure you're a virgin?" He was laughing like hell, shaking his head. Thank God. I was resurrected.

"I was, until last night, man. Besides, I read and dream a lot, Mitchell," I said aloud to myself. Yeah, I dreamed for this to happen, but fucking shit, the Kano had his own boy back home!

So it was like that. But at least, I was able to sleep in a five-star hotel, was able to eat in restaurants which did not admit anybody who did not wear an American-style jacket, or a barong Tagalog but hey, they had spares in their closet, in all sizes, and which they graciously lent to customers who weren't wearing any, and was able to taste, as if I hadn't really tasted them before: *cocktails or white wine, ham and mushroom hors d'oeurvre, fillet steak maitre d'hotel, red wine, vegetables in season, fruit Swedish, Australian cheddar, tea, coffee and liqueur.*

And at noon, I went home to eat lunch: *fish frito, pork sinigang, steamed rice and fresh kalamansi juice.*

Well, what could I say? The Kano was amused by me. Probably because despite all my textbook knowledge of everything, I still looked like a babe in his eyes. I was always interested in anything he put in front of me. *Oh, you're terrible, Ritchie, you're just terrible.* And I was blabbering. *Oh, you're too much Ritchie, shut up already and clean up your language, you're disgusting.*

Almost everything that I asked from him, he got for me: A Lacoste polo shirt, a black one, definitely the real thing, made in France, not Cainta; a pair of Levi's corduroy, made in U.S.A., not a copy by your friendly neighborhood tailor; a pair of Calvin Klein blue jeans, the one with red label, made in the U.S.A., not with brown tag, which was local; a pair of Adidas ROM, the green one, made in France; a pair of orange Crayon shoes with translucent plastic soles, perfect dancing in the disco, also made the U.S.A.; and a pair of high-heeled tan leather boots, made in Italy. *What's with all these shoes, Ritchie?* It was all new to me, paying by credit card. *Don't worry about it, Ritchie, I'll write them off as business expenses.* I didn't understand.

The Kano liked me to call him as the big boss, which I liked too, for really, he acted like one, like a chairman of a big company wanting to own everything. Including me. In return, I had done everything practically possible that I could offer him in my own little way. I was his lover, his waiter, his mistress, his paramour, whatever. I even clipped his toenails and brushed them with my toothbrush when we were taking a shower together. Talk about personal sacrifice, huh?

I really felt that I gave something back to Mitchell. Not just the backrubs and the sex. Something else beyond the physical. He told me that he saw in me, partly what he should have been when he was growing up in America and partly what he was when he was young. In his eyes, I was bubbly and sparkling, as if I did not have worries in life and was always aggressive, willing to take risks. *You've got guts, Ritchie.* When he was my age, he was already working and did not have time to enjoy himself. To him, it was as if I served him some potent liquor that made him re-live his youth again. *Your cum tastes like honey, Ritchie.*

Three days! Three days and two nights of earthly pleasures and delights. We didn't even go out of his hotel room much, except of course, to dine and to shop for my wish list. I wished it would never end. I prayed to high heavens, to the Lady of Perpetual Help, to St. Martin de Porres, and all the other saints that my mother used to pray to. But I came to my senses on the third day I was with him. While I was lying on his shoulder hollow after an afternoon of lukewarm lovemaking in front of the TV with the antics of Bert and Ernie on, he told me he was flying back to Chicago that night. Just like that. No warnings, no foreplay.

I just became limp. I knew that he was going to leave eventually, but I never had an inkling that he was going so soon. I hadn't had time to prepare myself for the end. I was having such a good time, why should I prepare myself? I hadn't felt at home with anybody that fast at all. I didn't want it to end right away. I didn't understand what was going on inside of me, but it felt wonderful. How could the Kano cut it short, how could he let it finish so soon?

I kept quiet. Later, I said it was okay, I could deal with it.

At the airport, I was left behind outside, looking at him through the thick glass walls that separated the outside from the check-in area, with a lump in my throat and sour taste on my tongue. He wanted to bring me inside with him, but the security guard, the one with the blue uniform and the armalite said, only passengers with tickets were allowed inside, ha-ha, laughing to my face.

So outdoors, amidst the throng of people who were sending off their relatives to Hong Kong and Kuwait to become domestics and/or prostitutes, the Kano and I said our goodbyes. *Hey, here is something for you. Open it after I'm gone, okay? Well ... Ritchie ... be good ... take care of yourself ... and write! You have my address somewhere, don't you?* He reached out for my hand and gave it a squeeze, and then he went in, walking to the check-in counter without even turning to look back at me powerless, hopeless, in the middle of the chaos of people sending off their loved ones abroad. I wanted to break that glass that separated the ones that were left like me, from the ones who were flying to their dreams.

I said to myself, so, that's all there is to it. A gift wrapped in pink paper. *An Yves Saint Laurent wallet with a one hundred dollar bill inside.* I'm rich! An admonition to take care of myself, and a hand shake. But I always had been taking care of myself! He didn't even give me a hug!

He was just a fucking tourist. *Hey Ritchie, how come they always shout Hey Joe, give me a cigarette, Joe! to me in the streets. Those cute little boys. What am I supposed to say to them?* Just don't mind them, Mitchell, or call out, Hey Pinoy, to them and for sure they are bound to shut their mouths up. He said he'd be back in about six months or so ... maybe. And perhaps we'll see each other then. Maybe. Why suddenly all these maybes?

Who did he think he was? It was as if nothing had

happened. As if we did not cross and share paths together. As if what happened was not really important at all. What about my dreams? Fucking hell, he was not the only Jewish Kano in the world.

I felt so self-conscious in front of all the people milling about outside the airport. I felt they were all staring at me, as if I had this big sign across my chest: JUST NEWLY USED, and on my back: CAN BE USED AGAIN. I felt just a bit more respectable than a condom. Unlike a rubber, at least I can be used again after being thrown away.

Back at home, my nephew, the fine arts major, said my face looked like it was just ravaged by typhoon. He would really like to paint it. I just looked at him without saying anything. I didn't understand it myself too. How come, so many days after the Kano had left, I smelled his perfume all over my body? Even after I took very long showers every day?

Afterwards, one day, you come to a realization that it doesn't matter at all. Just like that. As if nothing really happened to you. It happened to someone else. You feel numb. You start not to care. As if nothing has been lost in you, although deep inside, you know something was taken from you. You just can't tell anybody. You try to cover it. You try to hide it. You shrug your shoulders and say, life is like that. And then you're born again.

I wanted it back. Whatever it was that was lost from me.

Oh, I'm sorry. I fell asleep. It's this fucking disease. It always makes me tired. No matter how much I rest. I'm always exhausted, deep to the bones. Thanks for your patience, pala. I was talking in my sleep? Sori na lang, I hope I wasn't blabbering too much. Where was I? What happened to the Kano from Shakey's? No se.

After he left, I searched for him. It was like searching for a ghost. Everywhere I can find him, from honky-tonk bars of Manila to the sleazy hustler bars in New York, even in the classified ads of boy-toy magazines in Europe and Australia. I was there. Come to think of it, I came here to Chicago because of him. I agreed to go with Brian to the U.S. as long as we lived in Chicago. I didn't know what I was thinking, but I thought, maybe, I could catch an essence of him in Chicago where he told me he was from. For years, even though I had my life with Brian, I still went back to the streets. To chase phantoms of that long lost love.

Then I met Steven, another Jewish guy. A New Yorker. I don't know. I really have this penchant for Jewish guys that sometimes I am tempted to hang out in the steps of a synagogue, to ogle. I met Steven at a benefit for Chicago House where many of my friends who were sick were staying. So sad. They didn't have any place to go, they were abandoned by their families. Mostly Chinese and Vietnamese, and young, and one Filipino. It was a double whammy for the families. Not only did they learn that their sons are gay, but they have AIDS! Anak ng tinapa. The families just couldn't cope and turned their sons away!

Steven said I was his brown Ganymede, always pouring sweet wine into his silver chalice. It was like Mitchell all over again. This time though, the wine aged for six years. And then he fell ill, had a short battle with the disease and was gone. I was devastated of course. And now I've got it.

I had a full life though. But I don't intend to die, not yet anyway. If I do die soon, I could say now, I don't have any regrets. Back in the years when I roamed the streets, nobody knew about the fucking disease, much less how it was transmitted. All I knew then was, I was having fun with my power over the Kano I met in the streets. My only lament now is, I will just become a statistic. I know that more Filipinos are dying of HIV than any other segment of the Asian American community, so I guess I'm not alone. Nothing much is known about AIDS among Asians, even medically, and there are still a lot of myths. I remember hearing about an old Filipino doctor who believed that the virus only infected whites. He and so many others really thought it was like that. The height of irresponsibility, no?

It's all hush-hush. Just like when the adults in my family

were whispering at the dinner table when I was small and they didn't want children to know what they were talking about. Especially when they were talking about Tay Nonoy, a dapper bachelor uncle who always smelled of French cologne, and who gave scholarships to young men from our town in the province, to stay with him in his elegant house in Remedios in the old district of Manila. They all talked about him in muted tones. As if we didn't know. We'd seen him doing it with our errand boy, Nicasio, under the big sampaloc tree in our backyard.

Really, being a bakla, a homosexual, it does not exist in the macho-pseudo-Catholic community that is Filipino, even here in the America. One exists as a bakla only if you dress up like a woman and work in beauty parlor. To manicure the ladies' nails, beautify their faces and style their hair, even sometimes, to satisfy the insatiable sexual needs of their philandering gentlemen husbands. Bur apart from that? You exist, swept away under the living room carpet. Or to the underworld of dank movie houses, parks and thankfully, back home, the casas and bars full of young men fresh from the boondocks.

Nnnh, I am just so fucking weary. I need to get some rest again. It's this AIDS talk. It makes me sound preachy and political which I am not. You will stay of course, and wait for me to wake from my rest, won't you? Or perhaps you will come back again some other time and listen to my chattering about life? I hope you don't mind. You're very kind. I still have more stories to tell. And there's little time left.

**Bio:** *Eulalio Yerro Ibarra is a recent immigrant settling in Chicago on the shores of Lake Michigan with his partner of three years. His search for fertile ground to let his roots grow brought him to places as diverse as Australia, New Zealand and Europe. He was trained to cure animal deceases and also studied how a lamb digests its food, but is now working as a specialist to explain male infertility. Among the other hats he is wearing, Ibarra also the resident writer of* Tribung Pinoy, *a popular Filipino-oriented home page on the Internet; Ibarra is an aspiring* *web designer himself. His previous works have been published in* Passport Magazine *and* On a Bed of Rice, *an Asian American anthology of erotic fiction, published by Anchor Books in 1995. Eulalio Yerro Ibarra is named after his paternal and maternal grandfathers; he hails from Malinao in Aklan province.*

# HANG, MAN

## Nadine L. Sarreal

AT LUNCH HOUR one Tuesday in late March, a small crowd of people milled about in the garden square between the Hong Kong Immigration Tower and the Revenue Tower.

There were five or six Filipinas, amahs on their odd day off, eating rice with sweet-and-sour fish from Styrofoam lunch boxes. In far greater number, businessmen of varying nationalities sat here and there on the hard stone benches and along the sides of the large concrete flower boxes, taking in the noon sun, some of them smoking or wiggling their arms and shoulders to free themselves of tension. A very wrinkled and stooped Chinese grandmother scolded a young boy who ran ahead of her, his burdensome school bag bouncing on his back like a loose turtle shell. Two young Chinese women in identical navy business suits opened paper bags of hamburgers and Cokes, and spread their small feast between them. They tossed their dark glossy hair in the wind before tucking in. The day was cool, but it was the first time the sun had come out full-faced in a month. It had been a long winter, bitterly cold and overcast, and the people were out on this day to welcome spring weather.

Above this small garden, just outside the thirty-fourth floor of the Immigration Tower , a young man of twenty-eight or so stood carefully balanced on a narrow rectangle platform. He was washing windows. He wore a much-stained shirt and denim pants, black now with grime, and over this, a light cotton jacket. Around his waist, a safety belt was fastened which attached him to a metal rail on the platform. He was a laborer who had formerly worked on the new airport site with a team of other men from the Philippines, kabayan, whose main duty was to flatten and level the rocky ground that was to support commercial airline hangars. He was a family man, with six children back in the province of Cavite. In the months he had worked on the airport, he was able to send home a decent sum regularly towards the feeding and clothing of his four sons and two daughters. The youngest, a baby boy, was especially sickly, and his wife could not afford the medicines for the boy's asthma. He suspected, too, that she occasionally splurged on small pieces of jewelry for she had a secret fondness of sparkling ear clasps and fine gold bracelets. This suspicion gave him a tiny thrill of joy in the deep dark nights when he could not sleep, to know that with the strength of his bare hands and the perseverance of his heart, he could provide these things for his family.

To pass the time when he was not working and to hasten the onset of a good night's sleep, this young man sometimes sat for a few hours with his kabayan, drinking beer and whiskey. One Sunday evening, a month ago, they had been drinking a particularly cheap brand of whiskey. He became drunk quickly and his head began to pound so that he was easily roused to anger by the others.

Pare, who does your Mrs. dress up for these days? a town mate asked, jabbing him in the ribs and winking widely around the group. This man had just returned from a funeral in their barrio and had seen the young wife in the market wearing a bright new dress and leather heels. At first, the young man felt a burst of pride to know that his wife had new clothes and that she was looking well. It was the whiskey, though, he thought later, and his loneliness, that magnified the hoots and laughter of the circle of men around him. He reached for the kitchen knife on the table they all sat around. It belonged to one of the older men who used it to cut the strips of dried meat they chewed and washed down with the whiskey.

He was so quick and deft in his single thrust that the warm surprise of blood gushing from his town mate's belly seemed to scald his hand. He jumped up from the table, though the two sitting on either side of him reached out feebly to stop him, and he ran from the worksite. He fled the laborers' shelter, running into the cold night first on foot, then by train, and bus, and finally, he hid in a cramped building of shabby flats where other Filipino men and women -- maids, musicians, errand boys, waiters and prostitutes -- shared dark, dank quarters.

The young man heard that his town mate was treated for the stomach wound and the construction firm that held his contract sent him home with a small lump sum of cash. He envied this fate for it was far better than his life as a fugitive. Surely, he was being hunted by authorities although no one said anything of the stabbing to him. He became silent and withdrawn, carrying the weight of his conscience like a large invisible boulder. When he walked by policemen on their rounds, he felt the ice of fear riding up and down his spine. And he knew his town mate's circle of friends were looking for him to exact their own form of justice, revenge that would serve as a lesson to others, too.

It was difficult finding work in his circumstances. The construction firm would have reported him missing to the Immigration authorities by now. He chose jobs that put him out of public sight and kept him off the street. Sometimes he washed dishes and cleaned toilets for a couple of bars in Wanchai when the regular janitors took holidays or were sick. For this work, he rose early, four o'clock or so, to work after the last floor show had ended.

Today, the brother of a bouncer at one bar had offered him and two other men this job of cleaning windows. The two declined, looking away in shame when he accepted eagerly. Pay good money, ah. Little bit danger but I teach you how be careful, Sam Au had said. Must finish today, one day work only.

The young man hadn't realized he would be cleaning the Immigration Tower. As he swabbed at the glass panes, he worried that a clerk looking over a thick file on illegal immigrant workers would glance up as his cloth passed over her window. She would see his face, look down at the page she was examining and she would cry out, stabbing at the photo and then pointing at the window, Him! Him! Wanted for overstaying! Expired visa! Arrest him! This is what he feared, and fearing it greatly, he was able to laugh, chuckling repeatedly, shakily, at the irony of his situation as he adjusted the pulleys time and again, lowering the platform one more story closer to the ground. I laugh, he told himself, because I am a man. Tears are for women. He bit his lip to stop its quivering.

Once in a while, he turned from the windows and looked at the view below and across from him, the bustling pedestrian overpass stretching over wide parallel strips of busy road and the solid wall of high-rise buildings across the way. Between these buildings, he caught glimpses of green sloping mountains, their tops hidden in clouds. At first he had felt queasy at this height, his stomach rebelling at the unnatural altitude, but after a morning of mopping countless panes of dark glass he had gained some ease. Far beneath, he could see the square of tamed flowering bushes and well-contained grass patches amid the concrete expanse. He was careful not to lean over to peer more closely at the tiny figures of people. Sam Au had warned that the railing on the platform served merely as reminders to stand back and they did not ensure safety and protection. Always with belt, Sam advised. He himself was working the other side of the building.

The young Filipino father thought how pleasant it

must be to eat lunch in a small park on a sunny day. Why have I never done this before? he wondered aloud. He promised himself that tomorrow, he would wash up and change after his shift at the bar and he would bring a lunch and sit on one of those benches, warming himself in the sun. Maybe he could even find a pretty kabayan to pass the time with. Even if he sat by himself, he could watch other people in the square and imagine what they were saying, thus he would not feel alone.

\*

In the garden, the crowd was growing. People returning from lunch stopped to read newspapers on the last few minutes of their hour away from work. More school children pulled away from their smiling grandmothers and amahs who huddled on the benches, reluctant to return to the confinement of their cube-shaped dwellings. The two young ladies in navy suits had long finished their picnic. The neater one carefully gathered the wax paper and empty cups into the paper bag; she held the lot in her lap, meaning to drop it in the waste bin across the square on the way back to her desk. She and her companion sat close now, squeezed on both sides by old women stretching their aching feet before them. The young women watched children squat and tumble on a small patch of grass. One adjusted her short skirt better to show her legs for she thought they were quite shapely. She was almost certain the bespectacled young man reading a paperback on the bench directly across was covertly watching them, and she hoped he would narrow his focus on her even though her companion had a prettier face. The woman held the paper bag of lunch leavings on her lap, wishing he would look up again soon so she could smile at him.

Grandma, look! a small child cried from the grassy patch where he lay, dizzy from rolling about. He was pointing at the platform, perched like a lone barnacle halfway up the side of a glass ship. The child's grandmother glanced up, squinting, and turned back to her conversation with another grandmother.

Look, look, look! the child insisted. He jumped up from the ground and was pointing a chubby finger upwards. Look! he squealed, tugging at the old woman's sleeve.

Ai. ya! Quiet, ah! the grandmother scolded but she glanced up anyway and even with her failing eyesight, she saw the platform suddenly swing free from one of its anchoring ropes so that it hung precariously on one end. A large pail of murky water hit the pavement with a bang and splash. A long-handled mop followed directly. The movement of the long platform was larger than that of the lone man so it took a small piece of time before the old woman saw him, too, swaying just below the platform like a spider hanging from a thread of web. His arms and legs flailed wildly for a moment, seeking to grasp hold for safety. Then he hung still, resigned, aware of the strap around his waist.

As one, the people in the square, alerted by the child's cries, had risen to their feet, some of them raising their arms as if to clutch the man in their hands. They gathered in a tight knot in the middle of the garden and ripples of concern and alarm ran through them. Call the police! a British businessman shouted. No, no, call the fire department! an American voice corrected. Several Chinese men, including the one who had been reading, pulled out their mobile phones and simultaneously punched in 999 to alert the emergency center.

They waited and murmured among themselves feeling the sway of the dangling man, back and forth, just below the platform. The safety belt was hooked on the platform railing with a heavy metal latch. The crowd beneath him seemed to draw one breath when a wind swung him harder. God, I hope the bugger has a good ticker, the British man breathed softly. One of the Filipina amahs clutched her hands together in prayer, and her companions, seeing her, crossed themselves and stammered out Ama Natin and Hail Marys. Ai. ya! a grandmother moaned. Over the years, she had lost two sons in different accidents -- first in construction, and last year, her younger son had been crushed as he crossed the road in heavy traffic. Granny, the tall American man said beside her, he's got a safety belt on. He'll be all right when the ladder comes. She nodded without looking up at him but still she clasped her hands and shook them in a prayer of desperate hope.

It was several hours now past the lunch hour but no one left the garden to rush back to their piles of fax and phone messages. With one mind, the old women, the suited businessman, the Filipinas and the young women who had spread their lunch on the bench all felt their presence was necessary, their vigil crucial, to the hanging man's well-being. By watching intently and clutching their hands into fists, they believed they ensured his safety. They could almost taste the moment of deliverance when he would be lowered, glad and sheepish, to bask in their clamor of welcome and affectionate scolding.

In the distance, the wail of sirens sounded, and the men with cellular phones still gripped tightly in hand sighed with relief. Rescue was on the way. Hang in there, my man! the paperback man shouted up. Small children held hands and swung their joined fists back and forth, chanting, Hang, man! Hang, man!

A long, red fire truck whimpered to a stop along the street where traffic was backed up as the motorists had caught sight of the hanging man, too. Half a dozen firemen tramped into the garden, ordering the crowd to stand back, out of their way. A short argument ensued -- the firemen couldn't agree whether to lower ropes from the top of the building for the man to cling to while they hauled him to the roof, or to raise a ladder and carry him down that way. The glass panes the Filipino had been cleaning were not real windows in the sense that windows open and shut. They were merely glass tiles pieced neatly together to form a cover for a raw steel and concrete support beams within. Rope, rope! some people shouted from the crowd. The ladder! others cried.

The firemen decided to take the man down, and long folding ladder lifted out of the truck, slowly approaching the swaying man. The little boy with the heavy school bag saw how the man seemed to shrink back as the ladder neared, and he tugged again at his grandmother's sleeve, asking if the man feared the ladder. She hushed him and craned her neck further back to get a view. The hydraulic whine of the rising ladder came to an abrupt halt and the metal stairs froze several meters below the man. Oh no! the crowd groaned collectively. What now? What's wrong? The neat young woman found she had crushed her paper bag to a flat package against her chest.

Then, before their eyes, the man jerked suddenly and the sound that had startled him came to them, too: a cold, hard snap. The metal rail on the platform hung broken for an infinite second and then fell like a silent, rusty arrow. Immediately behind it, the hanging man followed, safety belt trailing and then leading, seeming to drag him along. The Filipinas murmured tensely that he appeared to hover first and then, feather-like, waft gently down instead of plummeting. Every heart froze and each person in the crowd felt an abrupt and irretrievable loss a split second before he hit the gray concrete -- not so much the loss of the man's life, for many people die this way in Hong Kong -- but the ripping away of the innocent trust, their foolish collective belief that by standing witness, they could have prevented tragedy.

The fireman scrambled under the ludicrously impotent ladder above them, a disembodied hand reaching out in supplication. They tore off their coats to soften his fall. Too late. Instead, they heaped the actual impact of brown skin and bone on the concrete. The wailing and praying, the screaming and shouts of hope in impossible despair, drowned out that one sound of a life ending.

*Bio of Nadine L. Sarreal: I believe I must be somehow related to everyone in the Philippines - by blood, marriage or adoption. Think about it. We, as a people, carry our family lines out long and far.*

*My stories are usually sparked by the spirit of a character that communes with me at a particular time. There's a lady at church I love to watch. She always sits with her family. Her husband is first in the pew, next to the aisle, and then the older daughter, then her, then the younger daughter. There's a way this woman moves -- a quick, unself-conscious stroke of her first daughter's hair, or how she reaches to straighten the younger girl's collar, or the way she squeezes her husband's hand during the sign of peace -- that draws my eyes to her. I think I know her, not her -- her, but her spirit, and her second level of awareness of her family, how she is connected to each member. I know that spirit and I feel drawn to it.*

*For someone who is at heart a small-town dweller, I have moved often and have lived in too many places. As a writer, I couple my inherent desire to stay put with my curiosity about other places and people to fuel my work. I believe a journey does not have to be long or far for one to travel well. It is the attention we pay to what is around us that counts in living fully.*

# THE HOUSE OF PRIME RIB

Jay Ruben Dayrit

RATHER SUDDENLY, my father decides to bring his new wife to America. Just like he suddenly decided to remarry only after a year after my mother's death. So I decided to call her Angeline. Not Auntie Angie. Not Iling. Filipinos and their silly nicknames. Bing Bing, Bong Bong, Ping Pong. Just Angeline. No title of respect nor affection. I do bring flowers though. Pink carnations, pretty but sufficiently trashy. Even though Brian thinks the flowers are a little mean-spirited, he kisses me softly and wishes me luck, frowning like he feels sad for me. I imagine he looks at his little students the same way when they have to get their vaccination shots.

We meet in the lobby of the San Francisco Hilton, a cavernous space with huge chandeliers floating like shimmering clouds. My sister Teresa and her neurosurgeon husband Alois are already sitting with my father and his wife on one of the puffy couches. The couch is so overstuffed it appears to be swallowing them whole. I smile and descend the short stairs toward them. They all manage to stand, freeing themselves from the couch, every one smiling so widely their eyes are tiny crescent moons. Angeline is mestiza and tall for a Filipina. A good five nine. So unlike my mother who was short and dark from working in the garden under the sun. Angeline's face is almost entirely hidden behind her wide rose-colored glasses and big gold jewelry. She wears some pink checkered Coco Chanel suit thing, probably a knock-off, an outfit my mother would have wrapped up and given away the very next Christmas. Angeline's contrived elegance is Imelda Marcos and Yoko Ono rolled into one.

I hand her the carnations, kiss her on the cheek with a convincing, "How nice to finally meet you ... Angeline." She thanks me and notes how well the flowers match her suit, which is not exactly what I had in mind. I hug my father and my sister and shake Alois's hand, stiff Austrian that he is. His pale blue eyes are distant and unnerving like the sky on a crisp autumn day. He and my sister are in town for the neurosurgeon convention at Moscone Center, where he will be presenting his invention, a tiny bolt that, once drilled into the skull, reads pressure and gas levels. Finally, a doctor in the family. Dr. Frankenstein.

"I like your glasses. Are they new?" my father asks, laughing a little. He seems pleased to see me, although a bit nervous, standing there in a red aloha shirt and khakis. She must have dressed him. My mother would have never dressed my father like a tourist. He's seen my glasses before, last year in the Philippines when I was looking after him, right after he had a valve in his heart replaced. Perhaps he just doesn't remember. Or perhaps he just has nothing else to say. When I was growing up, we'd go fishing every weekend, trolling around the barrier reef for hours, almost without saying a word, communicating only in subtle nods and perhaps a raise of the eyebrows ... for what does a father say to a son who didn't quite turn out the way he wanted?

"We're eating at the House of Prime Rib," Angeline says. "My son and his wife are waiting." Fly half way around the world into San Francisco, a city with great restaurants, only to reserve a table at the House of Prime Rib. My sister and I exchange glances. Seems like the only time we ever eat prime rib is when relatives visit America.

"Great," my sister says cheerfully, always the diplomat.

"We have to take two cabs," I say. "They won't take five."

"Do you want to ride with Dad and Angeline?" my sister asks.

"Sure," I say. She knows I have no choice. Bitch.

During the cab ride up Geary, I fill our stilted conversation with censored details about my life. Busy at work, putting in lots of hours. Copywriting is rather uninteresting, but good money. Still hit the gym though.

I leave out Brian, conveniently. I leave out the way we take naps on warm days, letting the sun stream down onto us from the open window, how the most enjoyable thing we do is eat Sunday brunch at greasy diners in the Castro, sharing a blueberry waffle with lots of butter, how he makes me laugh with stories about the children at Pacific Primary, the way he had them draw on blank postcards and mail them to their parents, the way they all walked to the mailbox and dropped the cards in one by one, standing on the tips of their toes. I leave all that out, all that would make me smile if I could tell Angeline and my father.

I look back and see my father and Angeline holding hands, gazing out the window at the transvestites strutting down Polk Street. Perhaps they just think they're regular prostitutes, only with really big hands.

They were high school sweethearts back in Pampanga, Angeline and my father, long before he went off to graduate school in Los Baños where he met my mother. Despite my father's thinning gray hair and the wrinkles on Angeline's neck, I can see them as they once were. Teenagers holding hands at the barrio fiesta, sharing a bag of roasted peanuts. My father, young and handsome and strong. Angeline, tall and pretty, the star of the girls volleyball team.

I look away, out the window at the Galaxy Theatre on Van Ness, neon lights coloring the wet sidewalk pink and blue. I can't decide if the ache in my chest is sorrow or anger. Whatever it is, I want to reach back and separate their hands.

At the bar inside the House of Prime Rib, we meet Mario, his wife Jonél, and their two-year-old son Omar. Mario has a thin moustache, the kind high school boys grow to make themselves look older, and Jonél has hair way too big for Asian woman. They shake our hands eagerly and tell their son to say hello to his new auntie and uncle. I cringe at the sudden acquisition of a nephew but am relieved when Omar defiantly shakes his head no. Mario and Jonél are both insurance adjusters. I try to imagine what exactly that might be, but all I can picture is Mario sitting in an office, adjusting the tint on a very large color TV.

We are seated at a round table, barely able to accommodate the eight of us. We all decide to order the same thing, prime rib, all except Alois, who orders the grilled salmon. "No spinach," he says sternly to our waiter. My sister happily explains that, once when Alois was very young, he fell ill, and all the nuns fed him for nearly two weeks was cooked spinach. And now, of course, he can't stand the sight of it. Sure enough, his salmon comes with spinach.

Alois is visibly annoyed, but before our waiter can correct his oversight, my sister has already quickly and cleanly exchanged her baby carrots for Alois's spinach. Pleased, he thanks her, discretely touching the small of her back.

Throughout dinner the conversation is polite, even lively, mostly centered around Omar. Isn't he cute? What a smart little boy! How clever ... as he discovers that kicking the table makes the silverware jump and the dishes rattle. Angeline says very little and laughs even less behind her placid smile, which seems permanently affixed to her face. Occasionally, she nods in agreement with my father or moves to adjust her enormous gold earrings.

No one confronts my father and Angeline about anything, like why they were in such a hurry to get married. If her first husband has been dead for nearly nine years, why couldn't they have waited just a little longer? Why were none of us invited to the wedding? Was there a prenup? What about the land on Guam or in Hawaii? In Hawaii, where my sister and I worked one summer nearly ten years ago, planting sapling balls of lychee, tangerine, mango and guava. What about those?

But it's not the Filipino way to ask such difficult questions, particularly when first impressions are so damn important. But I feel like saying, Fuck the Filipino way! It didn't work when Mom was dying, everyone so afraid to admit she might not be able to fight off cancer, everyone consulting priests when in truth, they should have been consulting lawyers. Her brothers don't speak to each other now, bitter over her share of the land outside Iloilo, believing a silent grudge and time will solve any problem.

"How do I get rid of this?" my father asks me, patting his small but noticeable belly. When we were growing up, he used to run six miles every day, from our farmhouse to the Farmer's Market and back. But since mother's death and his surgery, I gather he's been a bit inactive. "Sit ups," he asks. "How about sit ups?"

"Well, Dad," I say. "You can't really spot reduce. Running will help, but you should ask your doctor before you do anything cardiovascular."

My father pinches his love handles, chuckling. "I never used to have this ... but Iling feeds me well." Angeline raises her eyebrows and nods. My father continues. "Before I used to come home, open a can of corn and eat right out of the can. That was good enough for me," my father says cheerfully. I suddenly feel like crying, imagining him sitting in that empty house, eating out of a can, my mother's things packed away in cardboard boxes neatly stacked in what used to be my room. The only sound, the quiet ticking of his mechanical valve.

When the doctors told us they were going to start looking for cancer, my mother sat us down for a talk. The very first thing she said was, "Kids, if I die, you have to make sure your father remarries."

"No, no, no, no, no," my father refusing to listen. Though he tried not to show it, he was terribly scared, for it seemed she had always lived in his world, as if, before her, there was nothing.

"Mom, don't worry about him," I said.

"Listen to me," she insisted. "Your father cannot take care of himself. That's my fault. I spoiled him. Your sister has a rich husband. She'll be okay. And you ... you're smart. I'm not worried about you. But your father ... he needs someone to look after him, someone to cook for him, to clean for him ... He has his needs."

"We have to think about you, Mom, how can you get better."

"I might not get better," my mother said.

"I make sure he eats," Angeline says. "Old style food from Pampanga, like the kind we grew up with."

"Yeah," my father says. "I like it. She's a good cook." They look at each other briefly, and in that moment, as much as I don't want to, I see a little of my mother behind Angeline's glasses, something in the way she smiles at my father. And for the first time in nearly two years, two very difficult years for my father, I can see happiness in his eyes.

After dinner, we say good-bye. Mario is driving them back to Union City. Tomorrow, they are off to LA to meet Angeline's daughter. It is not a tearful parting, just a hurried one. Our family has gotten good at saying good-bye. We know we will see each other within six months. Before she died, my mother asked that we try to see each other more often. And now, Christmas is always just around the corner, and the Philippines doesn't seem so far away.

Mario's car pulls away, and my sister, her husband and I are left standing on the sidewalk outside the House of Prime Rib. "So what do you think of her?" I ask.

"God, she's boring," my sister says.

"I know, huh?"

"Even more boring than her son," Alois says. "We are

all relieved that dinner is finally over."

"I feel sorry for her though," my sister says. "Dad could never love her as much as he loved Mom."

As we walk to my bus stop, my sister reaches out, touches my shoulder and asks, "How's Brian?" I look at her, almost startled, as she strolls alongside me with her husband, her arm hooked into the bend of his elbow. I want to hug her for asking such a simple straightforward question, gather her small frame into my arms and squeeze her as hard as I can.

"He's fine," I say. "He said to say hi."

On the 24 Divisadero, I think about Brian waiting at home for me. When I get there, he will greet me at the door a little sleepy-eyed. He will ask me if I'm okay. And I will say "Yes, I'm fine." We will sit on the bed together, and I will tell him about Angeline and my father, about my sister and the neurosurgeon, and Mario and Jonél and Omar. We will crawl under the comforter together. He'll put his strong arms around me, kiss me lightly on the nape of my neck, and we will fall asleep like that, like we've done so many times before, so many times that I now find it difficult to fall asleep without him.

On the 24 Divisadero, I realize what my mother tried to tell us that day the doctors began looking for cancer. After a while, however short or long, six months or twenty-eight years, after a while it's not so much about the kind of love that makes you want to run across a field of wild flowers or see fireworks when you kiss. After a while, what matters are the ordinary things: mailing postcards to your parents, exchanging carrots for spinach, holding hands in the back of a cab, asking simple straightforward questions. After a while, it's about companionship more than passion. It's about making sure that everyone is safe and protected, that everyone, plain and simply, is looked after.

**Bio:** *Born and raised in Kolonia, Pohnpei in the Federal States of Micronesia, Jay Ruben Dayrit is a graduate of Yale University and the Creative Writing Program at San Francisco State University. While an undergraduate, he received the Peter J. Wallace Fiction Prize and the*

*James A. Veech Prize for Short Story Writing. His work has appeared in* Transfer, XY Magazine, Hot Lava, The Minnesota Review, His: brilliant new fiction by gay men, GenerAsian X Sumtin To Say/Behind Our Backs, *a resource guide published by the San Francisco AIDS Foundation. He is currently an Artist-in-Residence at the Headlands Center for the Arts. He lives in San Francisco.*

# BOY LEFT BEHIND

Ligaya Victorio Fruto

HE STOOD outside the bathroom door and was quiet, listening.

"Mummy, are you there?"

"Yes, son," I shouted above the splashing of the water.

He did not shout in response, but the patter of his feet running away to the sala was lively with joy.

When I entered the bedroom, he was the perched atop the low table.

"Get down!" I said, a little sharply, for the table was shaky.

He got down slowly and watched me rub my hair dry. He picked up the comb from the dressing table, then the brush. Gravely, he watched me use first one, then the other. I said nothing, and neither did he for a long while. Then he walked a step or two toward the low table and picked up a copy of *Esquire*. He thumbed through the pages listlessly, then turned to me.

"Mummy, are you going to the office?"

"Yes, son."

"But it is raining."

I looked out the window, deceived for a moment. "The rain has stopped."

"Oh, Mummy, you can't go now," he announced in uncertain triumph, "because it is Sunday."

"It isn't Sunday," I explained with patience. "Auntie has gone to school, and Daddy left very early this morning." I did not look at the little face. There was no sound save the swishing of the towel against my hair and the thick dropping of each turned page.

Suddenly, two short arms were about my legs and a small face was rubbing against the roughness of my robe.

"Mummy, take me with you." I picked up the small figure and kissed the serious face.

"I have told you a number of times that you can't go to the office. I have to work there."

"I will sit on a chair. I will read Daddy's magazine like you do at night. Then we can go to Lola's afterward." The promises were halted by a kiss. I laughed because I always laugh at a moment like this. Then I put him down for he was a heavy boy and would be ashamed of being carried.

"You know I can't take you with me. I have to leave the office for several hours and then what would you do? You would get hungry and then you would be cross and cry."

"No, no, no, Mummy! I'll never, never cry. I am big. I am so tall." he came up to my waist.

I laughed again and began to dress. "You are a big boy," I said between struggles with the buttons, "and I know you will be good. But I have told you many, many times that you can't go with Mummy. Not now. On Sunday, we shall go to church."

"With Daddy?" and his face grew a little bright.

"Of course!" I pounced on the brightness, and held it on his face with a hurried kiss. "We'll wear our new clothes and we shall take Tita with us and Lili and your aunties. Then we'll go to Libis and eat a lot of things."

His eyes were luminous with the pleasures of Sunday, and his little-boy face was cut by a smile. He clung to me again and made a noise which made me laugh with relief. Then he started to dance around me till I had to ask him to stop because the lamp jogged perilously on the table. He watched me tie my bow and smooth out my dress. He talked gaily, fast and furiously glad, of a number of things -- mixing the things we had done and the things we would do like bubbles in the cup of his joy.

"I know. Mummy, I know what we shall do. We shall get guavas and we shall have salt. And tell Daddy to buy me a donkey like the donkey at the cine. And I shall roll and roll like that funny man. Remember, Mummy? And Tita will be frightened, and Lili. And I shall say Stick-em-up! and they will cry. By golly!"

I turned around quickly. "What did you say?"

"I said buy me a donkey ..."

"No, no. The last one."

"By golly!"

"Where did you learn that?"

"That was what the man said—the man in the talkie."

"Oh," I said, and let the subject rest. He was quiet while I did my hair. I stole a glance at him when it was over, and he was looking out the window, fascinated by the slow ambling of a horse harnessed to a carratela. I stopped to pick up my shoes, but like a streak he moved and picked up the shoes before I could touch them.

"Thank you, baby," I said politely and he smiled.

"Will you come back soon?"

"Yes, dear, I'll come home early."

"Before I go to sleep with Lolo?"

I shook my head slowly. I did not want to make a definite promise. It always caught up with me when I did not live up to its absolute fulfilment.

"Well, perhaps a little late."

"But come home early. And tell Daddy to come home

early. I'll call him up on my phone and tell him to bring me a golf ball lollypop."

"And what do you want me to bring you?"

He thought a while. I knew he was weighing an apple against an orange and a balut against a chocolate bar. I offered no suggestions, enjoying his perplexity. Instead, I gathered up the things I would take with me -- my pocketbook, the magazine which I had to go through, two or three articles I had edited the day before.

"Bring me an orange and an apple and three pieces of bubble gum."

"Sonny, what a lot of things! Suppose Mummy has no money this afternoon!"

"Then buy me a stick of bubble gum," he settled promptly.

I laughed at his words, and he laughed with me. Then I stooped to kiss him goodbye. All at once his arms were about my neck and I had to sit down for he would not let me go. He kissed the makeup off my face and nestled against me. This is foolish, I thought, but I could not put him down. I gave him kiss for kiss, leaving lipstick all over his face.

"Get off, you rascal," I said at last. "See how Mummy looks now." He scrambled from my lap and laughed at the splashes of color on my face. I faced the mirror once more and tried to restore whatever bloom had been coaxed to my face by the things on my dressing table. He laughed like a pleased little savage and made fun of my hair. Then, once more grave, he regarded me.

"Mummy, you are very nice now," and I blushed because I was staring at myself in the mirror when he said this. I gave him a pat on the head, then I gathered my papers and pocketbook in a hurry, in sudden anxiety about time. He walked with me to the door, then on a sudden impulse, he stopped.

"Mummy," he said, and "portentous" formed itself as a word in my mind.

"Yes, darling?" I moved my hand up and down his

shoulder, wondering at the new idea in his head.

"I'll take you to the corner. Daddy always does and I am already big." The words rushed past his lips so fast that I could not even laugh at the preposterousness of the idea. When I could laugh, his face seemed so eager and small that I changed my mind. Instead I bent down to give him a kiss.

"You can't do that. I don't want you to go out of the house without Lolo or Auntie."

"But Mummy ..."

"No," I said firmly. "You can't even go downstairs. I forbid you to. Suppose a car goes by. No, no!" I said, almost shouting at the nakedness of the thought. He looked as though he would argue for some time, but my face was not smiling. He placed my hand on his cheek, then like someone renouncing a treasure, he let it go.

I walked quickly down the stairs. I heard his feet briskly running, so I looked up at the front window when I passed it. I knew he would be there, face glowing like a brown flower. He started to wave his hand and shout reminders of what I was to bring him. When I was several yards away, he called me, and I, turning once more, saw his face thrust out of the window. I had to go back.

"Put your head inside," I called to him. "And stay there. Didn't I tell you never to put your head out too far?"

"But Mummy, I forgot to tell you. Bring me a lollypop too. And I will call you and Daddy on my phone and we shall go for a long walk, ever so far. And Mummy," his voice was like a little dog following me. He said nothing new -- just the things he always said, but he brought out such well-known words like a new gem to lure me back. His face rose above the window sill like a brown flower in a wide pot and his smile caught up with me so that I had to return and wave and smile like someone bereft. Once his face disappeared, and when it came back, a small white piece of paper waved beside it. I knew, though I could not see very well, that this was the boat I had made before breakfast. His words sang out to me, following me still, faster and faster, wagging behind me, but I could not understand what he was saying. I thought: he must be lonely. Then I said to myself: that cannot be; he has so many playmates. He is just a baby, but he must grow up. And I thought of the time when he wouldn't mind going away, when I would not be the world to him. I thought: then he will not follow me about like a loveable feather which drifts up or down according to my pleasure. His face won't be at the window, lighting up when he can make me go back, when he tries so hard to be patient when I finally go away.

I heard one bus pass, and another, but I stood at the corner waving because he still waved his hand to me. Looking at the faint white of the little paper boat, I thought: he can't go on waving his hand forever. Someday he will not care, and he will not feel badly about being left behind. That will happen, I thought and the world will not end.

**Bio:** *Ligaya Victorio Fruto was born and raised in the Philippines. A teacher, she taught for many years in the mountain region of Baguio. She later worked as a journalist for the* Tribune, *a forerunner of the* Manila Times. *She has written two books,* Yesterday and Other Stories *and* One Rainbow for the Duration.

*She was married early but was widowed during the Japanese Occupation. She worked for the Philippine Foreign Service in Honolulu, where she met and married her second husband, Larry Fruto. She has one son from her first marriage, Ramon V. Reyes, who lives in the U.S. with his family.*

*"Boy Left Behind" was written by Ligaya a number of years ago as a joke when the literary editor of a rival publication asked her why she hadn't submitted stories to him in a long time. The piece was published in the* Philippine Free Press *(October 23, 1937) and won the Best Story of the Year.*

# THE LITTLE BOY
# WHO FELL IN THE PUKA

Edgar Poma

## GO GLENDA

*You go, girl.*

There seemed to be a voice inside her urging her on. Her lung power got stronger and her pitch got meaner as she berated one of her subordinates, a young v.p., basically shredding him like a piece of paper: "You totally screwed up the deposition by stating that our real estate tax service operation's earnings had dipped, without bothering to mention that its return on average tangible equity was a solid 26 percent. You were goddamned sleeping at the switch."

"It was a mistake I won't make again, Ms. Rivera," he said. He looked considerably relieved when she was interrupted by an urgent call and started yelling at someone else. When she got off the phone, she took another urgent call, summoned some assistants and gave them orders, then she laid into him again, as if there hadn't been a break. By the end, he was looking down at his polished wing-tipped cordovans and quivering.

Glenda was used to that. She had that effect on people. When she went on tirades, she was like a tennis player with a crackerjack serve: she put all her weight into it. And it made an impression because, though she had a sleek frame, she was quite solid. In fact, one reason she was feared was because of this muscularity: she looked perfectly capable of reaching over her desk, which was koa wood by the way, which she had shipped over from the Honolulu office to San Francisco, and grabbing someone out of his chair with one hand and shaking him like an uli-uli, a hula implement that dancers used as a rattle. Her Filipino father had been a boxer, a middleweight, so she was used to workouts and garage gyms and barbells. After her classes at Punahou, she did a few hours of bookkeeping several times a week for a small neighborhood spa in exchange for weight room usage. She lifted weights as an undergrad at Brown, where, rumor had it, her classmate, JFK, Jr., was knocked out by her stunning good looks, and asked her out. (She thought he showed off too much at one of the weight machines and turned him down. She thought, *'ey*, John-John, *no act*, which was a pidgin term that meant, *Don't even try to impress me.*)

At Stanford Law, she lifted. Back in Honolulu, where she got her first job as a litigator for a financial services firm, she lifted at Gold's. This was where she met, at age thirty, four years ago, her husband Scott. She really didn't need a husband, she needed a spotter, but she married him anyway. (She stopped using his Portagee last name, Castanheira, though, when a temp secretary wrote her name as Glenda Castanets on a report once by mistake and Glenda freaked out.)

When she was commandeered to Corporate six months ago, in the spring of 1994, she began her regimen of getting up at 4:30 every morning and going to a gym called Powerhouse near her home. Scott joined her most days, so they could spot each other.

At Corporate, everyone treated Glenda with absolute

deference. Even when the big boss came to her office to consult her, his nervousness and body language made it seem like he was the senior v.p. and general counsel, and she was the CEO. She even shouted at him, to his face, about a dozen times, when she was in Honolulu and since arriving on the Mainland. She was never hesitant about giving him stink-eye at board meetings. When she called his office that morning and told him that she wanted yet another permanent assistant, he said, "You know you run this company, Glenda -- you know you can do what you want."

"I was thinking of recruiting someone out of the Honolulu office."

"Okay with me. Getting a little homesick, huh?"

"Me homesick? *Me*? My friends back there are all losers. My parents have passed on from old age and illness. I don't keep in touch with relatives. They all think I'm a money machine and I'm tired of seeing them come to my door with palms out. The only person I'm still speaking to is my kid brother, but only because I feel sorry for him because he doesn't have any mettle."

Her boss quickly began to talk about something else, but she cut him off and said, "About the upper management conference being planned next year in Lihue: I hope you've decided to move it to another island."

"I've thought that one over. I suppose we can move it to Maui. But what's the problem with Kauai? I don't think there's any reason to be hurricane-phobic."

"I grew up there. I just don't like going back. And I'm not phobic about anything. Just move it."

When she finished with her boss, she took a teleconference call from their Geneva office, which needed legal advice on some critical acquisitions strategy. It was two-way, so they could see her and she could see them on a large-scale video display in her office. When she spoke, she was pleased with their attentiveness. When she got tired of feeling like she was watching a movie, she transferred the picture to her PC, and when she had to use her PC to bring up a spreadsheet, she transferred the picture to a little box in the corner of her screen.

When the meeting ended, she turned off the remote and called the Honolulu office on another phone line to offer a job to her former top aide, at double her salary and other incentives, like absorbing all relocation costs. But the aide said she was happy where she was at, and in fact had bought a condo on Dole Street with her sister and they were both volunteering after work for a sexual trauma victims clinic.

"Well, Beverly, I'm in a meeting right now," Glenda interrupted, "and don't have time to convince you to take the job or hear about your life, so just e-mail everyone there about the opening and anyone interested can fax me a resume. Mahalo."

Beverly did what she was told: the e-mail went out that G.R. wanted another flunky. G., unfortunately, was referred to in other ways when the news was spread word of mouth: "Imelda's looking for a new victim" and "Spam Musubi's looking for a new stroker." The latter moniker referred to the fact that in Honolulu, she once dispatched an aide to Foodland to get her some individually wrapped Spam musubi, and she was so absorbed in her work that she ate all them with their cellophane wrappers still on, and never noticed.

*

She was auditing some claims documents at her desk when she felt a tightness in her stomach, or was it her chest (she had overlifted earlier that morning, going kind of macha on the bench press, and Scott hadn't been paying attention because he was on his portable phone screaming at a colleague). So she had her secretary bring in some Advils, which she took without water.

The secretary said, "I was checking your schedule. You have that funeral mid-afternoon."

"I know. Don't remind me." She returned to her auditing. "Actually, I'm really too busy to go. I have so much to do and then there's that finance leasing division lawsuit. Why don't you set up a one-way teleconference thing so I can see the funeral, right? See if you can get a temp remote over there."

"Certainly. I can call for a dispatch this morning. I'll call the funeral home and the family for permission first."

"No, just do it. No one's going to notice the wire-up. It isn't obtrusive. Anyway, I'm paying for the funeral. Just go ahead and arrange it."

The secretary straightened up a stack of papers on Glenda's credenza and hung around, so Glenda looked up from her work and said, "Do you need something or what?"

"I just wanted to tell you how sorry I am that you know a child who's died. Was he or she family?"

She went back to auditing. "Nah. Neighbor's kid. Well, not a neighbor's kid. His mom's a Filipino lady who works as a housekeeper and cook for the yuppie couple across the street. I guess she had to bring her son with her to work because he didn't have anywhere else to go, like preschool. I guess she couldn't afford it or whatever. Anyway, he was a cute little boy. Four years old. I never even knew his name. All I knew was that when I came home from work, I would see him staring at me from the big picture window across the street.

"At first, I thought he just liked my BMW. But it was way more: he'd smile at me and wave. Every day, I would see him and it was like he had been waiting for me the whole time. And I sort of got used to him being there. I'd hate to pull all-nighters because I didn't want to disappoint him. Anyway, when Scott moved his jet ski and acoustic guitars and tools and all the other junks he had stored in the garage behind the house and I could finally get my BMW in there, I told him I preferred parking it on the street and throwing a cover over it and walking into the house through the front door." she looked up from the auditing and said, "Bring in the mail and I'll tell you how he died."

The secretary brought in a huge stack and Glenda went through each item, poring over the important things and scribbling notes, while tossing the junk mail over her shoulder into a trash container like Henry VIII discarding his prime rib bones.

Glenda continued the story, matter-of-factly: "Scott's been redoing the front of the house on weekends. We want to extend the porch and then later redo the front steps. So he and a buddy began work on the porch extension a couple of weeks ago. Last week, they had finished some framework and foundation, but there were still some pukas -- sorry, that's how we say holes in Hawaii -- on one section of the porch. On Halloween night, we kept the porch light off because we weren't giving out candy -- it's just our style. We had no way of knowing that the Filipino kid across the street was going to come to the house. His mom, apparently, was going to take him trick-or-treating in the neighborhood. But the "yupps" she worked for were having a dinner party that night. She could've prepared some stuff ahead, then gone out for a while with her son, because it got dark enough around 5:30 or so, but she didn't think there was enough time.

"So around 7:00, while Scott and I were having dinner, the kid must have asked his mom if he could just go across the street to ring our door. And she was so busy, she must have said yes, as long as he looked down both sides of the street before he crossed. It wasn't as if she could get away right then and there to watch him. So he came. He made his way up the steps and he got on the porch, but because it was so dark and the railing was down, he must have tripped or stumbled, then broke through the space between the wooden barricades and through one of the holes. He fell onto some pavement on the side of the house, hit his head and bled to death. We didn't hear anything. We didn't know what had happened until paramedics came. The mother had been looking all over for him and happened to spot his trick-or-treat bag, which was one of those plastic pumpkins with a handle, on our side lawn. It had separated from his hand when he fell.

"Naturally, we were worried about being sued, but the mom's legally unsophisticated and our attorney got her to sign a waiver. I told the mom I would pick up the funeral expenses. I heard later that the 'yupps' across the street had invited a few people over who had kids who were trick-or-treating, with an adult escort, in the neighborhood. The little boy asked if he could go along with them, but they told him no, because he was wearing a costume like one of the other little kids had on. Isn't that unbelievably selfish?"

She was in a bad mood by the time she had her next meeting, with the v.p. of human resources about impending staff layoffs. The v.p. recommended that all unified budgeted positions should be axed, except for all of Glenda's staffing requests, including an associate counsel position that was still vacant.

"Your needs are so important to the company," the v.p. said.

Glenda sniffed, "Well it's not like I have a lot of them."

*

Between meetings, Glenda called Scott at his office. He was an assistant CFO at a large accounting firm also headquartered in the Financial District. When Glenda was promoted, he got headhunted into the job after his wife insisted that he leave his position at Barnwell and move with her to the Mainland. When he got on the line, she kind of blathered on, sharing some gossip she had heard about a huge securities firm being shut down by federal authorities for bilking their investors.

He interrupted her and said, "You never do this. Is something wrong?

"I dunno. I feel kind of out of sorts. It's because of that funeral I'm going to today. Actually, I'm not going to the funeral. I'm going to be there by hook-up."

"What funeral?"

"What do you mean, what funeral?" She was furious. "The funeral of the little boy who died on our fuckin' lanai!"

"Oh, yeah. Right. I forgot. Bite my head off why don't

you!"

"Why don't you come over and watch it with me?"

"Are you kidding? I'm flying out in two hours. *Watch* it with you? I have one more slide show I gotta prepare. I have memos to get out. Anyhow, you knew the kid. I didn't."

"I know that. But I guess I thought it would be nice if you were with me."

He grumbled.

"I can send it over to your PC so you can watch it too."

"Send it to my PC? Some kid's funeral? When I'm leaving for London to close a $70 million dollar deal? Get a grip! Look, gotta go." he made the sound of two lip smacks.

She thought about the day that they had moved the last of their things from their home in the Hawaii Kai district and Scott had to remove his pricey custom-made copper weather vane from the roof. She never liked it; she thought it was too haole and pretentious, though it was a three-dimensional Hawaiian warrior figure standing on the arrow and it was extremely detailed. Underneath it was a fixed post of directional letters for west, north, east and south.

"What a pain taking this thing down," he said to Glenda as she held the ladder steady. "Maybe it'd be easier if we just called the marriage quits." She laughed. He didn't.

He said over the phone, "Love ya. And I'll see you in three weeks."

"Okay, I'll keep the front light burning bright." It was, inadvertently, a terrible thing to say, given the little boy and the puka and all. But she had forgotten completely. Then she said to him bluntly, routinely, "Scott, remember to wear condoms."

He was so busy and preoccupied that instead of saying his usual, "Oh, baby!" as in "Oh, baby, quit joking!" he simply said, "Yeah, got um."

\*

She had a late lunch sent up from the lobby restaurant, and seemed to finish it off in one chomp, like animals in cartoons. She was looking through a slew of documents and briefing books when her brother called from Hawaii. She put him on speaker phone. Alex said that he needed her help on a legal quandary that a client had stuck him with. He gave her the details and she rattled off an opinion. She could hear him typing her response verbatim on his computer keyboard.

Afterward, he sounded as if a tonnage had been lifted off his back and said, "Howzit?"

"Swamped." She was comparing balance sheets from different reports while she conversed. "Scott's going to be travelling again. Other than that, same ol' shit. So did you do any more thinking about running for that house district seat that we talked about?"

Alex moaned.

"What do you mean—" She imitated his moan. "If you have any inclination at all, Alex, you have to jump on it and line up your soldiers. You have to get the Democratic party behind you, raise funds and network even though that particular election is years away."

"*Humbug.*"

"Yeah. So? What do you think, there are election planners around like there are wedding planners? *Fo'get* it."

"I'm afraid of -- you know -- the thing about Dad. What if I get into politics and someone comes out with the whole thing to embarrass me? It's the only skeleton in my closet, and *Gods*, it's not even my closet, it's Dad's."

"Don't let that stop you. It's the perfect opportunity for you: you're young, well-educated, making good money, not ugly though it would be nice if you were taller, a little stunted in the relationship department but you might meet someone if you keep trying. At any rate, there's no better time for the Filipino-American elite, either: the population's growing, Ben Cayetano's governor. It's very rosy picture for Orientals in general."

"Asian," Alex said.

Glenda was annoyed, but knew she needed reminders of political correctness. "Asian," she said with an edge.

During her next meeting, she was distracted by one of the women participant's scent, which seemed like an expensive version of her mother's cheap Avon perfume. She thought about the time her parents visited her while she was at law school. She left them in her apartment, brought down a rice cooker from a kitchen shelf for their use, told them at what time and on which channel they could watch *Wrestling*, her father's favorite. Then she did her own thing.

The only place she took them to during their trip was the Winchester Mystery House in San Jose. It was a strange, four-story mansion with nearly 400 rooms. A widow, an heiress to the rifle fortune, kept carpenters and craftspeople adding to the house twenty-four hours a day for thirty-eight years because a medium told her that continuous building was the only way she could appease evil spirits of those killed by the Winchester rifle. Glenda's mother was a tad confused about the whole setup: when she saw stairs leading up into a ceiling, she said, "Niiiice, yeah?" Glanda's father was somewhat senile by that time, but was lucid enough to complain, during the tour, about being in a Pupule House or insane asylum. Glenda muttered, "Well, no, you're not in one ... yet." She wanted to push him into some airless isolated room that the Winchester people hadn't yet discovered and then board it up. She figured that since the house was goofy kine anyway, no one would know the difference.

She suddenly started to think about her brother. After Punahou, Alex went to the University of Hawaii and worked part-time as a management assistant at an office supply store on Dillingham Boulevard. He didn't plan to continue school after getting his B.A., but Glenda talked him into going to law school on the Mainland, at UCLA. She hoped that he had finally gotten aboard on her sky-high career ladder. But then he dropped-out at the start of his second year, citing boredom rather than intellectual inability. But even that didn't soften the blow of his withdrawal as Glenda's hands felt like they were slipping from her own ladder rung by rung.

"What do you wanna be, Alex?" she screamed at him

when he returned to Honolulu. "Pig Knuckles Rivera?" She was referring to their father, who was dying at the time. Originally, he had arrived by boat from the Philippines with other sakadas to cut sugar cane. He went on to California to pick crops, got restless when he wasn't in the fields and had too many liaisons with all the wrong women: Whites who were willing, but legally verboten because of anti-miscegeny laws or their whoredom, or Filipinos who weren't verboten for any reason but who were unwilling. So some older town mates forced him to pack his things and return to Hawaii. He was a tough guy and resisted them at first, but had a dream that his father in the Philippines wanted him to return to Hawaii, so he acceded.

Back on Oahu, he hustled his way into a job as a pipefitter at Pearl Harbor, while he tried to make it as a boxer. But work was too demanding and he never got anywhere with his big dream. In the early sixties, he returned to his hometown of Kekaha in Kauai and took over a flagging construction equipment rental business that would never, never revive. His only shred of sensibility was in agreeing with his wife about sending their kids, who were brilliant in school, to live with relatives in Honolulu and go to private schools on academic scholarships.

Alex sat through Glenda's ranting and said, "I don't know what I'm gonna do but I might go back to Office Depot." Which he did, where he got a job on the sales floor. He stayed in Glenda's condo at an exclusive building called The Waipuna and she charged him a lot for rent, until he worked up enough courage to say, "What do you think I am, some tourist? Can you at least give me kamaaina rate? I mean come on, Glenda. Be real." And she softened. And they got along much better.

But she nagged, which was her forte. And she did it so relentlessly that he went back to the Mainland inevitably and got his law degree and passed the bar, then got a job with a top law firm in Honolulu with Glenda pulling strings. She had basically gotten someone fired so her brother could take the person's place. He did reasonably well in the job, and after several years, Glenda planted the seed in his head about a political career.

When the meeting in her office was finally over, she checked the time and tuned into the funeral, which was in progress. She left it on the big screen for a while, then watched it on her PC screen. The whole thing was programmed so she could see shots of everything from different angles. So unless she punched a button on the keyboard to hold, she saw in twenty second increments scenes of the funeral underway: the priest giving the Mass, the half-filled funeral home, the flower arrangements ...

She returned a call from a reporter from a legal newspaper as she watched.

... and the family in the enclosed space off to the side, the mom shrieking hysterically (at which point, Glenda turned the volume completely off), the boy in the coffin. He was in his Halloween costume. Someone had placed candy in and around his folded hands. When she saw this, she felt like screaming with grief, which she, did deep inside, so loudly that her bones shook.

"That would be libelous to put it that way," she was telling a reporter calmly. "Interest rates imbedded in our product liabilities, and our ability to be on guard in rapidly changing financial markets. At year-end, the aggregate market value of our fixed income portfolio will be $1 billion in excess of its book value. No matter how much you try to dick it around, you don't have a story."

As Glenda continued to watch the funeral, she sent for, on an impulse, the v.p.-corporate communications, the company's p.r. expert. He came to her office right away, practically dashed over like he was in a track meet. She said, "I want to discuss two things with you. One, I saw a tape of the new proposal for the t.v. spot the other day and I liked it, but the rock music has got to go. Try, well, you know rap."

"I don't like rap. But you have to keep up with these things."

She had heard a woman rapper on the radio in her BMW months ago. The back-up vocals repeated "Go! You go, girl!" throughout the song, and somehow the words and the beat pounded in Glenda's head from time to time.

"Two, I have an associate in Hawaii who's thinking of running for public office. He's a little gun-shy, though, because of something in his past. I'll get to the point. His parents weren't the best. His mom taught school, but was gone a lot. She had developed some new method of teaching immigrant kids how to read English. His father, while the mom was on one of her trips, raped a 12-year-old girl some time back. The girl had a kid, a little boy, but she put him up for adoption and all the transaction records were burned. My associate's father is dead now. The girl died young, most likely from shame and humiliation, though she wasn't at all at fault for what had happened ..."

She was interrupted by a panicky call from a finance group v.p. who needed legal guidance regarding securitization. Afterward, she picked up where she had left off: "Anyway, the whole thing should be forgotten except for the fact that the girl's black hair supposedly changed color, turned red, after the rape, so there are a few old people in the small town where it happened who still talk about the event and keep it alive."

"Oh, so it's like folklore almost. Modern folklore."

"Yeah, right. You get all kinds of that crap in Hawaii. So my question is, can this harm him in any way later on?"

"Well, no. He shouldn't bring it up until someone does, which may never happen. If by some fluke someone dredges it up, the spin would be that here is this guy who overcame adversity, like his father's sins, and made something of himself."

She was pleased with this and rewarded him by suggesting that they have lunch next week. He knew, of course, that there was nothing more prestigious than to be seen having lunch with The Big G., who very rarely left her luxurious 25th-floor corner office for anything.

\*

She drove home in the rain, and when she parked in front of her house, she looked across the street. Her buddy at the window, perhaps the only person who ever really loved her, was not there. Her portable phone rang and she answered it while she picked up the newspaper covered in a plastic bag from the walk and went up the steps to her porch and got the mail and dug around in her briefcase for her house key. The caller was an attorney who had left her staff two months ago to accept an executive position for another company, in Atlanta, and who now wanted her old job back because she had just learned that her 30-year-old drug addict son had AIDS and she wanted to come home and take care of him.

*Go Glenda.*

"That position's been filled. Besides, you can't expect me or anyone else to bail you out of every difficult situation. It's not my fault that you made the wrong move when you left. You have to learn how to use better judgment in life. Obviously, you can't get any pointers from your son."

*You go, girl.*

After she got off the phone and closed the front door, she turned the porch light on and placed all her stuff on a table in the entry-way and took off her raincoat and checked the answering machine and went to the kitchen and made a small salad and heated a bucket of leftover hot wings (grilled, not fried) in the oven and had a slice of angel food cake and washed the dishes and kept the bucket instead of trashing it because it had a ½-off coupon on its face, and she went to the bedroom and got out of her suit and got into a baggy T-shirt and went to the bathroom and brushed her teeth with her Braun Oral-B Plaque Remover Deluxe, which Scott had given her on her birthday, and brushed her hair and saw up close in the mirror traces of red in her roots, so she wen ula, or rinsed, her hair until it was jet black again, then wrapped a towel around her head, and slipped on a bathrobe and went to her bedroom and sat on the edge of her bed and tried, with both hands, to

183

contain a heart that, after many years of keeping it on the mend, began to break into too many pieces.

*Bio of Edgar Poma: "The Little Boy Who Fell in the Puka,"* which won first place in A. Magazine's second annual Asian American literary contest, and first appeared in the Asian-Pacific Journal, encompasses some of my favorite themes: power, migrant farmworker history, sentimentality, a nagging undercurrent of loneliness, and a terrible unmasking, all the backdrops of Hawaii and Northern California.

My parents were born in San Juan, Ilocos Sur and now live in Sacramento, California. I was born in 1959. Some of my work is published in collections by Filipino American writers, Without Names (Kearney Street Press) and Flippin' (Rutgers University Press). My full-length plays, "Reunion" and "Little Train," debuted in San Francisco in 1981 and 1992, respectively. An essay, "Bresh," appeared in The Threeplay Review while I was an undergrad at U.C. Berkeley. I was selected by HBO for their New Writers Program in 1994 and received a California Arts Council Grant in 1995 for playwriting.

# *SUTIL*

Marianne Villanueva

I WAS LAST home for my father's funeral.

I say "home" even though I am an American citizen now, sworn in with a twenty piece Navy band in the grand ballroom of the Marriott Hotel on 4th and Mission in San Francisco. Yet, "home" for me was always that other place, that city James Hamilton-Paterson describes as "a parody of the grimmer parts of Milwaukee."

I've never been to Milwaukee, so I can't tell whether this is true or not, whether Manila really is like a parody of the city in the far north of this country (or at least what I imagine to be the far north, in a general region of the country I associate with heavy snow and Laverne and Shirley). But that it is different from here, of course. It is the differences I loved.

When I was last home, which was for my father's funeral, I slept with my mother in the big wooden four-poster in my parents' bedroom. This bed, handed down from my grandfather, was familiar and reassuring. It was of heavy wood, a wood that doesn't exist today in any Philippine forest, having been cut to extinction. It may have been called "molave". I am not sure of this, as I am not sure about so many things about my culture, which I think I received very young, too young really to understand context or value.

This bed had, instead of a box spring, a woven rattan underside to hold the one thin mattress. And on this mattress, lying next to my mother at night, it seemed to me I could still feel the contours of my father's body, he who lay in the coffin downstairs in the living room, unfamiliar now with the mortician's make-up.

Next to the bed were scattered newspapers, some even from the day my father had his last breakfast, only a few days before. My mother was too distracted to begin putting his things away, and I was glad. It seemed to me that if I stopped thinking for a moment, my father could still be alive. I saw his desk, his bifocals resting on an open page of his appointment book, his pens, the scattered photographs of his grandchildren. His shoes in the closet, his shirts and silk ties, his dressing gown and slippers -- all these were still in the room. Even now, as I write this, I see so much of my father, and perhaps because I am not in Manila, where he lived and actually died, it is hard for me to imagine him as really dead, and not just in some foreign city, some city that reminds a British writer of Milwaukee.

It was the cool season in Manila, and therefore we didn't need to run the air conditioner all the time. The windows were wide open. They were barred, screenless windows. From the neighbors' side yard only a few feet away, I could hear their help coming and going, hear the splash of dirty water being emptied onto the plants, hear the maids chatter as they hung up the laundry, which was clearly visible from my parents' windows.

An attempt had been made to shield us from the view of the neighbors' dirty kitchen. There were a few stunted mango trees and banana palms. But these were ineffectual.

If I paid attention, I might also smell dogs and chickens

-- everyone in Manila seemed to keep a menagerie of animals in their backyards, even here in the heart of the city. Everything was dirty and smelled good to me.

In the morning, the maids scrubbed the wooden floors with coconut husks and YCO wax. There was also the smell of frying bacon and fried eggs, fried sausage, fried fish. Everything here seemed bathed in oil, and the oil tasted good, too.

I'd lived for a long time in California. It had been years since I was last home. And I'd forgotten many things about smells and such. But once I was back home, I remembered everything again.

I had two brothers, both still living at home: one was a bachelor and was out all the time. The other was married and had a three-year-old son. The son and his yaya stayed in a room downstairs. My brother and his wife stayed in a room down the hall.

Sometimes, living in California, I forgot that I had brothers. They never wrote, and I heard all their stories second-hand, months after the events in the stories had taken place, usually from one of my mother's letters. Now, back home, it occurred to me that they must also have forgotten they had a sister somewhere in California. Their friends gazed at me with something akin to shock. Perhaps I seemed old to them. I wasn't so much older than my brothers, but in Manila it is still possible to go to discos and other such places well into middle age, and I hadn't done any of those things for a long time.

My brothers didn't say so much to me. We would meet each other at breakfast. One or the other would grunt. We would settle down to our meal. They would bury themselves behind the newspapers. Occasionally, someone would gesture to a maid for hot chocolate or calamansi juice.

The last time I was home, they had been very young, and so it was hard for me to accept this view of my brothers in coats and ties. I found myself watching them out of the corners of my eyes, as if I might discover a secret, lurking beneath the outlines of their suited shoulders. But I never discovered what it was, really. I ate meekly, head lowered. I couldn't bring myself to gesture to the maids. My hands remained ineffectual, hovering across the table for the butter dish which one of my brothers, with a snap of his fingers, would have summoned a maid for.

We ate breakfast in the same room as my father's coffin. It was a custom that the body could never be left alone, not even for one minute for the nine days of the wake. But because my father had been such a peaceful man when he was alive, even in death the sight of his coffin did not cause me any heart-rending stirrings of grief. There were tears, yes. But they were quiet tears, and flowed in private. At breakfast, we would just have breakfast. No one talked about the coffin or even referred to it. We knew he would be there for nine days. In a way, he was still with us.

I try to remember if my brother's wife was with us during these breakfasts. My married brother had met his wife at a party at which they were both very drunk. Afterwards, this brother, Ernesto, told my mother that the girl was pregnant. And of course, being the culture that it was, my brother eventually married the girl. Their son was born a few months after the wedding. They named him Miguel.

The first week I was back home, I rarely saw my brother's wife. She never came down for breakfast with the rest of us. She was always upstairs in her room, and sometimes I would see one of the maids bringing her up a tray of food. My mother never remarked on this, and so neither did I.

My third night back, I lay in bed sleepless, thinking. There had been a lot of people in the house that morning. The relatives from Bacolod had just arrived -- all thirty of them. And we'd had to feed them, of course. Now they were camped out in the living room, on chairs and sofas, determined, like the rest of us, not to leave my father's body alone.

After a long time, I fell asleep. Then, after what seemed only a few minutes, I woke again. There were unfamiliar voices I thought must be coming from the hallway. It took me several minutes to register a man's voice, heavy and slurred. Loud, too. I imagined my bachelor brother drunk, coming home from wherever it was he usually disappeared to at night. Finally it dawned on me that the voices were coming from my married brother and his wife. I don't know how I realized this: the voices seemed a new terrain, an undiscovered country. They were nothing like the mild figures I was used to glimpsing around the house. Perhaps I had a secret knowledge of them that I had been carrying around with me all these past few days, a knowledge that enabled me now to say with certainty: Yes, I recognize those shouts, those moans.

My brother bellowed; my sister-in-law pleaded. The sounds were shattering. My mother threw off the blanket in one quick motion, and from the way she moved, I knew she had done this many times before. That knowledge wounded me. I followed her down the corridor. There it was again: that shattering sound, my sister-in-law pleading, "STOP, STOP, STOP." My brother: "SHUT UP, SHUT UP, SHUT UP!" I saw my mother standing at the door to their room, ear pressed to the heavy wood, listening. I rested my hand on the door knob, saying, "I've had enough of this." My mother's quick pressure on my wrist: I had forgotten how strong her fingers were. The hold she had on me was tight and urgent. "Give them a minute," she said. We stood outside the door, listening. And it was suddenly very silent. So silent I might have thought the earlier sounds were a dream. After a few minutes, my mother and I went back together to the bedroom. Sleepless, we tossed and turned on the big bed, the one where only a few nights earlier my father's body had lain in the depressions of the mattress. For a long time, we didn't speak. We each lay in our cocoons of silence, as far away from each other as we dared. I looked at the water spots on the ceiling. It seemed to me that everything I had just witnessed had changed the whole context of my visit. Finally, I asked my mother: "How long have they been that way?" I thought of my brother as he had been, or as I remembered him from old pictures: he had been chubby and round, his favorite attire when he was five or six a

Batman suit. He had a favorite yaya named Ning, her complexion dark as a coconut husk, who my brother nevertheless called beautiful and whose breasts he loved to squeeze when he was only four or five. She would slap his hands away, laughing. "Sutil! Naughty!" she would say, over and over.

This was my brother now who was causing his wife to moan and plead: "Stop! No! No!" My hair stood on end. I could not sleep.

The next morning, I saw my brother at the breakfast table. But he looked normal, in control of himself. My sister-in-law must have slipped out somewhere. I looked for my nephew. He was in the garden, playing with his yaya.

"Miguel! Miguel, come here!" I called, insistent.

"Whadisit?" he lisped, walking to me with his little bow and arrow.

I held him close. He smelled of sweat and Johnson's baby powder. I looked at his face, lifted his chin with my hand. I tried to see something of my brother in the little boy. There was something, very slight: the black, curly hair; perhaps the pudgy cheeks. But I couldn't be sure. And I wanted to be sure.

My mother had told me that my brother hadn't been the first. This was something. And he and the girl had had relations only that one night, the night they met. Afterwards, when she became pregnant, we told my brother, "Get a blood test." But he refused. And now this.

The day continued, and everyone went about on their own business: my mother went out with friends; my bachelor brother and the married brother went to work. I asked the maids: did you hear anything last night? And they told me they were used to seeing glasses lying broken on the floor, or cracked mirrors.

That night there was a family gathering in my aunt's house. She lived in a suburb just outside Manila. We had to drive down the South Super Highway, which was crowded with commuter traffic and buses and jeepneys. There was a confusing intersection with an overpass, where there seemed to be a lot of pedicab stands and vendors' stalls, where the aroma of barbecued pork was very strong and mingled with the garbage smells from the street. It was also poorly lit, and in the shadows I saw figures darting in and out of the traffic, some with long poles balanced on their shoulders, others brandishing cartons of cigarettes at passing cars. After making a right turn here, we were suddenly in wide, well-paved streets lined with large houses and tall gates.

We were having dinner, and my brother and his wife walked in. They were hand-in-hand. He nuzzled her hair and cheek. She laughed. I looked at them and lost all my appetite. I thought of the little boy, Miguel, sleeping peacefully at home. This morning Miguel had bit his yaya on the belly. Why did he do that? Bad boy! we all scolded. The yaya had cried. There was blood. Her name is Imelda; she was a very young girl, from the provinces. Looking at her, anyone could tell she was not happy.

Later this Imelda came to me and asked for some money. I gave her some. Later I asked my brother: "Has she asked you for some money lately?" And he said no.

I remained two more weeks in my parents' house, with my brother and his wife just down the corridor, and for the rest of my time there, I didn't sleep well although there were no more disturbing sounds from the other room.

After the traditional nine-day wake, during which time we were successful in never leaving my father's body alone, even for a minute, and during which time our family entertained hordes of guests who came from as far away as Iloilo, we cremated my father's body and placed the ashes in an urn in the family crypt.

During all this time, my mother and I were unable to shed a tear. I kept busy making a list of all people who had sent us Mass cards. This task kept me occupied for hours at a time. We stacked the Mass cards on the dining room table, and there were six piles, each a couple of feet high. My mother ordered engraved cards, so that we could reply to everyone.

My sister-in-law continued to flit in and out, but she

was not part of the funeral arrangements. One day I was surprised when she joined us at breakfast. I found myself becoming unexpectedly talkative, talking about all sorts of people I really didn't know very well.

My sister-in-law came from a rich family. Lopez. Mestizo. She was very fair, much fairer than my brother, and she had porcelain skin and light brown hair that made her look almost Spanish. Her eyes, too, were pale and rather watery, as though filmed over constantly with tears. She had a wan way of moving, but I heard people say she loved to go dancing and was quite a good dancer. On nights when my brother was out-of-town, she went with a group of friends to the disco. She had married my brother when she was only nineteen, and already four months pregnant with Miguel. It was a mistake, the pregnancy. She'd only just met my brother. But people said they were both very drunk. So that was the reason for the tension in the family. And I cringed thinking of my father, who was always so so decorous and correct, lying awake at night, listening to glasses shattering against walls, listening to the low moaning sounds my sister-in-law made at night. My mother told me it happened all the time. But they were always sweet and loving the next morning -- no one could understand it, and so my parents just left them alone. But my brother's voice is slurred and thick, and though rather slow-witted, or because he is slow-witted, his anger is a scary thing which he knows very well how to use, striking with it (though I cannot imagine he has actually used physical violence, this thought is so repugnant to me I immediately shut it out of my mind) here and there and reducing my sister-in-law to that voice, that voice moaning "Stop! Stop!"

After three weeks, I returned to my house in California. It seemed I didn't sleep very well there, either. Nights I would lie awake in bed, thinking. Or, in the kitchen, when I had my hand on the refrigerator door, to open it, to pull out an opened can of evaporated milk for my coffee; a piece of Wonder Bread for my breakfast, I would be struck by something: a color, a wash of white, the way the bread looked in its bright red, white and blue Supermarket wrapping. I could imagine someone painting the primary colors, the wash of white that hurt my eyes. And then I would think of THEM, my brother and my sister-in-law, in that other place, that place of heat and complex smells, and I would stop in mid-gesture, not knowing whether I meant to tuck a strand of hair behind my ear, or to continue getting the milk or bread. Suddenly, the present would be overtaken by a vision of hot rooms, tangled sheets, and cracked mirrors. I saw bedclothes trailing to the floor, which was littered with shards of glass. The room would be empty. I would stand at the doorway, looking around for my brother and my sister-in-law, who I somehow knew were not there. I would see my reflection in the cracked mirror. In my mind I heard again the words of the yaya, gone so many tears, saying over and over, "Sutil!"

*Bio of Marianne Villanueva: I was born and raised in Manila, though my father owned sugar farms in Bacolod and we spent every summer there I was growing up. I am a graduate of the Ateneo de Manila, came to Stanford to pursue a Masters degree in East Asian Studies, and went on to receive a scholarship in the Stanford Creative Writing Program. I wrote a collection of short stories,* Ginseng and other Tales from Manila, *which was published by Calyx Books in 1991. My work has been anthologized in, among others,* Charlie Chan is Dead: An Anthology of Contemporary Asian American Prose, *edited by Jessica Hagedorn; and* Into the Fire: Asian American Prose, *edited by Sylvia Watanabe and Carol Bruchac. I live in the San Francisco Bay Area, where I work as a Program Administrator in Stanford University.*

# GRANDMOTHER'S SOUP

Fatima Lim-Wilson

FOR WEEKS, the rumors had set fires around Emi's once happy home, stoked by the flying embers of hearsay, word-of-mouth.

She would walk home from the wet market, her head held high and with her young son bobbing from the handwoven sling binding him to her back. The heat of gossip brought the flush of wild roses to her cheeks. Windswept whispers brought pearl cluster of sweat rising upon her brow. In spite of the heat of spiteful words all around her, her heart was icy cold. And that is how she managed to walk down those streets, looking proud and defiant as a rebel queen, propelled by the storm of her frozen feelings.

Just two years ago, she had walked down those streets, colorful as the basket of fruits she carried. Her produce was renowned throughout the countryside for each juicy orb of sweetness was carefully picked by her four older sisters on her grandmother's farm whose soil was reported to be steeped in honey.

Emi's load was heavy, but her laughter was feather light. Her peals of joy and singsong cries praising the freshness and ripeness of her wares slowed down even the most harried passerby who would suddenly have the need for her heart-shaped bounty. One of these was Ramon, a carpenter who had just reached the wise old age of twenty. He, too, with pride, carried his means of livelihood with him -- a wooden case filled with the shiniest carpenter's tools. Ramon boasted that he could finish a one-room shack in a day. He lavished his hammers and nails with polish as lovingly as a priest would look after his altar's statues.

As Ramon gazed at the winsome maiden before him, holding out in her tiny fingers an oversized jewel glazed with sap, he felt that with her beside him, he could build a castle overnight. Emi, in turn, could not stop staring upon his muscled arms and his sturdy legs thick as the branches of the centuries-old trees surrounding her grandmother's grave.

The parish priest married the two giddy lovers under a full moon so bright it seemed that a madman had set the sky on fire. Her sisters glared at their new brother-in-law without blinking once throughout the long ceremony. Through the intensity of their stare, they gave the clear message that he did not deserve their most precious princess.

All the townspeople came to dance to the music of the inebriated band and to feast upon the grinning pig turning slowly over the hot stones. Ramon carried his laughing bride over the threshold of their home which still smelled of freshly cut timber. In their excitement, they knocked down the baskets set by the door which were overflowing with gifts of rainbow fabrics, palm wine, and rice. Their bed hewn by the groom himself from a single molave trunk rocked all night. Ramon marveled over Emi's beauty as he would upon finding a rare piece of smooth, supple mahogany. She seemed to take on many shapes under his hands. Her long, black hair cascaded over him like the softest of leaves. Her ancestral wedding gown lay in an abandoned, reckless heap by the foot of the bed. Only the tortoise shell hairpins from her dead grandmother kept getting in the way, poking him when he least expected it.

What a blissful first year it was. Ramon worked like one crazed, building houses faster than the town's best gambler could shuffle a pack of cards. Emi's fruits were a sell-out. They seemed to have grown even sweeter with an aftertaste of a secret sin. Their sticky fragrance lingered on the mouth and air. Fishermen carried these big globes of fruit on board their vessels both for luck and sustenance. City bound adventurers gingerly wrapped the sugared moons in layers of old calendars. They packed them together with their scant belongings in the hope that their grand dreams would take the shape and scent of these fragile treasures. And, in the middle of the night, pregnant women moaned, frightening their husbands. They must have Emi's fruit now, sliced open like a many petalled flower glowing in the dark, its liquid honey spilling over their fingers and swollen bellies.

Soon, Emi herself was with child. Ramon filled the town with his houses until the structures spilled over to the next village. He had to spend more nights away from home but he always carried with his hammer and nails a basket of Emi's magic fruit and the brand of her kiss left upon his forehead, a searing mark that was invisible but potent. Ramon did not have wandering eyes until he saw the next village's seamstress who kept on fluttering before his field of vision, vivid as a cockatoo. It did not take long for gossip to come flying back to San Rafael that Ramon was laying down more than fallen logs. Emi gave birth a month early, her four sisters gathered round her, sad-eyed. She pushed in silence for many hours, her laughter stilled, and her grandmother's locket gripped between her teeth.

Ramon came back months later, penitent and feverish. The seamstress, underneath her plumage, proved to be as cranky as a crow and as dull. She had tossed his hammer and nails into the river as soon as she sensed his wanting to leave. He had swam for hours in the fast moving current, diving again and again searching in vain for his priceless tools. He came back, in the dead of night, shuffling his feet before the door he had built himself, bearing Emi's empty fruit basket.

Emi greeted him in her soft, musical tones. Instead of raising her voice or her fists in anger, she lifted the cooing baby into his eager arms. As Emi felt her errant spouse's hot forehead, Ramon silently thanked all the stars and saints for his caring and forgiving wife. Meanwhile, Emi was taking note that her kiss's mark had been buried under the beaked imprints of ravenous bird.

"Sit and play with your son. I will make grandmother's soup for you."

Ramon licked his lips. Emi had never shared the recipes of her legendary grandmother till now. As Ramon got acquainted with his baby, Emi kept busy over her big, blackened pot. Already, Ramon was forgetting the seamstress's scissorlike grip and anticipating Emi's melting softness. He did not notice Emi grounding her mirror into diamond bits which she mixed with her mashed fruits. She jabbed her fingers with his rusty nails pulled from the roof, squeezing her own blood over the broth. From the folds of her chemise, she picked angry looking ants and spiders and salt crystals of her hardened tears. Finally, she opened her locket over the simmering soup, letting loose her beloved grandmother's ashes which flew like rabid bats over their paralyzed prey. Ramon meanwhile threatened and pleaded with his son to play with him but the infant kept trying to crawl away.

Ramon did not find it strange that only he ate the soup. He thought, vain man that he was, that Emi was content to just sit back and watch him, filling herself with the wondrous sight of him who had wandered off for so long. The soup was as delicious as her fruits but even more so for it had a haunting scent that reminded him of Emi's fragrance in bed or after she had come in from gathering fruits from the rain. The unrecognizable bits and pieces that floated in the shimmering liquid seemed to embrace and caress his tongue just as Emi did in those first heavenly months. Just as he was getting full, his other hunger was growing. His sensations were reawakening to the wonder that was his wife.

But Ramon finds that he cannot move. He drops the bowl and wooden spoon, the spilled soup slithering away like a hunted snake. He, too, has fallen to the floor with an echoing thud. His blood seems to have slowed, held back by an insurmountable dam. His every muscle has grown heavy, heavy as if he is being crushed by the rubble of his remorse. He finds himself wanting to hold his wife more out of fear than longing, but his arms are soldered to his sides. Only months ago, he was hot with the fever of desire, but he is quickly turning colder and colder, harder and harder. The last thing he remembers is Emi standing over him, gazing at him as her sisters once did, unblinking. His son, oblivious to his agony, plays happily with Emi's empty locket.

The rumors, having lost the kindling of fresh scandals, have died down. No one ponders anymore the puzzle of Ramon's disappearance. Ramoncito, his son is doing so well in school, there is no question that he will someday be a doctor or a mayor. Place a hammer in his hand and he will drop it, clumsily, but set him in his great grandmother's farm, and he will scramble up the tallest tree, gathering fruit faster that the screaming monkeys. And he has such riveting eyes, like moons that are always full.

Emi still sells her fruits in the market although she has long stopped laughing or trying to entice buyers for even if they wanted to, they simply could not resist her offerings. They pay her quickly, muttering thanks. They shiver under her icy stare. The warm fruits that they shove quickly in their straw baskets throb like hearts.

The houses Ramon built can withstand the onslaught of the strongest typhoon or earthquake but they all have taken on this strange, slanted shape as if they were kneeling, begging for forgiveness. They also tend to invite unwelcome hordes of brightly plumaged birds who peck holes on the roofs. Only Emi's house stands tall as it was when first built by her lovestruck husband. No birds dare to rest within the shadow's breadth of her eaves.

Emi takes daily walks to her grandmother's grave. The

trees crowd above her like her anxious sisters. She waters the flowers by her grandmother's headstone. Silently, she sits for what seems like many hours on an odd-looking, wooden bench that has the breadth and width of a robust man. The moon glistens above her like one of her outsized fruits. In the glimmering dark, the bench beneath Emi grows arms that try but always fail to hold her. The bench seems to groan, burdened by something far, far heavier than her weight.

# DARK STAR/ALTERED SEEDS

## Linda Ty-Casper

THE QUESTION hangs over her, deepest in the dark house.
Instead of reaching for it, she turns, lines a leg along
the edge of the bed and tries to fall back to sleep ...

In the hospital when she could not sleep, she asked to
be allowed back to the Red Lounge where visitors sat coiled in
their chairs, during calling hours. Sometimes there were others
chasing midnight; sometimes, just herself. If the others were
Pat and Leah, they sat together in a tight el, puffing at cigarettes
while keeping each other company. When their minds drifted,
they each retreated to the kitchen, each carefully scrambled her
own eggs in compliance with the Unit's regulations about
taking care of oneself.

Still unable to fall asleep they sat waiting, sucking in
their breaths when the midnight shift came in. footsteps
carried along the ceiling and walls of the hall leading from the
nurses' station.

Leah said, Don't ever talk in the hall or the whole Unit

hears you. Don't even think.

Then the bed check. It's one thirty. If your doctors left a prescription, I can give you sleeping pills. Okay. Take a few more minutes, then try to get sleepy. Okay?

The staff was very careful not to change medication. If the prescription said buffered aspirin, they called the hospital pharmacy to ask if that meant Bufferin ...

She thinks there is a light flashing across the room. A fugitive sun stirring. But she sees nothing but darkness ...

Every fifteen minutes there was a head count at the Unit. A light was flashed into one's room, swept across the bed. When she was new there, she lay awake waiting all night to catch the flashes; fell asleep just before morning call at seven thirty ...

She thinks she hears a knock at the door though she knows there is none. She turns lightly. Now it is her back alongside the edge, lying so still so as not to wake him up. She lies still, counting her breaths, trying not to startle herself fully awake ...

The last night together at the Unit, she and Pat and Leah managed to stay up until three. They went to their rooms at lights-out, came separately at intervals, to explain at the nurse's station that the pills didn't work. I'll just go light a cigarette, then turn in.

A new woman came in earlier that night. By chance she was passing by while the woman's wrist was being rebandaged. She thought of telling Pat and Leah, but it would not help them to know. First time she had seen a slashed wrist. The stitches made her think of wire fences. She had taken pills. Twenty-nine because she did not know how many were required to die.

None of them knew. Or just didn't say. By some remnant kindness after all feelings were gone, they did not risk telling. Instead they repeated what their milieu therapist told them: You're terrific. There's a lot going for you. A lot of fun left in your life. You'll make it.

Usually they had neither the will nor the energy to repeat those lies to each other. All they could manage was quiet, with the day broken up by therapies: occupational, psycho, group, whatnot; and visitors. In between they sat at table in Rec Area, drinking coffee, smoking while the television flickered its pictures dimly across the room and emitted sound barriers.

She went to the Unit to work at overcoming her anger through self-esteem so she would not again turn that anger against herself, never swallow those dark stars/white seeds again.

Until eleven thirty on weekends they sat after the visitors had gone and the rap session ended, thinking, thinking ... It was possible to go beyond the walls of the Unit in one's mind, to go past the lake where the hospital incinerator stood like missiles on launch pads ... To go anywhere in fact without the staff walking alongside, without having to hurry back if all one had was a two-hour pass. One returned, however, to the same body, the same confining fears.

Privileges differed. Some could go only as far as the lily pads to feed salt-free crackers to the fish in the lake. Others were allowed to go into town and take coffee at DiCenzos. Get a chance to finger the pastas on the way out. Linger over the newspapers. They might have the same medication but under different names, though the same pill could keep one awake that put others to sleep. Curled the lips of a third. Some recovered quickly. Some stayed and stayed, with the same psychiatrist ... She got well ...

Did that make a difference? Was that the question that woke her up? That like a petulant sun hung above the bed, waking her up from a dream of beds. All kinds. With mattresses. Jiggly waterbeds.

She looked toward her husband's body unetched in the dark. It would be perverse -- like fighting medication or lying to one's psychiatrist -- to ask what kind of bed *she* had in her apartment. Did his body sink into that bed or was it held? Did it float above her? Did she ...?

She? Why do you say she? Does the other woman not have a name? You say it happened. Tell me what happened.

Her doctor wanted her to face having been abandoned. He threw his questions at her like a knife thrower, just missing skin but making flesh bleed inside, bruising the nerves. He was a reality psychiatrist. Her first was more of an analyst. Can you ever trust again now that you know husbands can come and go? He wanted to know why she faced life so intensely ...

She winces. `Like a tight fist sun is inside her, strangling ...

Her confessor said, Don't expect God to intervene, but take responsibility for yourself so you can find your own strength. If you feel powerless again, you will try to kill yourself.

Her friends said, Be happy he's back. He left but he returned. Life can be better. Forget what happened. You're a strong person.

He said, It's you I love. I loved you even when I was sick, and with her. It's a sickness. I'm over it. I'm back forever. Can't you feel I'm back?

Leah said, Forgive the expression. I've seen lots of shit but he takes it, telling you he loved you even when he was fucking her.

She thought, It's a never-ending hurt ...

Now, she is fully awake with the sun circling inside her, creating turbulence ...

As awake as she was that night Leah called at two in the morning. I'm ashamed to call but I'm bombed out of my mind. Do you still have pills? Throw them. Throw them please. Please. You're too good a person. Promise. I'll call again tomorrow. Promise ...

She lies on her back, stretched, with the sun burning its way inside her; singing awful litanies: That's not his body but his long shadow. Remember she was in the house. She lay in that bed ...

She tries to keep her thoughts free of fear; tries not to be waylaid by that imperious sun unravelling her inside. Why should she promise? She worked at finding peace in the Unit and she is not the one who is back there. Claire is back. Jim with the all-time high is back. Ben is back because he cannot admit he's an alcoholic. And Pat is back -- not at the Unit with the wall-size mural in which plants leafed and flowered -- but at the State Hospital ...

How long did a cure last? January seven she took the pills. Next day she was back at the Unit. February seven she was discharged because she was set on signing herself out, with or without medical advice. Now it's the third of March. Almost a month ...

Her milieu therapist said, When something hurtful and grave happens to a person it is right to go to a place to think, so peace can return; a place where that person can work at finding answers. You hear only of those who come back. Many don't. We don't see them again. One or two write back. That's all. But we're all trying to live with what other people have done to us and some of us are exhausted with trying. The chaplain said, We're subject to futility, we're not without hope.

Jim said, The Unit is a land cruise for those who cannot afford the Bahamas. Peter said it was the twentieth century monastery.

Then why is Pat back, at the State Hospital? She crashed on returning to her apartment. Missing the safety and the community of the Unit she took pills she had hidden in the pocket of her dress. Pat could have called her or Leah ...

Is that a lie? A twisted star?

It's hard to ask for help. Pat might have left so as not to disappoint the staff of her psychiatrist. They thought she was well. But Pat was collecting pills when the nurses were not looking, taking them from rooms while everyone was at therapy. Should she not have said something to the nurses? It is not betrayal, if it is to help ...

She stumbled into the wrong place at the state Hospital when she went to see Pat. They came at her from chairs against the walls, from sitting on the floor, from talking and visiting; circling her, then stopping at arm's reach. I feel like hitting someone, a man said, warning her to leave. But she did not know what to do; where to go. Wire was stretched across the back porch. A man came at her with both hands. He merely wanted to touch her hair and was satisfied. He turned to the others and said, I like her hair. It's pretty. The others began walking around her, at their separate and different paces. The sounds of their steps were like branches falling ...

Somehow she backed out of the room. Pat found her in the next unit. For a moment Pat did not recognize her. They're crazy there. They're not just depressed as at the Unit. Luckily they're drugged. Your coming must have awakened them. But they're gentle, too.

Leah had told her not to go visit Pat, but she came on an impulse. You act so unpredictably, her doctor said, trying to talk her into staying at the Unit. How can you have time to call me when you feel like dying?

She was happy and sad at the Unit. Happy because it was the only place *she* had not also been. Sad because in that place her world had shrunk to a few friends; new friends. Her milieu therapist said, You leave here by yourself with parts of all the others with you. You're never alone afterwards. That's what milieu therapy is all about.

They were each other's best friends, though they were not their own. Against regulations, she allowed Jim to summon his priest to her room. He was between drugs. His fear was at him full force and he believed her room was the safest place. When the priest came to confess him, he asked Jim, Do you want her here? Yes, Jim replied. She's my best friend. Jim wanted the priest to help him leave that place so he could see his son who was born after he entered the Unit ...

A shiver runs down her neck, along her back, recalling the man in the State Hospital touching her hair.

Is she pretty? Was that the question that woke her up? Then why did he leave? Every nameless, faceless woman; every young and jubilant face she meets becomes that woman. She. When he holds her now, she becomes her, too.

The sun refuses to set inside her, to stop its cruel circling. Her breathing stokes its fire. It starts flaming. A dark still unnamed flower. It chases her thoughts. They cannot give up their bitterness. She cannot feel his weight on the bed.

She pushes off the covers, clears her elbows. Perhaps he's not really there, has left the way he used to leave again at four in the morning in order to take her swimming at the Y before he went to work ...

Returning with his clothes, he had said, Claim me. Don't be afraid. I'll never leave again. But what she could hear was him saying when he left, I care for you but not as a wife. I wish you can understand that I love you both. She is a fine sensitive person. I wish we could all live together so you can get to know her. She's a lonely person who has only me. She can't make friends, while you have many. You can take care of yourself.

She looks towards him on the bed, as she gets up; wishes he were not there. But she is not afraid. She cannot think of anything that will make her afraid again. One day, she even went up to the pastor after Mass: I'm making a different sacrifice this Lent, Father. I'll try to be happy.

Can she be happy again? Can the mind, if not the heart? Can life be put back together again, assembled as good as new after it has been taken apart?

She checks the clock in the kitchen. One thirty. Leah would still be up. Never slept before two; mostly after three. Leah looked at the employment pages and wrote resumes in her head.

At least she and Leah are well. Low average, but something to be grateful for. By Easter, they who had become friends at the Unit promised a reunion at Marconi's as a reward -- for what she can't recall.

The floor is sticky as if it's midsummer. She lifts the receiver off the kitchen phone.

She has memorized Leah's number; Pat's and Claire's, Sarah's and Steve ... Steve was the one who said the doctors at the Unit were just as nervous as they were. Take away our I.D. wristbands and no one can tell us apart. She heard Steve was back at the Unit. He had gone back to work, gradually back into fulltime, then had to return.

Hello? Leah, I'm sorry to be calling but I know you're up ...

Leah? She's in the hospital. Do you know what time it is?

Which hospital? she asks quickly before she's cut off. Who is this please?

All I know is that she went to see a friend in the State Hospital and slashed her wrist. I'm sitting with the children. Good night.

She hangs on to the receiver. Its silence is that of that a large drum, skin held down to hold it taut and still. A terrible weariness is coming upon her; like sleep; it's not sleep. She slides down the wall until she is sitting on the floor the way she remembers Paul saying he found himself after he fired and missed his ear ...

Someone visiting at the Unit sneered, If you people really want to die, you can always kill yourself. Aim down your throat next time, Paul. Or take all your pills and chase them down with whiskey before shooting yourself. You just have to be brave enough to die. None of you, as far as that goes, are. You're still around. Failures.

She remembers Leah saying -- when someone asked while they were weaving baskets, Do suicides go to heaven? -- I'm here to be cured, not to go to heaven. It used to be myself and a bottle after my sons went up to parts unknown. Not anymore. Myself is good enough, with a few friends. Used to be I knew people but had no friends. Now I have.

She tries to remember other faces, other names, but the words jam in her throat the way a scream dies. The sun is blowing, a clarinet screeching out of her ears, trying to wake her up. In the Unit she could go down the hall and the nurses would try to calm her down with words, with medication. Be gentle with yourself ... In the Unit she could turn the plants at the windows, pull their green parts; whatever she needed to stall that turbulent sun full of shadows and altered lies ...

She begins to cry. The sun is a wild rock hurtling inside her. She pulls herself up to look out the window. The light from the stove reaches halfway across the floor, dividing it. In the cabinet over the stove is a tin jasmine tea behind the box of oatmeal. Underneath the teabags are the rest of her pills.

She finds the tin without turning on the light. It is cold in her hands. She opens the lid at the sink where she turns the water on, letting it run softly away. Then she mounds the pills in one hand, takes and swallows one ... It catches like a bit of bone in her throat. She cups water in the other hand, drinks, takes another pill which goes down like a perfect seed, watered ... waits to feel that she has put the quick and fugitive sun to rest.

**Bio:** *Linda Ty-Casper has published both short stories and historical novels, including novellas written in their own time. Her long-term purpose has been to present a compromise portrait of the Filipino. On accepting the Southeast Asia WRITE Award on behalf of the Philippines in 1993, she said: If a country's history is its biography, its literature is its autobiography ... which enables it to be the world's thoughts.*

*Most recently her stories have appeared in* The Boston Review, Michigan Quarterly, Kenyon Review, *and* The Southern Anthology. *Her novels have been reviewed in* Asiaweek, World Literature Today, Radcliffe Quarterly, Yale Review, Belles Lettres, Los Angeles Times, San Francisco Chronicle, New York Times, Hudson Review, Booklist, The Statesman, Women's Review of Books, *and others.*

*In 1995, Giraffe Books of the Philippines published a representative chapter from each of her eleven novels, as* Kulasyon: Uninterrupted Vigils. Dreameden, *a novel covering the EDSA People Power Revolution of 1986 had been co-published by the University of Washington Press and Ateneo de Manila University Press. Her work-in-progress, started as a Radcliffe Fellow, a novel of the Philippine-American War of 1889, is entitled* The Stranded Whale. *It continues her previous fiction of that period:* The Three-Cornered Sun *(1979) and* Ten Thousand Seeds *(1987) -- works interrupted by several novellas challenging the rule of Marcos.*

*She is married to Leonard Casper, noted critic and professor emeritus of Boston College. They have two daughters, Gretchen and*

*Kristina, respectively professors of Third World political science (Penn State) and of physical anthology (cluster of Northern California Colleges.)*

# A CERTAIN FAILING

Paulino Lim, Jr.

TO THE VISITING Filipino Priest it seemed a choice of failures, something that could very well happen to him.

Hence his reluctance when Father Mullens suggested that he attend the reunion of former priests and seminarians the weekend before he went back to Manila. "Listen, Carlos, these are your fellow countrymen. Folks back home might be interested," Father Mullens said, as he slipped into his Notre Dame sweatshirt for a morning jog on the beach. "You won't be the only cleric there, but they'll be mostly ex-priests and seminarians -- your religious order no less."

"I see what you're getting at, Jim, curiosity or duty. If I'm not curious about Filipino ex-priests in the States, then I owe it to my order to find out."

"Good enough reason for most people. Here's another, this you can't resist. I'll pay for your registration and lend you my car."

"I really wanted to go to Disneyland, but that's tempting. How far is the retreat house?"

"Not very far. It's in Griffith Park, close to the planetarium and observatory."

"Is that where they filmed the James Dean movie *Rebel Without a Cause?*"

Father Mullens sighed, "Oh you Pinoys and movies! That's how you get this cock-eyed Hollywood view of America."

"Can't help it. Like it or not, movies are your country's window to the world."

"Spare me the sermon, Carlos, especially since mine didn't go too well this morning. The folks were restless, couldn't wait to get home. The new football season opens today. Incidentally, that was a good homily you gave. The appeal you made on behalf of the victims of Mayon's latest eruption was superb. The second collection was the most generous I've seen in a long time. We're having tough times, too, you know."

"I've heard, IBM, Kodak, Apple, all laying off thousands of workers."

"Blame it on loss of will or lack of nerve. By the way, retreats for ex-priests are not uncommon here, but this also isn't your usual gathering of Ateneo or De La Salle alumni living in the United States."

"I know; they all failed in their quest to become priests, or remain as priests. So they meet to massage one another's wounded ego, just like the ex-tipplers of Alcoholics Anonymous."

"Ouch!" Father Mullens said, faking grimace at a judgment that perhaps seemed too harsh. "I really think you should go, meet other Filipinos. You might even meet someone from your novitiate class. Don't forget, for my dough and wheels I want a full report ..."

The following Friday, on his way to the retreat Carlos wondered what kind of report did Mullens have in mind. He recalled reports on the estimated twenty thousand former priests in the United States who had married. Not too encouraging was the figure for the Philippines, something like fifty percent of Filipino priests being married or had common-law wives. Only two other countries exceeded this number, Peru with eighty percent of rural priests and Brazil with sixty-five percent.

Carlos arrived in time for Mass. He had skipped the registration and orientation the day before when participants were flying in from cities as far away as Toronto, New York and Memphis. Waiting for the Mass to begin, he counted about forty men and six or seven wives in their dry summer attire. Dry he thought, not humid, that was one difference, no sweating even though the chapel was not air-conditioned. It could have been a chapel overlooking Taal Lake, ringed by houses of religious orders. He knew he carried the mental baggage of first-time visitors to the country, and tried to shake off the impulse to compare.

A tall and lanky American priest, Father Rattigan, entered, followed by three Filipino priests. "A very special welcome to this Mass celebrating the Feast of the Transfiguration," Rattigan said. His disarming smile made the impassive Filipino priests appear sullen as sacristans uneasy with the solemnity. At his homily he invoked the biblical moment when Jesus appeared to the three disciples with Moses and Elijah his face shining like the sun and his clothes radiant as light.

"Afraid for his life, Elijah was running away after he had slain the false prophets of Baal. He went to Mount Sinai and hid in a cave. There the voice of the Lord spoke to him: 'What are you doing here, Elijah?' Throughout this retreat I want you to listen to God's voice asking, what are you doing here? Go back to where your roots are. Listen to where God wants you to be."

Carlos smiled inwardly that Rattigan failed to mention whom the ruler Elijah was running away from -- Jezebel. Perhaps, he thought that the modern meanings of Jezebel might offend the women in the congregation who had married priests. Carlos applauded Rattigan's strategy which he himself used in sermons -- name the human faults, find the biblical analogue, and draw comfort from it. He felt at ease momentarily in the ritual of the Mass with its rhythm of remembrance and hope. But at breakfast he began to wonder, "Why didn't I go to Disneyland instead?" Too late, he was in debt to Mullens for acts of kindness money could not repay. He was eating scrambled eggs and toast and drinking coffee at one of the long cafeteria tables, his ears picking up unwanted scraps of seminary stories. He turned at the chorus of ahs and saw a man bringing platters of fried rice and sausage from the kitchen.

"Cholesterol!" someone exclaimed. Another said "What's a Pinoy without his sinangag? A few used their fork to beat a rap music rhythm on their plates while waiting for the fried rice.

Carlos shook his head. He must find a way to amuse himself other than watch the antics of former schoolmates enjoying a weekend reunion. Then he noticed the two men to his right, engrossed in conversation, oblivious to the raucous horseplay going on. One was thin, with a tormented expression, the other much older whose face had assumed the look of a father confessor.

"So, what are you doing now?"

"Well, I'm working as a lab technician at St. Mary's Hospital. I analyze all sorts of bodily fluids they send me, blood, urine, sputum, you name it."

The older man chuckled and said, "When I asked to be laicized, things were different. But I had already spent ten years in Nicaragua. That's where I was sent after ordination."

"This is interesting," Carlos muttered to himself, they're priests, not ex-seminarians.

"Perhaps your superiors thought you had already paid your dues."

"Have you tried other dioceses?"

Oh, several, including San Bernardino County where fourteen of the hundred parishes have no priests and one is managed by a nun. The answer's the same 'Get permission from your superiors.' My superiors say, 'Come home first, and we'll talk about it.' Go back to the Philippines, that's what they want me to do. They're really stonewalling my petition, if you ask me."

"So right now, you're an AWOL priest."

"More like a fugitive," the gaunt man said with a pained, wry look.

"Well, if you're not happy at the hospital, you can always go home. Easier said than done, of course. I myself don't want to go back."

"I know. My family's been here a long time. I was still in the novitiate when my parents petitioned my citizenship. My brothers and sisters are all here now."

"Including your sister who's a doctor?"

"Yes, but she can't practice medicine, hasn't passed the state exams. God knows she's been trying."

A commonplace among immigrants, Carlos sighed, expatriates who take on lesser jobs than they are qualified to do in exchange for a higher standard of living. At least he was getting an immigrant cleric's view. He knew of religious orders that had sent their best candidates to Fordham, Washington and Vancouver for advanced studies that would qualify them for the doctorate, being stung by the news their would-be priests were leaving the order. Now he began to wonder whether it was right to call them failures. After all he had been taught vocation was a calling, that God did the choosing of men and women who would do his work. There must be different kinds, a failure leaning towards success, or a certain failing that makes one contrite and another suffer.

Carlos checked his watch -- time for the first session. On his way to the conference hall, he found himself walking behind a man wearing dark glasses and a subtly coordinated attire of silk shirt, printed with leafy designs, and dark green corduroy pants. Something familiar about the man's gait made Carlos quicken his pace and catch up with him. He said, "Hello, don't I know you?"

The man slipped the dark glasses down his nose and peered at Carlos' name tag. "Afraid not," the man said, "but now you do. I'm Loni Fajardo."

"Carlos Beltran." The timbre of Loni's voice flashed a thought in Carlos -- this man's gay ... priest or seminarian, I must know, find out what he has to say.

"From the initials, Father Beltran is it?"

"I'm afraid so," Carlos said, both of them laughing.

"You belong to the majority here. You show up those of us who are no longer priests. Rest assured, however, we'll be praying that you persevere."

Carlos winced, as if someone was chastising him. Nothing Rattigan said at Mass had touched him the way Loni just did. Do I feel superior because I'm still a priest? Am I really looking down on these seminary drop-outs and ex-priests? He smiled ruefully. He had found a purpose for his being there. If he clearly understood why he was attending an event he had dismissed as Alcoholics Anonymous group therapy, it might turn out to be a retreat after all.

At the first conference, Father Rattigan again picked up the story of Elijah. Carlos noticed the hum of the air-conditioner and thought of the interminable brownouts in Manila. He wondered if his school in Alabang had installed the new generator before classes began. So distressing to have his teaching interrupted by a power failure, instantly reducing an algebra lesson to elemental equations: no light, no learning; no knowledge; darkness equals ignorance. He could not remember how many religion and how many math classes he was going to teach during the coming school year.

Carlos snapped out of his reverie when he saw that Father Rattigan had given the floor to another man: white-haired, chocolate complexion, athletic build. "I was in the cave for so long after I had left the priesthood," the man was saying. "Why did I leave? Work, work, work. I became prefect after ordination, got saddled with teaching and administrative duties. Then I took a sabbatical, earned an M.A. in religious studies at the Ateneo. After that it was again work, work, work.

I felt empty, fell into a crisis, left the priesthood and asked for dispensation. Shortly after, I came to this country. Twelve years I stayed in the cave, rough years, until one day some mysterious wind passed by ..."

Carlos felt the silence, a time-stopping stillness droned into the hall by the air-conditioner. Part of the conference agenda was group-sharing, a public confession driven by the sinners' need for exculpation and the listeners' appetite for gossip. Another unkind thought, he berated himself.

I'm fine, now, the white-haired priest was saying. I'm a psychiatrist at the Terminal Island prison, near Los Angeles Harbor. It's a volunteer job. I'm a missionary once again, you see, new job, same direction."

Loni Fajardo had taken the microphone and struck a ham actor's pose, beaming behind his dark glasses at the applause, the hoots and shouts, "Right on, Loni!"

"I am, was ... a gay priest, a contradiction in terms to some people, abomination to others. I'm still gay but no longer a priest, or am I?"

The cheering stopped, a few smiled, others looked puzzled. Carlos sensed that Loni's candor had forced the listeners to look within, find a self that he can recognize and feelings he can truly express.

"For years I lied about who I was. Desperately, I wanted to know God's will for me, what he had wanted me to do. The seminary training made it easy to deny my identity. As you know, this discipline comes from two sources, philosophy and theology. One forces the mind to stretch its capacity for thought, ideas and questioning -- to the limits which no words can express or answers suffice. Theology comes in to account for these limits and provide answers in the realm of faith. One stirs, the other quiets. One questions, the other reassures. But theology could not reassure me, could not provide me the answers I found in my consciousness as a homosexual."

My God! Such a heady confessional, Carlos thought, Loni's taking this retreat to a new level. Rattigan wants examination of conscience, this is examination of consciousness.

"It was like trying to know what makes a Filipino from the volumes foreigners have written about us. That includes Hispanized Indios and Americanized Pinoys. You have to find what it means to be a Filipino in the languages that we speak, Bicol, Tagalog, Ilocano, whatever."

Carlos was thinking, Loni, you make me ashamed of myself. I have to apologize to you.

"One thing I must share with you though. It's much easier to be gay in the Philippines than in this country! There we don't judge a man whether he's fat or thin, young or old, rich or poor. We judge him by how he measures up as a human being. For us Filipinos, that is the only norm for success and failure that matters. Thank you."

Loni made a peace sign and took his seat amidst thunderous applause.

**Bio**: *Paulino Lim, Jr. is a professor of English at California State University, Long Beach, and author of a scholarly monograph,* The Style of Lord Byron's Plays *(1973); an anthology,* Passion Summer and Other Stories *(1988); and a trilogy of political novels:* Tiger Orchids on Mount Mayon *(1990),* Sparrows Don't Sing in the Philippines *(1994), and* Requiem for a Rebel Priest *(1996). He is working on a new novel entitled* Ka Gaby, Nom de Guerre.

# JOY RIDE

Greg Sarris

THE SIXTEEN-YEAR-OLD girl sitting next to me uncrosses her legs.

"C'mon, Unky," she says, "let's go somewhere."

Streetlight hits her legs, travels up and down her skinny skin. My heart pounds. I know where there's a motel, a room I can get for twenty-five bucks. To the left at the end of Grand. Or maybe we could take a ride to Montecito Heights, park, and look at the view. Just up Pressly here and out of South Park, five minutes across town. But I can't turn. I can't stop circling the block, passing my house with its yellow porch light.

This girl is a ghost. This sixteen-year-old snapping bubble gum and tossing silky black hair climbed into my pickup to haunt me. She tricked me by the side of the road, turned her face from the headlights so I couldn't see who she was until it was too late. I want to drop her off, get rid of her now and forever. I want to go in and come clean with my wife. But she keeps talking, this girl, reaching with her painted fingernails, across the seat. Her words form the stories that are my life. Her breath is the same as it's always been, as long as I can remember, sweet bait hiding the sharp metal hook. She's an Indian, after all, nobody fishes like an Indian.

I've known them all my life.

Worse than niggers, my father used to say.

We'd see them on the streets, lots of times, down by the train station on lower Fourth. The men glassy-eyed, holding wine in paper bags. They'd sit in the shade under the trees, or against the gray stone building if it was raining, and pass one another the bottles. Women were with them, heavyset dark women with scarves on their heads. Sometimes even kids sat there.

"Lazy drunks." My father scowled.

For the longest time I didn't know what a nigger or a drunk was. I knew we were Portuguese, and that's about all. Niggers and drunks were something bad, like when he called me and my brothers no-good sons of bitches. Which we heard a lot. He was easily pissed off. He didn't mince words when he told us his life would be easier if he didn't have kids to look after. "Saddled" was the word he used. "Your mother up and died and saddled me with you," he'd say. He'd blow up if we questioned him about anything he said or did.

Like the time my older brother Frankie asked why he always drove into town on the west side. No matter where he lived, and we lived lots of different places, the old man would take pains to drive into Santa Rosa from West Seventh, past the old bottling plant and warehouses. The day Frankie asked my father about this we had circled the entire town, a good while out of our way. It was hot, a fall day after the prunes, and we were parked outside Ben's Used Clothing, each of us sitting in the back of Father's forty-nine Ford pickup with our summer earnings clenched in our hands for school clothes. The old man's grizzled face reddened as he stood alongside the truck. He looked up and down the street, and instead of shouting like he would at home, he whispered. "Frankie," he said, "do you know what a shame is?"

Frankie didn't answer.

"Give me your money," he demanded, and Frankie opened his hand, letting the crinkled bills drop into my father's fingers, which curled up like prongs on a garden trowel. "There, there," Father said, grasping the money. "You'll know what shame is when you go back to school in old clothes."

He bought my sister a dress that day with Frankie's money. It was a hideous thing, orange with frayed bows up and down the front and on the shoulders, and old lady's castoff. He didn't want Frankie to forget. He made my sister wear the dress day in and day out until Christmas. My sister never protested. She never said anything to him. She never said anything to anyone, not to me or Frankie or my older brother, Angelo. Never. She didn't talk, Marie. My father would drop sacks of potatoes or flour by the back door, sometimes meat wrapped in bloodied butcher paper, and she'd fetch in the things and quietly get to work, peeling or whatever. She was dark, what we'd later call Mediterranean-looking, and she kept her thick hair pulled back with a plain barrette on each side of her head so you saw nothing but her downcast eyes. She was a mother and didn't want to be.

Me and my brothers took off every chance we could, cut away from the house. When we lived on the Nunes dairy we'd skinny-dip under the willows in the irrigation ditch. Swimming in the cool green water, hidden from where anyone could see us, we had a world of our own that summer. No cares. No grouchy sister, no father complaining about every little thing we did or didn't do. The naked wienies, we called ourselves.

We lived on lots of dairies. Our father milked cows. Portuguese people owned many of the dairies, and he could get work, I guess, because we were Portuguese too. For a while, though, we lived on the Benedict place, harvesting and then pruning their grapes. It was when the old man was between dairy jobs, which happened all the time. Portuguese or not, he'd fight with a boss or co-worker and we'd be up packing in the middle of the night. There was always something wrong with someone. The Benedict job was rough. Long hours, sunup until sundown cutting and hauling grapes. A rush job because the sugar was just right for making wine. Only my sister didn't have to work with us, just like she never had to go to school. The boss, Old Man Benedict's nephew or something, said the best workers would stay on rent free after the harvest. Already our father was complaining about people. It was about the Indians who worked alongside us in the vineyard. "Watch them," he'd say. "They'll steal your full boxes of grapes faster than you can blink." He told us not to walk alone through the tent camp. "They'll catch you and tie you up."

Old Man Benedict, the owner of the place, was crazy, senile. He sat in a tall hay barn at the edge of the vineyard and mumbled to himself. Me and my brothers found him one day. We had a couple of hours of free time, while we were waiting one afternoon for the boss to deliver empty boxes. After hearing so much from our father about this loony in the barn, we wanted to check him out. Our father talked about him after supper one night. It was like a ghost story. We ducked along the grapes until we came to the barn. Then, taking dares, we went in. Angelo went first. He signaled us to follow, and coming through the ajar door, I saw the old man right away. He was tall, standing in overalls against the stacked bales of hay, his featureless face and bald head like a dull lightbulb burning in the dark barn.

He was facing us but I'm not sure he saw us. He put his hands in his overall pockets and spun himself around so fast I never had a chance to really see his face. Then he started moaning, half sobbing, like, and screeching in a high-pitched cracked voice. We tore out of there like bandits.

Father must've known we went there. He must've seen us across the field. He never said anything that afternoon when we started working again, but after dinner he called us to where he was sitting on the ground under a walnut tree. He didn't yell. He just looked at us, letting us know he knew where he had been, and talked like he was picking up a story where he had left off before.

"You see," he said, "an Indian lady hanged herself in that barn."

He told us in detail how she wrapped the rope around the roof beam and then placed the noose over her head and jumped from the hay. Like it was happening just in front of us. Then he said the Indian lady was mad. Betrayed, he said. Old Man Benedict had betrayed her. The Indians got mad. "He thinks they're still out to get him," Father said. "And they might; they'll get you when you're not looking. Cut you in two with a butcher knife. Worse than niggers."

Me and my brother went back to the barn after that. We made a game of it. We'd chuck rocks at the side of the barn and holler, "The Indians are coming, the Indians are coming!" and then tear back across the vineyard.

*

There's nothing but a bunch of Indians in there, "the girl said to me when we first passed my house.

She must've seen me looking. Maybe I slowed down a bit. I don't know. At that point, before she started talking, before she mentioned the Indians, she was just a dark-skinned girl who waved me down as I turned onto Grand from town. A couple beers with my brother Angelo and then home. That was the plan, and I was almost home.

I stopped when I saw her waving, and she ran around the back of the truck, came up and opened the door, and climbed in. "You're cute," she said. She wasn't even looking at me. She was still pulling the door closed. First I thought maybe she was a hooker, lost her way in these part from over on Santa Rosa Avenue. She was dressed like one, short dress and makeup and all. But then there was something about the way her Levi's jacket hung on her that made me think she was a kid. That and the way she chewed her bubble gum. She was fresh, excited, not cool and collected like the streetwalkers. She didn't ask me what I was up to. She didn't talk money. She got in the truck grinning, smelling bubble-gum sweet, like any girl wanting a good time.

I know lots of women check out my decked-out Ford Ranchero. Clean, with mag wheels, the whole thing. Maryann liked my truck, the girl me and Angelo met in the Fiesta Club. And I don't look my age, thirty-eight. So why not, why wouldn't this girl take a look and want to go for a ride? Of course, until she started talking, I had no idea she was sixteen. She looked older.

She faced straight ahead for the longest time, so I couldn't see what she really looked like, the details of her face. We were halfway up the block when she finally turned and I could see her. She was dark, like I said, and beneath the silky hair cut in bangs over her forehead, her dark eyes slanted up, Asian-like. She looked different, like maybe part Chinese or Filipino. Her eyes caught the streetlight, and then the same light was in her smile and then down her legs. "You're cute," she said again.

First things first, I thought without thinking. Which is what a man like me does in these predicaments. He goes on a kind of automatic pilot to save both his home and his desire so that one doesn't cancel the other out. Get across town, at least out of your neighborhood, where you can sort these things out while both are still in your hands. Get out of South Park, I thought. But already I had turned again, onto Grand, where I live, and when I saw the house with its yellow porch light and heard her mention Indians, things changed. Tricky, the way she turned her face away in the headlights and then showed herself only when the light on her face and body blinded me. Never mind the slanty eyes, the part Chinese or Filipino. She knew who was inside my house. She's one of them.

Indians in there, she said.

*

That's what my brother Frankie said years, ago, outside the sagging tent by the water. I was fourteen. The three of us -

- me, Angelo, and Frankie -- standing there in the dark. "She's in there," he said. "The Indian." My teeth started clattering, and I looked away from the faint light showing through the tent flap. I saw the moon spread in a wide light over the river. It was late summer and the river was low, motionless, but looking at it just then I thought of the water below the moonlight as wild and bottomless.

"Remember what I told you," Frankie said. "Remember the plan." He was talking to both me and Angelo, but without looking at him, just hearing how he was talking, I felt he was addressing me in particular. My clattering teeth must've shown my fear. That plus the fact I was the youngest and hadn't done anything like this before. You each know what to do?" he asked.

I looked away from the water. "Yes," I answered.

How could I have forgotten, even scared as I was? He had drilled us all day with his plan. How he was to go in first and then signal us if things were all right. How Angelo was to watch the path from the road for anything coming. How I was to keep an eye along the river and on the tents a few hundred yards beyond this one. We practiced a bird call, a short, then long whistle we had to use if someone was coming or if something went wrong.

All during lunch break we went over the plan and practiced our whistle. We walked down to the water, scouted the area around the tents. "That one there." Frankie nodded. Even while we were working, picking prunes off the hot dusty ground, Frankie kept talking, monitoring for us to work close to him, away from the others. Which was unusual, I mean for Frankie to be talking while we were working. He wanted us to work as hard as he did, focus on what we were doing. He was our boss, since Father seldom worked with us in the crops these days.

Father had settled permanent on the Gonzalves dairy, just south of Santa Rosa. He mellowed. He didn't pick on us the way he used to. I figured it had something to do with my sister leaving. He had a fit, ranted and raved around the house these days, calling her every name in the book. He smashed the pies she left sitting on the sink, threw pots and pans. Then he got quiet, calm and stayed that way. What could he do? She was over eighteen -- nineteen, actually. She met this guy, Manuel, another Portuguese. Actually, she saw him, this guy walking up the road by the mailbox with peaches-and-cream skin and golden hair that was curly tight as a black person's. She walked out, apron on and everything, introduced herself, and never came back, not for her clothes, nothing.

Me and Angelo took over the cooking, since we were the youngest and had been around our sister the most. We couldn't bake pies or make anything fancy, but we got by with the basics: spaghetti, fried chicken, eggs. No one complained. Frankie took jobs after school, first in a grocery store, then in the shoe factory, where he made good money. We were poor, nothing like the rich kids who played sports on the school teams and got elected to class offices, but you'd never know it by looking at Frankie. Pegged Levi's, black wing tips, pressed new shirts, everything those kids had, Frankie had too. And he was a star athlete, with letters in baseball, basketball, and football. I guess you could say Father's lesson years before struck a chord. Frankie wasn't going to be ashamed ever again.

All kinds of girls liked him: blondes, brunettes; rich, poor. But he was strange in this department. Not the blonde whose father owned Satter's, the tony clothing store uptown. Not Christi, the redhead who drove out to the dairy in a Mustang convertible for six weeks trying to find him. He liked Angie, this plain-looking Mexican who didn't go to school. And the Toms sisters, big Indian girls who lived out by the coast. Girls tucked away in places a regular guy couldn't find. Work camps. Indian reservations. That's what Frankie liked. He sniffed them out. Like Rosie, the whore. He went nuts over her. Where did he find her, unless he went in that place on West Seventh? Who would go there but an old man or Frankie? He'd dress up every night after dinner, late when he got home from work. I watched him comb his hair with Vitalis and slap cologne on his neck. "Albert," he said to me once, you know what Rosie says to me? She says, 'Frankie, I can't take it anymore. Stop.'" He grinned at me? His teeth white, a dimple in his cheek, and I pictured him showing this Rosie the same grin.

He had to work hard for the clothes and things he wanted. And he bought me and Angelo stuff too, clothes, baseball mitts. And there was more to his working hard. He had this thing about outdoing everybody, and he wanted me and Angelo to be like him. So it was unusual, like I said, for him to be going on about his plan while we were working that day in the prunes. Even if it was about women.

He had talked all week about this girl in the tent, ever since we started work. "She's just right for you two," he said to me and Angelo after work the first day. "She's working here with us, but I'm not going to tell you who he is. It's a surprise." He went to see her that night and for three or four nights afterward. I think just talking, because there was no way for him to get alone with her without someone looking out for him. Then one morning he told us it was OK, he had the whole thing planned out with her. He was serious when he talked, as if it were about work or sports, and I felt like I had nothing to do but keep up with him and go along with the plan.

All week I tried to figure out who the girl was. Since it was a surprise, I imagined someone special. I knew she was Indian, because the tent was in the Indian camp by the river. So I narrowed it down to two girls: a light-skinned girl who was older, Frankie's age, or the girl with long black hair who wore low-cut blouses in the orchard. She was older too. I picked the light-skinned girl. Angelo picked the one with long hair. With my knees shaking and my teeth clattering, I started picturing the light-skinned girl inside the tent, lying on a blanket just beyond the flap. Then Frankie turned and said, "Her parents are upriver drinking, but they could come back any time. Watch close, you hear."

Standing in the willows close to the water, I kept thinking of that girl. I kept my eyes open, where I was supposed to, along the river and the other tents, but I kept seeing that girl. Even after Frankie came back and traded posts with Angelo. And after Angelo came back and traded posts with me. Going into that tent, crawling through the flap, I expected to see her, her light skin, maybe just a sheet or blanket over her.

So I was surprised.

Not because it wasn't her, but because it wasn't any girl at all. It was a child, a kid who by the look of her couldn't have been more than twelve years old. She was stretched out, resting back on her elbows, an army blanket covering her to the neck. I was so shocked, I forgot what I was thinking. I froze there on my knees, face to face with her.

"Well, what are you waiting for?" she asked. "Take down your pants." She slid the blanket off her body so I could see all of her. Below the kids face, with its pudgy brown cheeks and chipped-tooth mouth, she was a woman. Curves. Breasts. I felt my insides turn. Waves of warmth rolled and broke in me.

"C'mon," she said, stretching her foot with its chipped pink toenails to touch me. "C'mon." Her voice was deep, husky, not like something you'd expect from a kid with that face. It came from her body, which knew more than mine at the point.

Then I did a crazy thing, something totally unnecessary. I took off all my clothes. I mean my shoes and socks, shirt, everything. I guess I saw her naked and figured I had to be the same way. I wasn't thinking, like I said. When I stood up to slip off my Levi's, my head hit the top of the tent, nearly bringing the whole thing down, kerosene lantern and all. She laughed. I looked at her face, and that's what I kept seeing, focusing on, when I moved to her. It made sense to me, even when I touched her, excited as I was. And all along, until after, when I felt from her body something older and more powerful that her face had hidden.

I jumped up and felt the cool air where I had been with her. I gave out our bird whistle, loud and clear, perfect pitch. I thought of water. I crawled out of the tent, naked as a jaybird and dove into the water.

I swam madly. I made it to the other side without coming up for air. I ran up the sandy bank and stretched my wet body in the cool night air. I touched my toes, reached over my head, but when I looked, when I focused across the water to where Frankie and Angelo should have been waiting, I saw people, Indians, coming down the path from the other tents. A couple men and a woman, I think. One of them was carrying a flashlight. I ducked into the willows and started downriver, toward the place Frankie had parked the car. Then I saw him and Angelo waving from across the water. I dove in, swam across.

"Stupid fool," Frankie said as I got out of the water. "What in the hell's wrong with you?"

Him and Angelo turned and started finding their way to the road through the brush. I followed and didn't realize how badly I had cut myself on the twigs and stuff until I saw the bloody gashes on my legs and arms as I rode home naked in the backseat of the car.

My first thought was my clothes. My shoes and pants. Not that I didn't have others, but I wanted my clothes back. That's what I kept saying to myself. Me and my brothers worked only two more days at that place. I never saw the girl. And with both my brothers pissed at me, I did nothing to ask about her. "It's just a damn good thing we didn't get caught," Frankie reminded me.

We moved on to another place, north of Healdsburg. More prunes. Lots of Indians and Mexicans. Frankie found a Mexican girl, and me and Angelo found ourselves waiting for hours in the dark for him to give us a ride home. One day after work, Angelo said he wasn't going to wait. He decided to hitchhike back to Santa Rosa. I went with him. We got a ride into Healdsburg, but then no luck. We walked across the Healdsburg Bridge, tired from work and fifteen miles to Santa Rosa. "Let's go sit on the beach for a while," Angelo said. So we did, for about an hour, until it started getting dark. Then, on our way through the parking lot back up to the road, I saw the girl. She was looking straight at me from the passenger side of an old Rambler. "Hey," she said.

Angelo was up ahead. He didn't see her. I only half stopped, but it was long enough to hear her say, "Meet me here Sunday morning." Then she rolled up the window.

I felt there was something urgent in her voice, something she couldn't tell me just then. Like maybe her parents caught her that night, found my clothes, and gave her some kind of cruel and unusual punishment. Or maybe she was pregnant. I thought all kinds of things in the days ahead. But like I said, I wanted my clothes back, and I kept thinking maybe that's what she wanted -- to give them back to me.

I never told Angelo I had seen her, that she was sitting alone at the Rambler he had walked past. I didn't tell Frankie either. Sunday morning I was there at eight sharp. I don't know why I picked eight. It was like a church date or something. I had to get there. And it was church folks who picked me up on the highway and took me clear to the Healdsburg Bridge.

She was sitting on top of a picnic table next to a barbecue grill, a kid in Levi's and a faded sweatshirt. She blew a bubble with her purple gum, popped it loud in her mouth, and half smiled. I felt funny again, the waves rolling inside my body.

"My clothes," I said.

She laughed, throwing her head back, showing her soft little neck. "Man," she said, "you're nuts."

I felt embarrassed, remembering how foolish I had acted that night. But when I looked at her, I saw her mind wasn't on that night at all. She wasn't thinking of what I just said, she was looking right at me. I looked across the beach to where the river was dammed, the water wide and smooth. There wasn't a soul in sight. An occasional car clunked above on the bridge.

We went below the dam, away from the main beach, where the river continued its course. I followed her inside a grove of willows. We sat in the sand, facing the water. She didn't say anything. I smelled her grape gum. She tapped her fingers on the top of her knee. I looked at the river rippling in the morning sun through the leaves. I thought of my clothes again. Then she said, "This time keep your pants on."

I saw her after that, lots. Same place, same time: Sunday mornings, Memorial beach, in the willows below the dam. Her name was Mobile. She lived with an aunt in Healdsburg, close to the river. I never learned much more. She wasn't talkative.

Each time I wanted to ask her about my clothes, what happened to them, since I figured out this time I'd never get them back. I'd go over the whole thing in my mind when I left the house each Sunday. Standing on the highway with my thumb out, I pictured myself asking her. Then I'd get there and couldn't say a thing. She was just a kid, but she had the power to embarrass me. All she had to do was make me think of that first night.

I'd get nervous sitting there with her. Once, when I felt jumpy, I snapped off three willow branches and braided her a necklace. She liked that. It broke the ice, made things easier. After that I started giving her presents, packs of grape bubble gum, once a cheap silver bracelet. Now, when I left the house on Sundays, I wondered what to get her.

Then one day she disappeared. She didn't show up. It was well into fall, colored leaves fell all around, and the dam was down. I waited until noon, when a couple Mexican families fixed their towels and things on the beach and sat looking at the scummy river bottom where the water had been all summer. I thought something had happened to her, trouble. But then something else told me she just got tired of the affair, called it quits, went on to see somebody new. I thought of that first night, not of my foolishness but of Frankie and Angelo in the tent with her. How many other guys did she have in her life? She was no kid. She was a conniver who tricked me. I was dumb. I clutched the dollar-ninety-eight red carnations in my hand and headed back to the highway, relieved, thankful I hadn't told my brothers about her and that she was behind me now.

But I kept thinking about her. I wanted to find her just

to sit there, so she wouldn't have anything on me. I went back twice but no luck. Then the rains came. I got busy with school and things and hoped I'd never see her again.

Other girls came into my life. A few more summers passed. I blinked and found myself graduated from high school. The Vietnam War was on. Me and Angelo got high numbers in the lottery. Not so for Frankie. He went and got killed inside his first month of action.

If my sister's leaving the house cooled off Father, Frankie's coming back in a flag-draped box froze him. The old man didn't talk for a month. He'd milk cows, then sit in front of the TV without the sound on. Then one day he started talking, all this stuff about how the world was upside down. "Hate everywhere," he complained. "All people do is hate." He started doing nice things around the house, making homemade ice cream, washing and ironing the curtains. Since I was the only one left at home, no one else ever had the benefit of knowing his kindness. I figured since we had seen Marie and her two kids at Frankie's funeral, he would pay her a visit and make up with her. But this never happened. About two weeks into his change, he took a gun to his head and left his brains on the metal stanchions inside the milking barn.

I went to live with Angelo and his wife, Toni. Since they had only one-bedroom apartment, I slept in the front room on a sofa, which wasn't that comfortable, not to mention their kid, who cried every other hour of the night. Angelo got me a job with him at the cannery, driving a forklift. Full time, permanent. "It's just you and me now," he'd say, which made me happy to be with him, lousy old sofa or not.

We got to drinking, me and Angelo, after work. At a place in Sebastopol, near the cannery. First just on Fridays, then, before long, every day. I was just eighteen, but somehow I never got questioned. Angelo said I wouldn't. He knew the bartender. He knew practically everybody there, a lot of the guys we worked with. I had a hard time at first. I was what you'd call a cheap date, since I hadn't been a drinker and got buzzed so fast. Shots of tequila, beer chasers. It's a lot if you're not used to drinking. After a while I got so I could keep up.

One night after we left the bar, Angelo didn't drive back to town. He drove into the hills above Sebastopol. "What are you doing?" I asked. He didn't answer me. He spun his truck onto a dirt road and parked where he had a view of the lights in the valley below. "What's going on?" I asked again.

He looked at the lights a long while, then reached under the seat and pulled two beers. "Here," he said, handing me a can. He raised his can toward the lights. "For Frankie," he said.

I looked at my can, pulled the lift top, and toasted.

"You know, Albert, I used to bring chicks up here," he said, turning to me. "Yeah I did." he looked back toward the city. "Wasn't it great when we were kids, running free with Frankie, nothing to do but pop the babes? Shit, it seems so long ago." He kept rambling on, but I knew then what Angelo was up to. He didn't want to go home.

True, him and Toni weren't happy. They fought all the time, mostly about his not coming home. I saw her point. There was a baby, after all, and Angelo should've been responsible. But you had the feeling that if she hadn't gotten pregnant, they would have split up. They had given up liking each other long ago.

Things got worse. Angelo started gambling: five-card stud, blackjack. Not at the bar in Sebastopol, but in that dive in Granton where you were likely to get a knife in your back. Especially over matters like cards. And women, yes women. The women were nothing beautiful in there. Indians and Mexicans who looked as if they'd been drinking too much, too long. At least that's what I saw when I glanced around the dark bar. But I didn't look too long, lest one of those guys in there thought I was checking out his woman. Like I said, they'd dust you over cards or women. They were mostly Mexican guys, a few Filipinos. The Filipinos were temperamental, hot to start arguing, worse I think, than the Mexicans. They gambled hard, serious. I watched Angelo's back. I watched him lose his shirt night after night, leave the bar with his empty pockets inside out of his pants.

Then he started with the women there. First some Mexican he gave twenty-five bucks. He drove off, left me in the bar for an hour. Second time around I wasn't going to stand for it. But it was more than my impatience with him. Actually, my anger when he slipped out of the bar with a broad-built Indian prevented me from putting together certain facts. Like the woman's features and the silver bracelet on her wrist. Then I flipped.

Even though I drank, I watched my money. I never played cards. I saved for a truck. That night I paid some guy to give me a ride. "Thirty bucks," I said. I didn't want him to say no. and sure enough, there was Angelo parked on the dirt road above Sebastopol, all the lights below him.

I flew to his truck, pulled open the door. "You son of a bitch," I said, "get out." I said, "get out."

He got out, standing unsteadily. "What ...?"

"I'm tired of you!" I screamed. "Go home and tell your wife what you're doing, man. Or just end it. Get it over, Angelo. Just leave."

"Where?" he asked. He sounded as if I was asking him to leave that spot on the road, as if he didn't get the bigger picture about his marriage. He shrugged his shoulders.

"Leave," I said, and this time I meant for him to leave that minute.

I gave the driver another ten bucks.

"You want this bitch?" Angelo asked. "Is that It?" He was gesturing over his shoulders to his truck with his thumb. The driver, a good sized Mexican, stepped toward Angelo. Angelo looked at him, then glanced back at me. He started laughing. "Go ahead. Take her. She's seven months pregnant," he said and walked off with the big Mexican.

I waited until they were gone, until the taillights vanished beyond the apple trees. Then I climbed in. I don't remember what we said, me and her: a few words, maybe. My mind was white light, blank. We were in a truck, no back seat, so she turned on her side.

Afterwards, things started to fill the vacuum that was my head. Features, the bracelet on her wrist, why she didn't show up at the beach ever again. Then from out of left field, I asked her who the father of her baby was.

"Guess," she said.

She had the same girlish smugness I knew from her before, even though now she was grown. She must've been about sixteen, but she was large, older-looking, like twenty-five or so. She was the kind of heavy you see on some women where you can't tell if they're pregnant just by looking. Her clothes were dark, baggy.

"I don't know," I answered her. "Probably some Mexican."

"Nope," she said, shaking her head, as if I was guessing which hand had the M&M.

"Some Indian?"

"Nope."

"A black guy."

She started laughing. "Nope you're the only nigger I know, and I ain't been with you for some time. How long? You and your brothers, you're the only niggers I know."

Nigger. First I thought she was just slamming me. But then something changed when she brought up my brothers. Something about the way she said it. "What do you mean?" I asked.

"Nigger Marie," she said.

I thought she was referring to my sister, her dark skin and wavy hair. But just then I thought of something, even before she said it. My mother, who I never knew, was named Marie too.

"Yeah, my aunt, all of them, called her Nigger Marie. Then she died and everybody felt bad."

"We're Portuguese," I said.

"Part," she said, "like I got Irish in me. But your father too! You're all part nigger."

I thought of mentioning our name, Silva. I thought of other things, like the way lots of Portuguese, even Italians, are

234

dark. But I said nothing.

Later, when my mind settled on this moment in my brother's truck, on those days in the weeks and years ahead of me, I would think of a lot of things. Like how a Portuguese could be a black person: you know mixing with the Moors and all. Or how a black person could be a Portuguese, mixing with a Portuguese. It could happen either way or both. I'd never know in our case, since there was no one to ask. Maybe my father didn't know. But I'd think of him, and all of us, during these spells of mine, about his meanness when we were kids, and his driving all around town so we'd always come on the west side. And my sister, how she stayed locked up, hidden, until she saw someone like her and took the chance of her life by asking him to let her go with him. And me and my brothers, even if we didn't know this part of the story: Frankie with his out-of-the-way women, who could never put him beneath them. The whole picture of our past looked different to me. It was the picture our father couldn't escape, even with his short-lived kindness, until he blew his brains out.

But that night, sitting in my brother's truck with Mollie, I flip-flopped to make sense of things. Nothing came up but anger, anger and something else. Anger because this girl, this woman, got me again, took me senseless. I was mad at myself now, but it was something more, something that made me mad. I couldn't stop feeling Mollie's tight, swollen stomach in my hands or seeing her dark pleated dress thrown up, covering her face. It was my story, my particular version of what plagued everyone in my family, my shame.

*

My wife, Anna, is a good woman. Honest, devoted, hardworking. She loves our kids. She loves my family: Marie and her kids and husband, Angelo and his kids. She's strong, keeps the peace. She's held us up and half the neighborhood too. She loves me. She's everything I thought she was the moment I met her, though she'd be hard pressed to say the same about me.

About two weeks after my skirmish with Angelo, I moved out. It wasn't over Mollie, the Indian girl. Me and Angelo never said a word about that. And I never saw her again. In fact, I made a point of avoiding Indians. I'd look the other way if I saw an Indian woman coming. I moved out because the fighting between Angelo and Toni reached the pot-and-pan-throwing stage, and I didn't like being in the middle of it.

I got my own place. It wasn't much, a studio in a converted motel way down Santa Rosa Avenue. But I fixed it up good: new curtains, art posters, and a couple of plants in macramé holders. With the money I saved while living at Angelo's, I bought a car, a sixty-eight Mustang I cleaned up and polished to a bright blue, like the sky. I felt good, kind of like I did when I was in high school. I quit getting drunk. I led a clean life. I met nice girls at local dances, like the girls I dated in school, clean, the kind that reminded you of everything you were doing every step of the way.

Seemed like there were lots of girls, dates at the movies, concerts. I wanted someone permanent. I wanted to settle down with someone, not get married, not for that. Then I met Anna. Like I said, the moment I saw her I knew she was special. A girl in clean white tennis shoes, wholesome, with long dark hair that wasn't curled up or teased like other girls around her. She wasn't rich. You could tell she was from the country. But she did her best. She made me think of myself, or the way I wanted to be.

It was at a dance, one of those at the union hall. Even though she looked as if it was her first night out, she seemed to know people. She talked to the regulars, women you saw there week after week. Like the Toms sisters, the big Indian girls Frankie used to fool around with. Those girls smiled at me all the time. I figured they knew who I was, that I was Frankie's younger brother. But I was wrong. When I went up to them to get them to introduce me to Anna, they asked what my name was. They didn't know me from Adam. I figured they told

Anna all about me. But again I was wrong. Anna knew nothing. I told her both my parents had died, not much else. She told me she never knew her father, and her mother took care of somebody's kids on a dairy. She was boarding with an old maid in town while she was doing homework and taking classes at the junior college. She wanted to have a preschool. We talked outside the union hall until dawn, until the gray morning light showed the empty gravel parking lot all around us. We couldn't get enough of each other after that. We fell fast and heavy so fast that when she told me she was pregnant I didn't know what to say or do. I should have told her right then and there I'd marry her. I just didn't think of it.

Once, after the news, she took me to meet her mother, at a dairy in Sebastopol. A tall woman in her midfifties answered the door. But that wasn't her mother. I blinked and an Indian woman was standing where the blonde had been. That was her mother. A clean tidy-looking woman, but no doubt Indian. The dark woman had us in and served us tea in fancy cups. I couldn't believe it, that this fair-skinned girl I loved came from this woman. But why not? I had been so careful not to bring up the details of my family that I never asked about hers. I watched as she hugged this woman good-bye and kissed her hard on both sides of her face. I heard the way she said "Mama," loving, for all the world to hear. I had always thought we were alike, me and Anna, more or less like orphans with no ties. But just then I saw we were different; she wasn't like me at all. On the way home that day I asked her to marry me. I told her we'd have a big wedding for all our families to see.

You dream and plan, plan and dream -- and then there's life, the everyday way of the world. It's like ivy. It looks pretty at first, the way it climbs a tree. Then it takes the life right out of the tree, strangles it. You have your firstborn and it's the most beautiful thing you know, so beautiful you decide to have the second one, which you didn't plan for, even though you can hardly afford the first. Then the third and fourth appear, but it's all right because your mother-in-law moves in and helps with her social security check. You open your eyes and realize you're too far under water and haven't taken a breath of air for some time. You learn to live without breathing.

Angelo never quit his wild ways, not with his second wife and not with his third, who was Indian. Once in a while I'd have a beer with him after work. But I'd leave when he got too out of sorts with the drinking. I never understood why he even bothered to get married. He angered me. One night, after a couple of beers with Angelo, I was coming home and came upon a car parked off the road half in the ditch. Clearly there was no danger, but what caught my attention was a head on the passenger side, someone slumped down. It was dark, quite late maybe nine o' clock. I was going too fast to stop. I pulled around the corner, then came back up the street behind the car, slowly with my headlights out. Why I turned off my lights I don't know. Maybe I sensed what was going on. But when I walked up on them, two kids, I was stunned. Not that they were butt-assed naked but at their wild abandon, the madness that left them oblivious to the dark figure standing over them outside the car.

My heart thudded. My knees shook. Somehow I made it back to my truck. But I had a hard time making it back to my life. It was like a first kiss that tells you there's more you could do, even if you weren't thinking about it before. It was like seeing a naked girl for the first time. I started staying out for that one extra beer. I flirted. I fell more than once. I hated facing my life. Worse, I hated seeing Angelo, whose life I detested.

*

"Nothing but a bunch of Indians in there" this girl said to me as I drove past my house. "Don't stop," she said. "Don't stop."

A bunch of Indians in there. In my house, yes. Not just my wife and children and my wife's mother. It doesn't stop there. It goes on. Now my mother-in-law's brother, the Indian preacher man, and half his congregation pack in our house every night with their Bibles and prayers for our sins. And when Jeanne, our oldest, got cancer, it wasn't just the old preacher and his troupe of hand tremblers but all the Indians in the neighborhood. They came out of the woodwork. Long-lost relatives like the Toms sisters. Yes, turned out Frankie's big girls are Anna's cousins. Everybody's connected to everybody. Seemed I'd leave the house to take a breath of air and then come back, only to find the space I left filled by another Indian.

So after this girl mentioned Indians, after I collected my thoughts and made it around the block once, I figured she was a relative of some kind, that her family was visiting my wife. Then she started on this Unky business. I wasn't the only one who had done some figuring. So had she. She knew who I was.

I've heard Indian girls call their uncles and other older men relatives "Unky." It's sweet, respectful. Not this girl. And she talks openly with me about her life, about stealing and getting in trouble, as if I'm a kid, just another guy. She doesn't care who I am.

She doesn't care about anybody. She goes on and on about people and things. But I've stopped listening. I stopped after she talked about her mother, after she called her a low-down whore, after she said her mother had screwed every man in the country, that she'd been doing it since she was a young girl living with an aunt near the river in Healdsburg. "People say she took ten Mexicans at a time into the willows there," she said. "I've heard them say that, that she was just a kid and doing that."

Something turned in my brain, rolled, and came up right. No white light, nothing emptying my better senses. No rage, like when I went back to Healdsburg time after time, or when I got into it on that dirt road with Angelo that night.

I wanted to drop this girl off.

But where? If I drop her off in front of the house or a

hundred miles away, it's all the same. She'll be back. And what's to keep her from blabbing about riding around with me? No matter how you look at it, it's not right. I didn't go straight home. Already she's got me on that score. I bit the bait: her short dress, the naked legs on the street. Now I can say I don't want her, and I don't, but what do I do? She's a mean girl, vindictive, no doubt. She could talk. Each time I pass the house, I make things worse. I can't stop circling.

"Cmon Unky," she keeps saying. Let's go someplace."

Not a motel. Not up to Monteceto Heights. Maybe for an ice cream. But even that isn't innocent. I'd like to throw her like a stone out of my sight. I picture her as a small hard rock in my hand, and I'm tossing her with all my might, like when I was chucking rocks with my brothers at an old barn, when I didn't know any better.

**Bio:** *Part American Indian, Filipino, and Jewish, Greg Sarris was adopted at birth and raised in both Indian and white families. His grandfather, Emiliano Hilario, was a Filipino from Panay who married a California Indian woman (Coast Miwok), Evelyn Sarragossa.*

*Sarris is the author of* Mabel McKay: Wearing the dream *and* Keeping Slug Woman Alive: Essays Toward a Holistic Approach to American Indian Texts. *He is the editor of* Rattles and Clappers: An Anthology of California Indian Writing. *Formerly the elected chief of the Miwok tribe, Greg Sarris is a professor of English at UCLA and lives in Los Angeles.*

*His novel,* Grand Avenue *published by Hyperion (1994) and Penguin Books (1995), was adapted by Greg Sarris for an HBO movie co-produced by Robert Redford. Sarris's contribution to this anthology, "Joy Ride," is a chapter from* Grand Avenue

# MY LOST HERO

Lee Respicio Colomby

THERE ARE many factors that contributed to the complicated relationship I had with my father. For one thing, the bonding that normally takes place between a parent and a child never happened in our case since I was almost four years old before we met. Several months after my mother and dad took their vows, my young and impetuous mom discovered that she was not ready for married life: it was getting in the way of her dream of becoming an actress-slash-dancer and she packed her bags and left to pursue her destiny. That my mother had no training (and not much talent) was of no consequence. Even the fact that she was pregnant with me at the time, did not prove a deterrent to her departure. My mother was a determined, headstrong young woman who was on a mission to succeed. Marriage would have to wait.

This was how I came to crisscross America several times before I was born -- a passenger, as it were, of this impulsive dreamer. When her time came due, my mother simply put her quest on temporary hold, and headed for her nearest relative, who happened to live in Cincinnati. However, before I was two weeks old and able to lay claim to being an Ohioan, we were on our way again -- my mother resuming her pursuit of fame and glory. The next three years were spent traveling from place to place, staying only as long as an occasional dancing engagement lasted, or until mother earned enough money, doing odd jobs, so we could afford to move on.

I was growing up thinking all kids slept on Greyhound buses and brushed their teeth in depot washrooms.

When mother heard a rumor that any dancer who could do a descent time-step had a good chance of finding work in Chicago, the Windy City became our destination. It took a month of auditioning before she landed a job and we were down to our last five dollars. Preparing to step out on the stage of the Club High Hat, mother declared, "This is my last stand. I'm either going to make it here or quit." She wouldn't have long to wait before she would come to a decision about her career.

A Chicago gangster named Rico found himself attracted to the new chorus girl who was doing high-kicks before an appreciative, if unruly, audience and asked for an intro. Mother flatly told him she wasn't interested, but Rico paid no attention. He returned night after night to catch her performance. Tokens of his affection, in the form of expensive pieces of jewelry, began arriving at her dressing room. Mother was highly tempted to keep some of these gifts; living on a dancer's salary wasn't easy, but she was afraid to do anything that would encourage the enamored racketeer.

After one particular show, Rico made his way backstage with something besides jewels -- a proposal of marriage! Mother's career came to an abrupt halt the minute she turned him down. After all, she already had a husband. This news sent Rico into a rage. He threatened to kill her and then himself on the spot. Waiters and bouncers tackled the distraught suitor in an attempt to restrain him as mother bolted out of the club and headed for home. I have a distinct memory of his breaking down the door of our apartment, brandishing a large gun. Someone had the good sense to call the police, but as they were carting Rico off, he vowed to return. Leaving everything behind except what could be packed in one suitcase, mother and I took our permanent leave of Chicago in search of a safe harbor.

That safe harbor turned out to be my father. Reliability and dependability were his middle name. He had settled in New Orleans and when my mother and I turned up on his doorstep less than a week later, relating our harrowing tale, my father gathered us in his arms and welcomed us home.

Although my mother was very beautiful and quite a charmer, I prefer to think that the sight of me, his only child, brought about my parents' reconciliation. Whichever was the case, I was suddenly a member of a bona fide family living in a story-book house located across the street from a park where clover swayed back and forth in a field of green grass as a gentle Louisiana wind swept over thém. I spent many hours looking at this wonderful view from my bedroom window, happy in the belief that I was here to stay for the rest of my life.

And for a little over two years, my high-spirited mom, my steady dad and I had a wonderful life. Friends of my parents flowed in and out of our home and, for the first time, I had friends of my own, too. Sometimes as many as twenty of us would head out for a day at Ponchatrain beach, or a picnic/tennis outing at City Park. I loved our extended family, but my favorite thing to do was go to a drive-in movie with my mother and my dad -- just the three of us -- in my dad's second hand, steel-gray Dodge. My parents would sit in the front seat and I'd have the back seat all to myself where I felt safe and happy with the two people I loved the most in the world.

Sometimes my dad would do the grocery shopping for my mom and he always asked me if I wanted to tag along. We'd drive to the chicken farm where my father would silently watch the birds strut their stuff until he'd spot the one he wanted for dinner. To indicate his choice, he'd lift his eyebrows, ever so slightly, in the bird's direction. It was as if he was bidding on a precious object d'arte at an auction and lifting his eyebrows was his secret signal. My dad and I would often go for a ride in the Dodge to listen to the music of the big bands on the radio. He'd drive through the wealthy section of town where the homes were stately mansions. He'd ask me to point out my favorite and then he'd smile and say, "That's the one I'm going to buy for you and your mom someday." My father and I were on the verge of becoming the Number One father-and-daughter team when my mother gave birth to my baby sister.

Fortunately, I started kindergarten shortly after my sister's arrival and was spared having to remain in the house to witness the underserved attention I felt she was receiving. I was suffering from sibling rivalry, but I was also confusing my jealous feelings towards my sister with something else that time -- something that would have a lasting effect on the relation between my father and me.

I remember the exact moment. My father was a railroad employee and his working hours were determined by the train schedules. He had just left the house to go to work one day as I was returning home from school. Ordinarily when we'd meet on the street, he would lift me high in the air and swing me around. When I ran to greet him that particular day, he hardly looked at me, almost shoved me away, and quickly continued walking down the block. What had happened? I couldn't comprehend the moment. From that time on, my father would never greet me in public again. Whenever I asked what the matter was, he avoided my question. I attributed this terrible change in my father's behavior to the arrival of my baby sister, but there was another explanation.

America had just entered into war with Japan and my family, who was Filipino, was being mistaken for the enemy. To white America, Japanese and Filipinos were indistinguishable. I found out many years later that a few days following the bombing of Pearl Harbor, my father was beaten by a group of men "avenging" the sneak attack. Beatings of this sort were not uncommon. In an attempt to avoid further incidents, the Pullman Car Brotherhood Union or the War Department, issued badges showing a brown hand clasping a white with the words "American/Filipino" written underneath in bold letters. My father had left heart-broken parents in the Philippines to come to the United States at the age of seventeen because, as he put it, he saw a "brighter light" shining for him in the United States. He never mentioned whether he thought that light was dimming as he reluctantly clipped on his new badge of identification.

I was becoming aware that my father was different from other Americans. Up until this point, I thought he was interchangeable with the all-American prototype John Wayne. I had never noticed that he was shorter, darker, and spoke with an accent. This new knowledge made me uncomfortable. Complicating matters, was the fact that my mother was a beautiful, American blonde. That my father and my mother were different from one another was another aspect of my family that had escaped my attention. Disapproving eyes everywhere now seemed to be staring at us. This was especially true in New Orleans where segregation was still a way of life. "Colored" and "White" signs had always been prominently displayed, but up until the declaration of World War II, I hardly took notice of them. They seemed to have nothing to do with me. I attended an all-white elementary school, ordered ice-cream sundaes at the lunch counter any time I had a spare quarter, and tried on hats in department stores like everybody else. Everybody who was white, that is.

Perhaps if war hadn't been declared, I would have gone on believing my father was just like everyone else. Perhaps not. However, once I discovered he could be mistaken for the "yellow" enemy, those "colored" and "white" signs came to represent barriers posted as a personal warning. The nastier and more vociferous the propaganda depicting the Japanese in newsreels and cartoons became, the more ominous those signs grew. I began to believe I was in grave danger. My father seemed the only person to blame for my new and terrible predicament.

To spare us from insult and, perhaps even harm, my dad stopped sitting with the family whenever we rode the trolley; he discontinued our shopping trips together, and stopped participating in many of the things a family ordinarily does. As a six-year old, I didn't know how to feel. On the one hand, I was relieved when my father wasn't around because then people didn't stare at my mother and sister and me when we went out. On the other hand, I felt as if my father was deserting us, leaving us to fend for ourselves. I felt hurt and abandoned. I wonder now how hurt and abandoned my father must have felt.

It was about half a year after President Roosevelt declared war against the Japanese before Filipinos were allowed to join the American armed services. My dad enlisted in the U.S. Navy. He was thirty-seven years old and served with various Motor Torpedo Boat Squadrons, assigned as a cook. Many Filipinos entering the military were relegated to the rank of cook or stewart. My dad would have preferred combat, but he accepted his position with his usual quiet resignation and took the opportunity to become a first-rate chef. Years later, when he would come for a visit to my home, he always prepared a sumptuous feast of adobo or ampalaya or spaghetti made with Chinese glass noodles. This is still my favorite "pasta" dish.

Along with millions of other servicemen, my father was constantly being transferred from one stateside base to another with my mother, sister, and me relocating each time my dad received new orders. I remember running to catch a train that would take us to the city where my father would be arriving after an overseas tour of duty. Men in uniform had top priority when it came to traveling accommodations. For civilians, it was usually a long-wait or a stroke of good luck that got them a ticket. This went on for the duration of the war. I was traveling throughout the United States, living the life of a gypsy once more. This time for different reasons.

I remember our family's reliance on the Filipino "grape-vine." If my father received orders to report to a particular base in the United States, he would contact a Filipino who lived in that city to find out where we might find living accommodations once we arrived. Not everyone would rent an apartment to a Filipino or a "mixed" family. Between this and the housing shortage caused by the war, we'd sometimes wind up living in a really awful place. We stayed in a log cabin in Fall River that had no hot running water or bathtub. In San Pedro our temporary home was a transient hotel near the docks. We rented a furnished room in Seattle that had a bed with a feather mattress that looked great until I lay down to sleep. The mattress and I would sink into the springs and come morning, I'd wake with circles imprinted over my body. More than a few apartments had roaches or pests of some kind. In Providence, the only housing we could find was next to a fire station. I don't think any of us got a good night's sleep during our two month's stay. My mother used to say, "If the bedbugs don't kill us, the siren will." I wish I could say these difficult times bought our family together. The pressures of war, of moving from location to location, and of being perceived as "different" began to take its toll on all of us. I began to wish my father didn't have to live with us anymore. Life was easier when he wasn't around.

A year after the war ended, I got my wish. My mother and father divorced. My dad rented a furnished room near the section of Brooklyn where my mom, my sister and I had settled, but I rarely saw him. I was preteen now and involved in my own activities. My dad had also signed on as a merchant seaman and was out to sea a great deal of the time. His ship would dock in the New York area occasionally but whenever he was in port, he would bring my sister and me presents from places such as, Egypt, Germany, Japan, Viet Nam and Spain. Spain was my dad's favorite place to visit. He said everyone there was polite and treated him with respect.

I don't know where all the silver bracelets, embroidered blouses, boxes with the secret compartments, or any of the other gifts he brought us over the years have gone, but I still have the Bulova watch he gave me for my twelfth birthday. The curved glass is missing, but if I wind my watch, it still runs.

One of the last "meetings" between my father and me, before he retired and left the mainland to live in Hawaii, was when he boarded a New York City bus on which I was traveling. I could tell he saw me; he raised his eyebrows ever so slightly when he looked in my direction. He didn't sit down on the empty seat beside me. Old habits die hard, I guess.

In Hawaii, my father met and married a lovely Filipina woman and they had a wonderful son. Through the years my father's new family and my husband, son, and myself communicated often by phone. However, it would be almost twenty years before I would see my dad again. He was in ill health and my sister and I travelled to Hawaii to visit him. I hardly recognized my father. He was eighty-six years old and frail. He cried when he saw us. By this time my consciousness had been raised and I no longer saw his tears as a sign of weakness.

I watched my father interact with his wife and son. I listened as they told my sister and me about their life together and showed us their photo albums with pictures of my father looking on proudly as his son took his first step, made his first communion, graduated from high school, and did all the other things children do to make their parents proud. I couldn't help but compare how little time my dad and I had spent together when I was young. If I added all the isolated days and scattered weeks and months to the years we shared in New Orleans, it would be no more than six years. I was happy my father had found happiness and contentment and had a child to whom he could give his love and kindness. I tried not to think of what I had missed.

Two years after our visit to Hawaii, I received a call informing me my dad had died. The news was not unexpected. Still, it surprised me that I felt little sense of loss. It wasn't until about a year later that my father's death finally become a reality for me. I had dragged out a carton of photographs from the back of my closet determined to sort out the hundreds of snapshots I had accumulated throughout my life. Among the pictures, I found several of my father taken when I was a child. At first, I didn't realize that the man in one particular snapshot was my dad. He appeared to be no more than twenty-five years old and was so handsome, it surprised me. He is standing in our back yard in New Orleans looking as if he had just stepped off the cover of *GQ* magazine. He is wearing a sports jacket and a lighter colored pair of slacks. His shirt is open at the collar and he looks as dashing as any movie star I have ever seen. His black hair is combed straight back and the sight of this triggered the scent of the pomade he wore -- the label on the jar had an art nouveau sketch of a man and a woman in profile. Looking at the snapshot now, I notice my father is not looking into the camera. He's smiling at something or someone off to the side. Could he have been smiling at me? Lots of memories begin to come back: my dad reading the latest monthly supplement to his subscription encyclopedia, his speaking four languages (Ilocano, English Spanish, and German), and humming the song, "Ramona", as he putters around the house. I recall the lilt in his voice when he spoke in his native Filipino dialect. To this day when I hear Ilocano spoken, I turn expecting to see my father.

In a picture that I took with my Kodak box camera, given to me for my seventh birthday, my father is dressed in tennis whites and looks like a brown prince. Looking at the photo, I can feel the piercing New Orleans' sun; the scent of the magnolia trees in the background filters through my memory. I also recall the look in the eyes of some men who showed up, seemingly from nowhere, and stood, menacingly watching our Filipino group. After a while my father went to the men and they went away. I don't know what he said. He never discussed things like that. We all left soon afterwards, also. No tennis game was played that day.

Those men had the same look in their eyes as did some of my classmates, the ones who decided my father was a foreign enemy in their midst. They whispered to me that the Klan was keeping watch on my family. They assured me the

Klan knew everything about everybody and if the Grand Dragon didn't like something someone said or did, he'd send hooded men to kill them in the middle of the night. I remember having a nightmare about being stuffed in a barrel as full moon shone above. In my dream I have been shot by an arrow, of all things, and can see where it has pierced my back. I remember waking in the middle of the night, wanting to call out for my father to come and protect me, but I didn't. I had begun to doubt that my dad possessed the ability to keep me from harm.

Looking at those pictures, I realized why I felt no sadness when I received the news of my father's death. I had lost my father years ago when I was a little girl -- when he stopped greeting me in public, when he could no longer ride with me in safety on the trolley car, when he thought it best not to visit my class during Parents' Day. My father, that dark prince, who let me win each time we played tennis' my father, that dashing handsome, young man in the picture, who took me to drive-in movies and read me the Sunday funny papers; my father, that loving man who taught me how to make fudge with walnuts; my father -- that man who could have been my hero had our paths crossed at a different time, at a different place, had died -- for me -- when I was a little girl.

**Bio:** *Lee Respicio Colomby was raised in New York and is a second generation Filipino-American. She received her Bachelor of Arts from Antioch University. She has studied acting with Lee Strasberg and Uta Hagan and has appeared on stage and television in New York and Los Angeles. She has also been a theatrical agent and run a successful antique business importing merchandise from England and Scotland. Currently she is a partner in a television and film production company.*

*Lee has always had an interest in writing. When she first arrived in L.A., she began selling scripts and special material which enabled her to become a member of the Writers Guild of America West. However, she become disenchanted with her efforts as she was not achieving personal satisfaction and went on to other pursuits. It wasn't until recently, when she began an inquiry into her Filipino heritage, that her interest in writing was rekindled. Her investigation has had a tremendous effect on every aspect of her life and given her a sense of wholeness. She feels her American/Filipino experiences are something worthwhile putting on the page.*

*She is a member of the Board of Pamana/PARRAL, Pilipino American Reading Room and Library and a member of the Filipino American National Historical Society (FANHS), chairing the committee, Pinoys in Entertainment. She participates in as many activities that revolve around Filipino history and culture as she can fit into her schedule and is enjoying every moment of her involvement. She has been happily married for many years and is the mother of a wonderful son.*

# CONFESSIONS OF A DAWN PERSON

## N.V.M. Gonzalez

"YOU ARE correct about starting out early," said the taxi-driver who was taking us to the airport.

The traffic on EDSA was unusually light, it was true. But hardly were we the only ones on the road. At the departure lounge, there was already a crowd. Were these perhaps midnight people?

I am a dawn person. At first light is the best time to get started on anything, let it be reading a new book or escaping to the provinces.

Escaping I most certainly was not, but returning. Romblon is my birthplace. This would be my first visit in I don't know how many years.

To get to other parts of the Visayas, you took either *Nuestra Señora de la Paz* or her sister ship *Nuestra Señora del Carmen*. Romblon has been an obligatory port of call on the Central Visayas route. The gods of commerce had a soft spot for this little town that Recoletos had built.

Not only did they raise a church and a convento but also a belfry with a hundred and three steps, not to mention a tribunal or town hall. In the town square was a fountain. Its centerpiece was an Immaculate Virgin Mary statue mounted on a globe with a straggle of islands. The devotion to her had remained undiminished over the years. For honor guards, she had been provided with lions, their mouths hung open, for the fountain had long gone dry. Get closer a little more and look at the noble beasts in the mouth and all you'd see would be the grain in the wood.

On its tall, concrete pedestal in the middle of the plaza I found, of course, the Rizal of cherished memory. He stood handsome there in his great coat, his two books at his feet, alongside thick-soled bluchers. But why the uncanny feeling that the monument had risen by some four or five feet? I must have been quite little when last seen loitering about the vicinity, with a bag of peanuts in my hand.

As a boy I lived here for a few years with my grandparents. Out house was some distance from the town center, by the seawall that people called "Morro." The name was from way back, when Moro piracy had been rampant all over the Visayas and southern Tagalog provinces.

A reminder of this is Fort San Andres which, now with all the wars over has been converted into a weather station. Except in my memory, its brooding presence has been effectively obliterated by a rank of galvanized sheet-iron roofing painted light green, like banana leaves.

From the Tugdan Airport, we had crossed by pump-boat to Romblon harbor; this did not take more than two hours. Which seemed all the time that I needed to reach the shore where a treasure chest of childhood and youth had been buried.

I was four when my parents left Romblon and settled in Mindoro, two days by sail away. Although a wild frontier in those days, particularly notorious for malaria, it had been an alternative to Mindanao, the home base of pirates scarcely a century ago. It was only when a Boy Scout Troop in Romblon was organized that Fort San Andres acquired an importance to us: as a platform for semaphore practice, for nothing was more ideal than the banquettes of the forts. With troop mates waiting for our messages at the wharf three hundred feet below, we established lively exchanges on quite a number of subjects. The list could not but have included how one obtained a safe-conduct to the future.

My uncle was the first in our family to leave. Although only a junior in high school at this time, he displayed quite an impetuous desire to see the world. In fact, it was not too long after his departure that Alaska, New York, Chicago and Seattle became household words to us. Place-names like Bang-og, Alad, Agpanahat and Lonos withdrew to the margins of our consciousness and might have even dropped altogether had they not been important in our day-to-day activities. It could not be denied, of course that we have come by then under the aegis of empire. Only imperial language counted from now on.

Into the blue, sparkling waters of the bay we rode, heading for the anchorage. Cloud-strewn shadows draped the islands that girded the harbor. The marble quarries of Kahimos Cove caught the sun like a sieve, making the dark coconut groves look somewhat startled after having been graced by barbules of light.

I was missing something: a wireless tower that the government had built on Binagong Hill. This was now to our right. What had happened to it? Why was it that all I could see was only a ragtag troop of wind trudging up the dry grass, on the shoulder of the hill?

Finally, we tied up at Bagacay, deep in the cusp of the bay. I had not forgotten how I had dreaded the place, for it was where during the cholera epidemic of 1927 the stricken town buried its dead, wrapped up in the sleeping mats they had died on and then taken them away as fast as graves for them could be dug. You could be saddened greatly by that even after all these years.

But more painful to me was the loss of the tower, for it had been my tower. I had written a story about it that not a few readers had become fond of, so I had been told. They saw themselves in the character I had invented, Roberto Cruz, who climbed the tower step by painful step to the very top with only one purpose in mind: to ascertain for himself whether it was true that once when the tower had been struck by lightning, the shaft at its tip had split. I had made it all up, of course: that bolt of lightning and Roberto Cruz's iron resolve to know, to seek the truth. You held your breath as he made his ambitious and -- for a boy his age -- and dangerous ascent. His success did not end just there. He made sure he had a record of it in his notebook. "It is true," he said.

And what a contrast to my fiction the tower in actuality had now become. It had crashed to the ground in an August storm, I learned; and, thereafter the locals had set upon it as vultures do carrion. Steel rods, bolts, and all -- these were collected for scrap.

And did the poblacion's old cemetery meet a similar fate, perhaps? A hundred years ago, a five-foot stone fence had surrounded it. The coral had come from the floor of the sea. But where was this wall now? Where did the graves go? I had to know. Grandfather was buried there.

I searched for the cemetery in the blistering heat. A row of houses concealed the wall, I discovered. In an excess of fancy I had once said to myself I should wish to be buried there someday, upon a shelf of stone. There had been nothing morbid in the thought, only a deep sense of belonging. But what, now, had been all that feeling for?

A small crowd had been following me around, and everyone was generous with information. In Suba District, where I had stayed during my sophomore year, I found the wood frame where I had lived. It was terribly weather-beaten. I had carried around its image wherever I went, an amulet that protected me from harm. Now there I stood before the real house. Its boards, gray and proud, bore no signs of ever surrendering to the elements; yet one habagat season seemed all that was needed to tear the entire structure down and reduce the whole neighborhood as well to shambles.

"Oh, don't I know this house too well," I told the old woman who, smiling, met me at the doorway. "Are not your stairs made of narra wood? Is there not a large piece of galvanized sheet-iron roofing directly over your wood-stove?"

"You once lived here?"

Her delight did not escape me. "Many years ago, yes," I said, suddenly embarrassed.

To enforce the quarantine during the cholera epidemic of 1927, sentries had to be posted at nearly all street corners. Late one afternoon, I climbed the roof, safely reaching that section over the wood-stove. Before me lay the stricken town, heart-broken.

From the deck of a steamer that had called at Romblon at this time, Rizal wrote in his diary, "Este Puerto ... es hermoso, pero triste y solitario." He was returning to Manila from his exile in Dapitan.

The statue at the town plaza, like most Rizal statues, had its back to the church, the facade of which had been quite ruined. In any case, both facade and statue shared a melancholy difficult to dispel.

I couldn't help calling Bishop Salgado's attention to this the minute we reached his compound down the road that skirted Binagong Hill. Had I broached the subject less directly, I might have been better rewarded. As it happened, all he said was, "Yes, little by little, we should try get the old facade back."

He did not elaborate, but I believed him. He had quite a record as a builder and a man of action. In his compound were a seminary and lodging facilities for visitors as well as a dormitory. Years ago, there had been nothing there but coconut trees leaning against the water and listening to the sirens of Bang-og Island singing their plaintive balitaw on the wind.

We were guests of the Mingua family at Talipasak. The word stands for the spatter of water from numerous springs in the hillside. The Mingua sisters, although busy at their jobs in Manila, had remained devoted over the years to the place. Their mother had bequeathed it to them: three hectares of coconut trees fronted by a beach and with Tablas Island in the distance.

We were three nights and four days there. During the evening, we had for our front yard -- and all to ourselves! -- Tablas Island in silhouette and the star Venus, in full spate at that time of year. Passenger ships and lesser craft of all sorts on the Manila-Iloilo route passed in review before us, aglow with festive lights in parade, worthy of all engkanto stories you might remember.

We had company on our last day; the place had been chosen as the site for a family reunion. A boom-box was quickly installed and we were overwhelmed by the music and the ranting of the dedicated San Miguel beer drinkers. Only as evening deepened did the noise subside somewhat, and the clan members dispersed reluctantly to fetch their sleeping gear. Nearly all of them preferred to put up their tents by the water's edge.

We managed to turn in early ourselves but were awakened, perhaps by the brightness of the moonlight. An other-worldy beauty seemed to have possessed the night, now with the quiet restored. We sat up awhile by the cottage window to enjoy the silence and peace.

Into our field of vision in the moonlight came a familiar-looking figure of a woman between sixty and sixty-five, from her stoop and gait possibly the eldest of the Mingua sisters. We followed her every stop closely; she made it easily across the yard.

To reach the clan members' camp required going around a pandan bush richly girded by shadow. There the figure precipitously lingered and then was wrenched away by the night.

Neither the Mingua sisters nor anyone had been up and about at the hour. I was able to ascertain this much by the next morning. I had asked and asked, indeed even as we waited for the pump-boat for the return to Tugdan.

"Oh, but that could only be Mama! Of course, that was Mama!" said Mina. "Every so often she comes to see us. Your visit has pleased her very much.

*Bio: N.V.M. Gonzalez was born in 1915 in Romblon but grew up in Mindoro, later the setting of much fiction, like the stories in* Seven Hills Away, Children of the Ash-Covered Loam, *and* Look, Stranger, on This Island Now. *A selection is available in* The Bread of Salt and Other Stories *(1993). His most recent critical essays are in* Work on the Mountain *(1995) and* The Novel of Justice *(1996). "Confessions of a Dawn Person," one of ten short stories in a new collection,* A Grammar of Dreams *(1997), is about a balikbayan's return to the scenes of his childhood and youth after a sojourn of several years in America. For his writing, Gonzalez has won many honors, including the Republic Award of Merit (1954), the Republic Cultural Heritage Award (1960), the Jose Rizal Pro-Patria Award (1961), and in 1987, the honorary degrees of Doctor of Humane Letters from the University of the Philippines.*

# BRIDE

Alma Jill Dizon

THERE IS almost no dusk in the sub-topics where the sun drops into the ocean. At 7:30 p.m., it is warm and dark with the kind of moist breeze that makes thin-blooded island people shrug into jackets and sweatshirts. Billowy clouds roll over the Koolau Range and break apart, spreading out to allow star-filled gaps as they float south. An ominously yellow moon hangs low on the horizon and unnerves some of the stragglers that hope for a seat on the back-sliders' pew. Inside the church on Palama Street tonight, they wear their most formal dark clothes still creased slightly after repeated ironing. Now and again, there is a whiff of naphthalene. They have pried the children out of bell bottoms and slid them whining into slacks and dresses. Only a minimum of gold shines and most of it in the teeth of the older members. No one wears leis, and the only flowers indoors are chrysanthemums with a few hopeful lilies.

The old man sits in the front pew while the mourners and the merely curious file past the open coffin at the front of the church. He stares blankly and doesn't seem to notice the few old women in black who shiver and sob like Catholics in agony. The middle-aged parishioners also escape his attention as they store up their gossip for later, whispering now in muted tones to match their mourning.

In his head, he hears his own voice softly repeat over and over, "*I am Candido. I was born in Ilocos Norte and came to Hawaii to work in the sugar fields. I am Candido. I left my wife and children behind. She died. The children grew up. The war began and ended. I am Candido.*"

A baby's insistent cry scratches and prods at him, interrupting his thoughts. Through the glass on one side of the church, he can see his eldest grandson, Dennis, walking slowly back and forth. The younger man soothes a screeching infant. The grandfather wonders, dazed for a moment, whose baby it is and then returns to his internal monologue.

"*My daughter, Carmen, came with her children after her husband died. She is a nurse. She lives in Pearl City. I am Candido. I live in Waianae in a plantation house.*" He blinks slowly, tempted to shut his eyes but suddenly too aware of people who might think he is napping. "*Dear Nora, I never told you. I am seventy-four years old.*"

*

There was no land at home just as there had been none when he was born in the midst of revolution. So when the American sugar cane companies came looking for field hands, he joined the line that formed in the village square. They were led into the town hall where most of them had to sit on the floor. Blankets hung over the windows, and he felt a little anxious in the darkened room. Then flickering pictures high up on one wall caught everyone's attention. There were a few scenes of Filipino sugar cane workers already in Hawaii. All dressed in white with their tools in hand, they came out of their small houses and gathered by an irrigation ditch. Then the field hands smiled and waved as they strode one by one past their friendly overseer. In other sequence, workers carried a statue of their patron saint in a joyous procession. Someone cried out in the audience just then, recognizing a relative. The film ended with a series of now-rich Filipinos in linen suits with boaters and canes while spectators cheered in appreciation.

He didn't want to leave his family behind, but he promised them and himself that he would send money and eventually return wealthy. Yet while the sugar cane companies paid the boat fare, he had to buy everything at the plantation store, and he soon found out that the money he earned bought little there. He renewed his contract after his first three years were up. In the meantime, he sent home what he could until his wife died of typhus, and the children scattered to live with various relatives.

His wife was already dead and buried for two months before he received the letter from his cousin, Clara. He felt like he was floating, suspended on air instead of water. The raw edge of missing her had already passed. In years that followed, he went through a period of visits to Hotel Street. Once a month, he would make the day-long journey in the back of an open-bed truck that wove in and out of the gullies on the narrow road to town. Studying his friends' faces and bodies, he saw his own there. They had all been slight of built but now they had thinned down to hollow, the skin hanging from their cheekbones and their chests caved in. The sun had blackened their skin, so that the odd grey hairs shone whiter on their temples and napes. They wore their best clothes, but their shoes remained rust-colored from the soil.

The Pinoys went into town to find women in all their varied shapes and sizes. On the streets and in the shops, they could see shortening skirts and unpinned hair. Blondes populated the cinema, but the tinny sound and unending grey could not compete with the taxi dancers. For ten cents, a man could whirl around while touching Japanese, Portuguese, and even blonde and brunette haole girls. Each dance vanished quickly into another one until he had spent nearly all his wages.

According to his friends, there were also brothels with

women who looked very much like the taxi dancers though with less clothing. He wandered by there one day, but Kaiulani Elementary down the street had just let out, and those peering children's eyes shamed him. It wasn't so much that his own children might look like that since their round eyes and skinny legs had grown fuzzy in his memory. Rather, it was that children strained his sense of duty in a way that he couldn't explain. On the corner stood a Chinese crack seed store, and he darted inside. After carefully studying the candy jars of salted plums and dried lemon peel, he bought a nickel bag of sugared ginger strips and walked back out into the sunlight past a cluster of boys.

There were a handful of Filipinas in town that were allowed in with their husbands and children. If they had daughters, they watched the girls carefully. All the girls had chaperones, even if it was only a ten-year-old brother. There was a reason for the high fence around Kalakaua Intermediate. After much thought, Candido's friend, Manong Guillermo, a man already well into his thirties, approached the parents of a twelve-year-old to ask for her. The father spent some time debating the matter with his relatives before they asked and received $10,000 that Manong Guillermo scrimped and borrowed. Then he had to wait for her to turn eighteen.

He told Candido that he felt like Jacob, laboring seven years for Rachel. He had loved her so much that it only felt like a few days. The allusion unsettled Candido, and he was anxious for this friend who looked too much like himself, too much like the other waning men to ever be anything else. Candido reminded him of how Laban hid his elder daughter, Leah, beneath the heavy wedding veil instead and then told Jacob to work another seven years for the younger daughter. But Guillermo laughed and said that the family only had one girl, and they wouldn't give him one of their boys instead. Then his smile hardened, and he said that they must give her to him. He had stayed away from Hotel Street and had proven himself a hardworking man. And why should they humiliate themselves, selling their daughter more than once?

Once a month for six years, he rode into town with gifts of vegetable and fruit that he respectfully offered to the mother. Then, he would sit on the couch opposite the girl who sat in a chair. But the family did renege. They wanted to marry the girl off to a merchant's son, and besides, she wasn't interested in this man who was almost as old as her parents. Candido soon heard about what happened next. It became one of those stories that everyone knows in a couple of sentences. One afternoon, Manong Guillermo knocked on the door, and when the mother tried to send him away, he pushed her aside and stabbed the girl once in the chest, burying a knife up to the shaft. She screamed and dropped, moaning and convulsing, dying as he held her for the first time.

Guillermo made no attempt to run away, and everyone said that it was a good thing that it happened during the day while the men were out or he wouldn't have survived. He received life in prison and remained there until his death some thirty years later. Candido tried to visit him once, but Guillermo refused to see him.

*

The Japanese men sent for picture brides, and Chinese families arranged marriages. There were so few women around from any country. The Chinese who had been there the longest had some Hawaiian blood from the first generation when the only women were Hawaiian. But after a series of epidemics, there were a few Hawaiians left, and other immigrants wanted their daughters to marry among their own. Besides these problems, the plantations separated the workers into camps specifically for Japanese, Filipinos, Koreans and so on. Candido was in the added bind of being Protestant. In Waianae, he had begun listening to Protestant sermons that a Tagalog preacher gave in the sugar cane worker's language. He had been open to a change in religion since the Church owned most of the land around his hometown before selling it all to one family. So even if he had met an available Filipina, she probably would have been Catholic, and he wouldn't have been able to marry her.

Some Pinoys had lovers who were men. Most of the homosexuals that the police picked up were Pinoys. The Ilokanos said, binabai, and the Hawaiians said, mahu. Candido felt embarrassed, but he couldn't understand why the police should bother them. True, it was a sin, and he didn't understand their desires, but he understood their hopelessness. The preacher harangued, all fire and brimstone, but Candido thought that hell stretched out from the present until his death, and it looked like all the days he had already spent bored with other aging men.

Carmen arrived on a steamer in Honolulu Harbor with three children who tore about and terrorized their grandfather, cheating at every game they played. His daughter looked nothing like her mother nor even like his. Instead, her long waist and bony frame mimicked the men in the family. She had studied and worked in Manila where she met her husband, a lawyer, who died during the war. Maybe it was from watching loved ones die at home and strangers in the hospital that had given her a talent and a right to assess people instantly. "How much do you make?" and "How old are you?" were normal enough questions, but "Why did you only bring bananas?" in a scolding voice to a visitor who was too much for Candido.

His daughter and her family found a place in the Pearl City near the military hospital. They drove to the country to see him from time to time, bringing pots of pancit noodles and sausages that Carmen stuffed at home. Her eldest, Dennis, grew less hyperactive and could sit in a rattan chair on the lanai while his grandfather talked story. Then one day, Carmen said that the boy had found a girlfriend, a Korean girl who attended a Catholic school. Candido had never seen himself as prejudiced, but the weight of too many possibilities overwhelmed him. He began to wheeze and hyperventilate. They made him lie down and brought him weak tea while he raved.

But why after so many years had he begun to hope

again? It was only after the war that the Philippines received a belated nationhood, just as he at last received the right to apply for American citizenship. Some years later, Congress voted in Hawaii's statehood, and Candido's worth as an eligible bachelor began to rise. When his cousin, Clara, wrote after another ten years to say that she knew a girl from a good family who was interested in marrying him, he knew that this young woman could only want to immigrate. Carmen almost growled when he told her and muttered darkly about the four M's that all Filipina nurses knew in Tagalog: "matanda, mayaman, madaling mamatay" -- old, rich, and soon to die. But his cousin, to whom he had sent money and gifts during emergencies, pressed the matter, saying that she only wanted to find him a good wife in these last years of his life. And there were other old-timers with younger wives around him since a difference of thirty or even forty years didn't matter if a man could provide for a woman who had even less. He reasoned that this was the way of the world, and if a woman chose to leave, she could do so, but she would have to find her own means, which were almost none. But he was too ashamed to send a recent photo of himself, so he sent an old one, obviously old, in which his steady and unsmiling gaze sat frozen over a borrowed pinstriped suit. For effect, he had held a borrowed felt hat and cane as well. He had been good-looking at one time and not too small for his generation.

Nora's letters were friendly, and in her Polaroid snapshot, she lifted her chin and smiled sweetly, revealing crooked teeth and an overbite. She was healthy, liked to cook, and nineteen. When she agreed to marry him, he sent her a plane ticket, met her at the airport with an armful of leis, and wed her a week later in the church on Palama Street. She wore a short, satin wedding gown with a lace collar around the throat that her grandmother had embroidered and beaded for her.

When he first stood before her with his sagging skin and dulled hair, she stared. Then she looked away, her unfocused eyes sliding over faces and walls as if they were all the same. He realized then that the old style of his photograph hadn't really sunk in until she saw him. But she had agreed to the marriage, and now she went through with it. In their wedding photograph, she held her glassy eyes a little too wide open. She couldn't smile. The reception was much larger than he had thought it would be, and he enjoyed seeing old friends who had moved to town. It was only months later that he understood how humiliating it must have been for Nora. He found a stash of coaxing letters from her mother and Manang Clara, saying that it wouldn't be for long, and then she could have anything she had always wanted. He tried hard to please her and then wondered if she felt sorry for him, so old and with his old-fashioned way of talking.

She said she was lonely in the country, but his pension wasn't enough for them to move closer to the city. She cried sometimes for no reason that he knew of, but she also fed him and started weeding between the bitter melon and sweet potatoes in the small garden behind the house. It was a small, dark blue house that sat on low stilts with slats in a diamond pattern to keep animals and children from roaming beneath. The breezes seemed to whisper through the single-walled building, but they were never enough on hot days to ease the heat that baked into the tin roof. Sometimes, she became short-tempered, especially on Kona days when the heavy air sank down around her, and the clouds took all afternoon to build up into a fierce rain. But then she regretted it and would give him a quick peck on the cheek.

He wondered if she imagined someone else when he made love to her, but he never asked, and he supposed that she never would have confessed to such a thing. But he didn't want to know, either. She would close her eyes, and he would kiss her lids.

As her belly swelled with his child, she brightened visibly, talking about her baby who would be an American. He was embarrassed but also proud. Everyone might think that he was too old to be with her, but he wasn't too old to father another child. He didn't daydream about a boy that would play baseball or a girl who would take hula lessons. He had already watched Carmen's children obediently fulfil these expectations. More so than the flesh and blood grandchildren, this son-to-be was a miraculous extension of his own faltering body. He would study his thick, cracking toe nails and the age spots on his hands before looking for her to feel the baby kicking. A young man tried to sell him life insurance, but he laughed it off. Even if he did die unexpectedly, he believed that Nora would find another husband to provide for her. He trusted that the family would take care of her until then, and she and the child would always have a place with them regardless of Carmen's doubts.

After two days of labor and the birth of a boy that they named Lawrence for *Lawrence of Arabia*, her favorite movie, the young mother was no longer the same girl. She would sit and stare at the shrieking infant while Candido tried to press him into her arms. She did manage to breastfeed the baby, and he put on weight. For a few months, the young mother ate constantly, and her pre-birth cravings became post-birth ones. One day, he brought her an expensive bag of California navel oranges, and she peeled them one by one, sucking on each section. By nightfall, she had eaten all four pounds, leaving only the peels and membranes in the plastic bag.

Disgusted at last with her still heavy stomach and thighs, she went on a strict diet that worried Candido. He thought the breastmilk might dry out if she overstarved herself. At night, she would inspect her stretchmarks in the shower and complain bitterly about them through the bathroom door. She had always been reluctant to show herself to him, and didn't want him to see these marks either. She just spoke about them. She didn't want him to touch her anymore, and at night, if he accidentally grazed her, she would grumble about the stickiness of his skin. One day, he came home and found a neighbor's wife outside the door, scolding him about the baby who had been screaming for a while as if abandoned. He went inside and found Nora, her face purple and swollen, hanging by the neck from the kitchen rafters. In the bedroom, the baby lay silent in his wet diapers, exhausted from crying.

\*

Dennis comes up to Candido and stands before him with the baby until the old man realizes that it is his son and he should take him. The grandson places the baby in his arms with the small head supported just above one elbow. Then leading him to the reception line, he stands to the left of the elderly man and steadies him while the mourners pass one at a time. They shake Dennis' hand because they can't shake Candido's. Instead, they pat an arm where they can or squeeze a bony shoulder. They stroke and coo sadly over the infant, now tranquil and spent after his funeral-long squall.

A girl in a dyed black dress that barely covers her panties shakes her long hair while speaking to Carmen on Candido's right. "She's so beautiful in her wedding dress. She looks just like the first time I saw her."

"It was the only dress that hid her neck," Carmen replies.

Candido did not listen to the service, and now that he looks about at the calmer expressions, he wonders what niceties the young minister has managed to say. Nora gave up Catholicism without any obvious regrets, enabling Carmen to say crisply that the girl could sell her faith in the next life as easily as in this one. But in the end, this conversation eased funeral arrangements that no priest in town would have agreed to. Reminded of the double barriers to a Catholic ceremony -- suicide and no final rites -- the now elderly minster declared a Protestant service possible since no one could know if the distraught girl had called out to Jesus just before her death. But it was the old minister's son who wrote and delivered the sermon. The new preacher speaks in English and more gently than his father though with the increased authority of a seminary degree. Candido, however, no longer cares about the possible bickerings of the pastor and the rest of the congregation in their deacon's meetings. The Waianae branch of the church closed some ten years ago, and he only comes to

Palama Street at times like these.

*Bio: Alma Jill Dizon was born and raised in Honolulu where her father's family has resided since 1924. After a year at the University of Hawaii, Manoa, she studied in Spain before completing her B. A. at U.C. Berkeley. She went on to get her Ph.D. at Yale, writing her dissertation on Rizal's novels. Some of her favorite writers are Pablo Neruda, Nick Joaquin and Toni Morrison. Now a writer and teacher of languages and literature, she lives on the West Coast with her husband. When not watching independent of foreign films, they spend their free time throwing frisbees to the dog, gardening, and looking for Elvis on the Web. One of Alma's on-going projects is a series of stories dealing with Filipino immigrants and their families in the U.S. from the 20's through the present.*

# ACKNOWLEDGEMENTS

In all cases, unless otherwise stated, permission to reprint previously published work has been granted by the individual authors. We are grateful to the magazines, publishers, and photographers listed below for their support.

F. Delor Angeles: "Grandma and Spanish Women" from Southwestern Review

Luis Cabalquinto: "The Fog" from *Philippine Graphic*, won second prize in the

1992 Short Story Contest; photo by Archie Reyes.

Alma Jill Dizon: "Bride" from *Pinehurst* Journal and *Yomimono*.

Ligaya Victorio Fruto: "Boy Left Behind" from the Philippines Free Press.

N.V.M. Gonzalez: "Confessions of a Dawn Person" from *A Grammar of Dreams*

University of the Philippines Press.

Vince Gotera: "Returning Fire" from *Into the Fire: Asian American Prose*,

Greenfield Review Press.

Eulalio Yerro Ibarra: Photo by Arnold Frasco.

Paulino Lim, Jr.: "A Certain failing" from *The Philippines Free Press*.

Veronica Montes: "Of Midgets and Beautiful Cousins" from *The Yellow Journal*;

Edgar Poma: "The Little Boy Who Fell in the Puka" from *The Asian Pacific American Journal.*

Mar V. Puatu: "Valentinus" from *The Girl with One Eye.*

Greg Sarris: "Joy Ride" from *Grand Avenue*, Penguin Books. Copyright 1994 by Greg Sarris; photo by Jerry Bauer.

Eileen Tabios: "Negros" from *Bamboo Ridge* and *Mobius (The Journal of Social Change)*;

Lilia V. Villanueva: "My Family/My Gang" from *Bad Women: Writings by and About Asian American Women*, Beacon Press.

# ABOUT THE EDITOR

Cecilia Manguerra Brainard is the author and editor of over twenty books including her novels, *The Newspaper Widow*, *Magdalena*, and, *When the Rainbow Goddess Wept*. She has also co-authored a novel entitled, *Angelica's Daughters, a Dugtungan Novel*. Among the books she edited are *Fiction by Filipinos in America*, *Growing Up Filipino: Stories for Young Adults* and *Growing Up Filipino II*. Her *Selected Short Stories* will be released in 2021.

Her work has been translated into Finnish and Turkish; and many of her stories and articles have been widely anthologized.

Cecilia has received a California Arts Council Fellowship in Fiction, a Brody Arts Fund Award, a Special Recognition Award for her work dealing with Asian American youths, as well as a Certificate of Recognition from the California State Senate, 21st District. She has also been awarded by the Filipino and Filipino American communities she has served. In 1998, she received the Outstanding Individual Award from her birth city, Cebu, Philippines. She has received several travel grants in the Philippines, from the USIS (United States Information Service). In 2001, she received a Filipinas Magazine Award for Arts. Her books have won the Gourmand Award and the Gintong Aklat Award.

She has lectured and performed in worldwide literary arts organizations and universities, including UCLA, USC, University of Connecticut, University of the Philippines, PEN, Beyond Baroque, Shakespeare & Company in Paris, and many others. She teaches creative writing at the Writers Program at UCLA-Extension.

She is married to Lauren R. Brainard, a former Peace Corp Volunteer to Leyte, Philippines; they have three sons.

She has a website with her blog at ceciliabrainard.com and another blog at cbrainard.blogspot.com.

## Published books by PALH (Philippine American Literary House)

*Acapulco at Sunset and Other Stories* by Cecilia Manguerra Brainard

*Benedicta Takes Wing and Other Stories* by Veronica Montes

*Contemporary Fiction by Filipinos in America*, edited by Cecilia Manguerra Brainard

*Fiction by Filipinos in America*, edited by Cecilia Manguerra Brainard

*Growing Up Filipino: Stories for Young Adults* edited by Cecilia Manguerra Brainard

*Growing Up Filipino II: More Stories for Young Adults* edited by Cecilia Manguerra Brainard

*Please, San Antonio! & Melisande in Paris* (novellas) by Eve La Salle Caram and Cecilia Manguerra Brainard

*A River, One-Woman Deep: Stories* by Linda Ty-Casper

*Woman with Horns and Other Stories* by Cecilia Manguerra Brainard

**Kindle Titles by PALH (Philippine American Literary House)**

**Fiction**

*Acapulco at Sunset and Other Stories* by Cecilia Manguerra Brainard

*Awaiting Trespass* (novel) by Linda Ty-Casper

*Benedicta Takes Wing and Other Stories* by Veronica Montes

*Contemporary Fiction by Filipinos in America* edited by Cecilia Manguerra Brainard

*Fiction by Filipinos in America* edited by Cecilia Manguerra Brainard

*Growing Up Filipino: Stories for Young Adults* edited by Cecilia Manguerra Brainard

*Growing Up Filipino II: More Stories for Young Adults* edited by Cecilia Manguerra Brainard

*Magdalena* (novel) by Cecilia Manguerra Brainard

*The Newspaper Widow* (novel) by Cecilia Manguerra Brainard

*Out of Cebu: Essays and Personal Prose* by Cecilia Manguerra Brainard

*Please, San Antonio! & Melisande in Paris* (novellas) by Eve La Salle Caram and Cecilia Manguerra Brainard

*A River, One-Woman Deep: Stories* by Linda Ty-Casper

*A Small Party in a Garden* (novel) by Linda Ty-Casper

*Vigan and Other Stories* by Cecilia Manguerra Brainard

*When the Rainbow Goddess Wept* (novel) by Cecilia Manguerra Brainard

*Wings of Stone* (novel) by Linda Ty-Casper

*Woman with Horns and Other Stories* by Cecilia Manguerra Brainard

**Nonfiction**

*Cecilia's Diary: 1962-1969* by Cecilia Manguerra Brainard

*Fundamentals of Creative Writing* by Cecilia Manguerra Brainard

*Magnificat: Mama Mary's Pilgrim Sites* edited by Cecilia Manguerra Brainard